GETTING
OUT OF **DODGE:**
PERIL 2

A novel
By
Ruby Barnes

Print Edition

Licensed by Marble City Publishing

Copyright © 2013 Ruby Barnes

First published by Marble City Publishing in 2013

All rights reserved

ISBN-10 1-908943-25-4

ISBN-13 978-1-908943-25-5

For Adrienne, Alannah and Eoin,
without whose support
Ger Mayes would never have made his comeback.

Other titles by the same author

Peril

The Baptist

The Crucible Part 1

Allen's Mosquito - The Crucible Part 2

The New Author

A walk in the park

The sky is heavy. Dark purple clouds reflect on the lake's rippling surface. Here and there an aquamarine gap opens in the sky – maybe a portal to the troposphere? I could do with someone beaming me up there, right now.

'Look, Ma, look!' A small boy at the far edge of the water points at a drake terrorising all the other ducks, wings beating as it chases.

The mother pulls her son back by the hand, trying to keep him away from the edge as he hurls chunks of bread at the uninterested, overfed recipients. Two swans glide through the ducks and seagulls swoop in for the spoils.

Plastic wheels on tarmac and a rush of air. A youth on rollerblades flies past the bench where I'm sitting. He moves like a speed-skater but looks like a thief, woolly hat down tight under a hoodie.

'Fecker!' shouts another mother as the youth swerves deftly around her pushchair.

Ah, the serene beauty of suburban Dublin.

'You okay, mister?' she asks.

I look up. She can't be long out of school. She's talking to me but I have no words to share.

'Jesus! What's happened to yer face?'

My hand goes to my cheek. My face, my whole body, is sore to the touch. I must look a sight, it was quite a beating.

She shakes her head and walks on.

'Feckers, the lot of them. Feckers,' she mutters to the world.

Sean Walsh Park contains everything I hate about this country. I should have left two weeks ago, with the first taste of freedom. Now look.

Across the lake a youngish man in a tracksuit walks cockily, phone to his ear and a beer bottle in one hand. He downs the last of the beer and hurls the bottle into the bushes. Then he switches off the phone and slips it into his jacket pocket.

The little boy feeding the birds turns and runs into the man's arms. I'm too far away to hear what the mother says but, from the body language, it's where have you been or who were you talking to. The man ignores her and runs to the water's edge with the boy. They look across the lake and see me watching, so I turn my head.

I don't know how I got here, but here I am. It has something to do with this *thing* between my legs. Everything to do with it.

A breeze picks up and rustles the plastic bag at my feet. I look into the wind and see lads loitering at the far entrance to the park. Even at this distance they look foreign. Something about their trousers. They're the Romanians. Friends or enemies, I'm not sure. Is this their doing? It could be, doesn't matter now.

The bag rustles again. I have no idea how I came to be here, can't remember. I don't deserve it. This time I tried to do the right thing. My intentions were good.

A shout makes it upwind from the mother with the pushchair. Two uniformed guards struggle past her at the other entrance. A man in a dark jacket follows and then the wiry, brown-suited figure of Detective Inspector Andy McAuliffe. I can smell his cigarettes in my memory.

Andy, I should have taken your advice and got the hell out of Dodge.

Before they reach me I have to know what's between my legs. But I think I already know and so does Andy, somehow.

The bag is oozing something onto the tarmac. Clear fluid with traces of pink. I open the top of the bag with both hands and my favourite fragrance wafts out. When a woman wears that, it means she's mine. The scorching sun, sea and sand of the Mediterranean, as the ad says, with a hint of butcher's shop.

I put my hand inside and let my fingertips touch, then stroke. Her hair is soft and fair. I always loved her hair.

Day 1 – Release

Two weeks earlier…

'You're going nowhere, Mayes.'

The veins in Delaney's temple look fit to burst. His over-muscled torso is some kind of obscene exhibit and his facial acne looks infectious.

Delaney isn't the first but hopefully he'll be the last syringe-wielding maniac to threaten my liberty. Just how I'm going to get out of this, though, isn't immediately clear. Fifteen stone of pumped-up white trash, a needle full of smack that's likely HIV loaded, plus the promise of a good rogering. Just a regular day at the gym in Portlaoise prison.

Stand my ground, that's what I've learned. There's not much else for it unless I want to play kiss chase with Delaney around the bench presses.

'Fuck off, Delaney.'

His top lip curls back to reveal a gummy smile and the hand with the syringe swings at my shoulder. There's no stand-off, he means business.

I block his arm at the wrist and just manage to hold it back. Delaney gives a chuckle and things go black for a second as his other fist impacts the side of my face.

I keep a grip on the wrist but have to drop to my knees. From somewhere behind him there's a crack of metal on bone and Delaney's head falls on my chest. He slumps to the floor, the syringe arm goes limp and I let go his wrist.

Officer O'Mahoney gives Delaney a prod with the end of his baton but the thug is out for the count.

'Well, Ger. Let's get you out to the office before this eejit wakes up.'

My head is still spinning as O'Mahoney escorts me to my cell to pick up the sports holdall containing my stuff. There's not much to show for nine years. A couple of dog-eared paperbacks, a wedding ring too small to fit on my finger and a small pile of letters explaining why I don't have the right to wear that ring any more.

A few of the other cons jeer as I'm walked out front and one or two call a farewell. The serious inmates pay no attention to Ger Mayes, accidental drug smuggler and lightweight criminal.

'Prisoner Delaney seems to have hurt himself in the gym,' O'Mahoney says to a young officer who unlocks the first gate for us. 'Have a check on him. Don't go alone.'

'Will do.'

O'Mahoney is the senior around here. Mid-forties, getting a little heavy and ready for early retirement. Just like me.

The gate clanks shut behind us.

'Prisoner Mayes, for release today,' O'Mahoney says at the second gate.

The lock releases with a buzz and a flash of red light.

O'Mahoney escorts me to the governor's office.

'So, Mr Mayes, we're parting company.' Governor Treacy makes a steeple out of his fingers.

I just nod. Treacy hasn't done me any favours. And he hasn't aged well. While I've been stuffing my face with the culinary delights of the prison kitchen, and rounding out nicely, our governor's wrinkles show the stress of every staff assault, escape attempt, death threat and inmate murder over the last decade. His darkest hour was when a woman visitor managed to smuggle a budgerigar in her knickers.

'As you know, the minister has considered you for remission and, taking your good behaviour into account, granted full…'

Blah, blah, blah. Treacy is so boring. It's a formality and nothing I do or say now, short of attacking the governor or O'Mahoney, can jeopardise the outcome.

Scared is how I feel. Nine years without a visitor, except for legal eagles. TV in the common room and the occasional newspaper have been my only windows onto the Ireland of today. Not even my wife – my ex-wife – came to visit. All tucked up cosy somewhere in Dublin with a new husband and my child.

'Mayes?'

O'Mahoney nudges me in the ribs.

'Answer the governor, Mayes.'

'Sorry, could you repeat the question?'

'One thousand and ninety-eight euro. A cheque for a thousand and the rest in cash. Correct?'

'That's right, Mr Treacy. That's right.'

He slides the envelope across the desk and I pick it up. It should be more but they've kindly used some of my money to provide the clothes I'm wearing for release. Dunnes Stores fashion for the middle-aged man. Cardigans must be back in style.

'…and with no small thanks to Officer O'Mahoney here.'

He's right there. We've been in this room before, the three of us. O'Mahoney has always told it straight. Whenever one of the heavyweight cons deigned to acknowledge insignificant me with a spot of delegated violence, O'Mahoney always saved me from the worst of it. More recently a couple of freelance toughs, like Delaney, tried to banjax my 'good behaviour' but

O'Mahoney has his ear to the ground. He's been my guardian angel.

I turn to O'Mahoney and he shakes my hand. The governor frowns.

'Yes, well. That's all, Mayes. I trust we won't be seeing you in here again.' He stands, walks around his desk and looks me straight in the eyes, up close. 'I personally never thought you belonged in my prison, Mayes. But after what you did…'

He shakes his head and I see O'Mahoney suppress a smile.

'There's a little reception party waiting for you outside, Mayes. I don't want to see you on the six o'clock news this evening. It won't take much to get the minister to change his mind. He didn't want to release you but rules are rules. Mr O'Mahoney, you may escort Mr Mayes from the prison.'

I look at Treacy's rounded stomach and have an urge to belly-bounce with him. Instead I give an embarrassing little bow and turn, O'Mahoney's hand on my elbow.

The air is cool as we cross the prison yard. Each of the soldiers on guard in their watchtower turns and the barrels of four assault rifles aim at my head.

'They really want to shoot you, you know,' O'Mahoney says. 'You made them look pretty stupid, back then.'

I'm happy to get across the open space in one piece.

'And watch out for *An Garda Síochána* on the outside,' he adds as we approach the main gate. He spits out the Irish words.

We walk into the shadow of the walls and his hand raises a card to a security reader but I intercept it.

'There's something I need to know, Mr O'Mahoney.''

He drops his hand.

'Call me Bill. You're a civilian now. Ask away.'

'Well. I just wondered why you've looked out for me, all these years?'

O'Mahoney rubs his chin with a hand and looks back at the prison building, then he turns to me.

'It's an old story. I joined the guards before the prison service. There were some shenanigans with evidence in a trial and I wouldn't play along. So they drummed me out of the force; for being too honest.'

I nod. I understand honesty. I don't do honesty but I understand it.

'Singlehandedly you delivered An Garda Síochána the biggest humiliation in their history. For that I'm personally grateful and, for that, you've deserved my protection.'

My guardian angel is a twisted, bitter man. But an honest one.

We proceed to the gate and I can hear a clamour of anticipation outside.

'Say nothing, Ger. Best of luck.'

I feel O'Mahoney's hand on my shoulder, then his touch is gone and the gate locks behind me.

Fame

Blinding light. Through squinted eyes I see a crowd of people thrusting microphones. A couple of news cameramen too. I look behind me but no one else is there, just the battleship grey prison door. It's my party.

'Gerard Mayes, your first day out of prison after nine of a twelve year term for *Offences against the State*. What are your plans now?' An overenthusiastic young man with a chiselled profile thrusts his microphone under my chin.

'A Chinese takeaway,' I say.

The man is elbowed back by a tall blonde woman I recognise from the TV. What the camera never shows are her long and slender legs.

'Judge Curtin described you as Ireland's worst ever criminal.'

I remember the judge saying that in his summing up. It wasn't a professional compliment.

'Yes.'

'Do you regret your crimes? What about your victims?' shouts another over the woman's shoulder.

My hand goes nervously to my head and strokes where the ginger thatch used to cover it.

'Erm … it was a victimless crime.'

'Are you saying that drug dealing has no victims?'

'No.'

'So what are you saying, Ger?' the woman at the front asks.

She's orange with makeup for the camera. I haven't slept with a woman, of any colour, in nearly ten years.

'I'm saying I wasn't a drug dealer.'

'What were you?'

'He was just a drugs mule!' some wag shouts from the rear of the huddle.

'No! That makes it sound like…'

'Like what, Ger?' the blonde says.

'Like I smuggled the stuff in, up me hole.'

'Jesus!' the wag shouts.

'Cut! Cut!'

The cameras and microphones drop away as the full Mayes effect comes into force.

After a few minutes of embarrassed shuffling I'm left with just my orange lady friend. She pulls out a packet of Silk Cut, offers me one and lights us both up with a cheap disposable lighter.

The sun has ducked behind a cloud and I relish the heat of the smoke.

'Roisín,' she says and offers her hand.

The thin fingers are cold.

'Ger.'

'Yes, I know who you are, Ger.'

We pull on our cigarettes like old partners in crime. She shivers as she exhales.

'You made a right hames of that,' she says.

'What? My fifteen minutes of fame?'

'Don't worry, it won't make the news. But I guess that was the outcome you were looking for.'

She blows smoke downwards and tilts her head towards me. I catch a whiff of scent amongst the tobacco, something expensive.

'Really, off the record, what are your plans now?'

'Well, I'm at a bit of a loose end, if you've a couple of hours.'

It's like I haven't been away. Old Ger still has the magic.

'Don't flatter yourself.' She laughs and pushes a few loose blonde strands back behind her ear.

But I know she thought about it, if only for a split second.

'I'm heading to Kilkenny,' I say and take a long drag. 'That's my grand plan.'

'Kilkenny? The quiet life then.'

'The quiet life.'

'I wouldn't mind trying that. Sometimes.'

She seems serious. It's difficult to tell what she really looks like behind the mask of make-up. I'm getting crazy ideas. Ten years in the company of men is a long time.

The theme tune to Hawaii Five-0 starts to play from inside her handbag. She pulls out a phone about half the size phones used to be, lifts it to her ear and turns away for a few seconds.

I look down at my Dunnes Stores special outfit. Then at her legs. I can see the muscles in her calves. She turns back and catches me leching at her.

'Look, I have to go. If you ever want to tell your story, the real story, call me.'

I take the business card thrust at me.

'Um, any chance of a lift to the train station?' I give my best cheeky grin.

'No offence, Ger, but you're a man just out of prison after ten years. I'm not getting into a car alone with you.'

I feel the wind blow in and out of my open mouth. This is the warm welcome of society.

'There's a bus stops just there.' She points to the kerb across the street. 'It'll take you straight to the station, then there's a coach to Kilkenny. Do you have money?'

I pull the notes and cheque that Treacy gave me from my pocket.

'Here. They won't take a note on the local bus.'

She scoops a few coins from her purse and drops them in my hand.

'See you, Ger.' She turns and walks away. The indicator lights blink on a snazzy red coupé parked over the road. After a few steps she turns. 'Call me. When you're ready.'

~

I study a timetable on the bulbous middle of the bus stop pole but the bus is late.

An old lady with her shopping trolley stands a respectable distance away; a veteran of riding public transport into town with ex-cons.

The bus finally arrives. Short and dumpy, like a cross between a van and an ambulance.

Granny elbows past me, all determined bone and gristle, and flashes a pass at the driver.

'Two-forty,' he says when I step up.

I fumble the coins into the plastic tray.

The ride takes all of a few minutes with just one stop for the hospital. I could have walked it, easy. But Portlaoise doesn't seem to be the sort of town where people walk.

The cars. I recognise all the makes but the different models are smoothed, distorted versions of memories. Granny scowls at me across the gangway and purses her shrivelled mouth. I see the driver eyeing me in his rear-view mirror.

'Final stop,' the driver calls out and swings his bus into the station.

I'm the last one off and thank the driver. He nods.

A queue is shuffling aboard the coach in the next bay. The sign says Carlow – Kilkenny – Waterford.

Students throw their oversized bags into the luggage compartment. A young woman struggles to load a pushchair, her left arm occupied by a wriggling infant.

'Here, let me help.' I take the buggy and slide it in.

The woman, little more than a girl herself, takes the burning cigarette from her mouth after one long drag and throws it in the gutter.

'Thanks, but I could've done it. Do it all the time.' She balances the child on her hip and gives me a once over. 'You just out?'

'Uh huh.'

'Nice clothes,' she says and laughs, climbing onto the bus.

I follow her on, close behind. Her skirt is too short and she has a tattoo on the inside of one ankle.

'Fifteen euro, sixty-eight,' says the driver when I tell him Kilkenny.

That's one week's wages in prison, the robber.

The coach is pretty full. Lots of died blonde hair framing hardened female faces, young and old. These are the visitors of Portlaoise Prison.

One of the older women looks straight at me then turns to her neighbour. The muttering travels up the coach. Oh, they know who I am, right enough.

Just one seat free, next to the short-skirted tattoo girl. She's probably the only person on the bus who doesn't know my story. The baby is bouncing on her knee.

It's sweltering hot and stuffy, the breath of fifty smokers mixed with cheap perfume. I take off my jacket and cardigan, and stash them with my bag on the shelf before settling into the seat next to the girl.

'I never saw you,' she says, turning to me as the baby tries to stand on rubbery legs. 'Never saw you in the visiting.'

I look at her.

'My dad's in,' she says. 'Armed robbery.'

Lower lip out and nod with respect.

'What did you do, then?'

'He's Ger Mayes, love,' says a fake tanned woman, turning around from the seat in front. 'You know, the drug smuggler.'

'You mean, that's him? How much was it? Five hundred million euro?' The teenage mum is in awe. My infamy transcends the generation gap.

Heads turn in other seats. I feel the heat rise up my neck and the scar down my breast bone begins to itch.

'More than that,' shouts another. 'But by the look of him he's all spent up!'

Whoops and caterwauling right down the bus. I feel like a male stripper rejected by a raucous hen night. One on one I can handle them, but not an entire coven.

My hand goes to Roisín's calling card in my shirt pocket. She's right, people are interested in the Ger Mayes story.

I sit back, close my eyes and take a long, deep breath, wishing it all away. Things quieten down as they realise they'll not get a rise out of me.

The coach ambles out of town and then hurtles along country lanes, trees brushing clean scratches across the dirty windows. Ireland has built a twenty-first century motorway network but our route neatly avoids it, criss-crossing from the Midlands into the South East. The heave of the vehicle on dips and bends lulls me into a dribbling, nauseous doze.

In Carlow town the coach bounces to a stop and lets out a sigh of pneumatic relief as the female hardcore disembarks. We remnants enjoy a few minutes of spaciousness until the seats fill up again with students from the Institute of Technology.

Roads I remember as race tracks, cars vying for overtaking rights, are virtually empty of traffic. The coach driver throws us around slow-moving farm machinery on half blind bends.

Paulstown looms and, no one being at the designated stop, we don't even slow, thundering along the deserted village high street. Ten more minutes and we cross Kilkenny city limits.

The river stretches out, way down to the left, Kilkenny Castle standing sentinel. Nine years is a long time for Ger Mayes but a mere cough in the life of this old place. Narrow streets of terraced cottages are packed around the churches and graveyards. Built for workers at the now defunct shoe factory, these days home to the older and poorer generation. This is where I will set new roots.

'MacDonagh Junction, next train to Dublin leaves in ten minutes,' the driver's voice says over the coach speakers.

My holdall rattles when I pull it down from the overhead shelf. As well as convict memorabilia it contains my pills; the cocktail of Smarties I need to keep a stranger's heart beating in my body.

There are murmurs from the few remaining convict relatives as I make my way down the aisle and off onto Kilkenny soil. No welcome party here. A Garda car is parked haphazardly up by the station entrance but it's not for my benefit. Probably an unruly bunch of stags on the incoming train.

Things don't look busy on the short walk to the top of town. The pubs all have room vacancy signs in their windows. It's Friday afternoon and things should be ramping up for the weekend. I choose Slaney's and wander in.

'Looking for a room?' a middle-aged woman behind the bar asks as she gives me the once over.

'Uh huh. For a few days,' I say.

Her eyes take in my bag and the Dunnes Stores demob outfit. She nods.

'Come on through and see if it suits,' she says.

I follow her through a part glazed door marked Residents Only and up a narrow staircase. Everything is pine clad, like a sauna.

'Number four should be free.' She turns at the top of the stairs, towards the front of the building, and reaches for the handle of a flimsy looking door.

The room has low ceilings but it's bright, lit from a window that overlooks the street.

'You have a bathroom in here. Well, a shower room, anyway. If you need more towels or anything just let me know.'

The fittings are budget but everything is clean. A double bed. Compared to what I'm used to it's the Ritz.

'How much?'

'How long did you say for?' She looks at my bag again.

'A week. Let's say one week.'

My landlady rubs a stray dark hair on her chin.

'Bed and breakfast, we don't do evening meals. That'll be two-fifty for the week.'

I run my tongue over my teeth. After nine years of earning fifteen euro a week it seems like a lot of money, but really it isn't.

'And you can use the washing machine,' she says. 'If you need it.'

'Okay, I'll take it.' I'll have her ironing my shirt before the week is out. 'Will you take a cheque?'

I take out the cheque book my solicitor posted to me a week ago. Her hesitation has me wishing I'd asked Treacy for more cash.

'Or I can give you fifty now and the rest later?'

She looks at my cheque book, my name printed there, and decides.

'Cheque will be fine, Mr Mayes. Will you be settling here, in Kilkenny?'

'I will. Mrs…?'

'Mrs Slaney. Call me Rita.'

If she shaved that chin, and plucked her upper lip, she'd be a handsome woman. In a room, alone with me.

'There's a pen over there.' She points to a flimsy looking table in the corner.

I stumble over how to fill out the cheque. Do people even still use the things?

'Thanks,' she says exchanging the cheque for a bunch of keys. 'Breakfast at weekends is half eight 'til ten, in the lounge bar. After-hours entrance is at the rear, the Yale key, and the other is your room.'

'Thanks, erm…'

'Rita.' Then she's gone.

I'm so crap with names.

A commotion out on the street draws me to the window. Pink rabbit ears, a dozen or so pairs. A hen party, down for the weekend. I sit close up to the glass to see more.

Quite a selection of women milling around in semi-drunken confusion. Three are clearly sisters and one of them is the bride; the girl who looks like she's been starving herself for weeks to fit into a wedding dress. Mum, aunties and a few friends. Plenty of candidates.

They don't walk into Slaney's though. It'll be the Kilford or Langton's for the likes of them. Maybe Kilkenny hasn't lost its magic after all. I have an urge to get out on the town tonight.

Bells chime from the tower over at St John's. One, two, three, four. I almost forgot, have to get down to McDonald before he shuts up shop for the weekend. I pick up my holdall and leg it out and down the stairs.

'It's definitely him,' Rita is saying to a guy at the bar as I pull open the half-glazed door. She looks at me with an open mouth.

'Ger. Call me Ger. See you later.'

John Street is static downhill with traffic. A cyclist races along the wrong side of the vague white line, swerving in when cars come up from the bridge. I have to step off the narrow path and into the road to get around the smoking pink bunnies down by Langton's.

Italian restaurants are everywhere. Or at least restaurants with Italian names. A woman with a tanned face and Slavic eyes looks out of a window at me as she adjusts a menu board. The Romanians have prospered.

Eateries give way to pubs closer to the river and the faux antique look is well employed. I can gauge the clientele inside the pubs by the class of smoker hanging out on the street. None of them look like me.

The bridge looks well. It's been re-paved and the stone parapets sand-blasted. It wasn't in such good repair when Renée, my ex-wife's best friend, stepped out over the edge with my baby in her womb. The night my world fell apart.

'Sorry,' a voice says.

Something presses up against my foot. It's the pneumatic tyre of a child's pushchair, the tread bald. The snotty kid passenger looks up at me with a gappy grin.

'Hey, you're the fella off the TV! Fair play to ye!' the mother barks, her thick arms flexing on the pushchair handles. A tribe of small beings swarm around us, likely previous occupants of the vintage perambulator.

The woman wheels the tyre over my foot and walks on. Happy families.

Oh, Renée. There could be no happy ending for us.

Infamy

McDonald's offices are in Lower Patrick Street, a struggle through crowded tourists on narrowing pavements. Young couples in hopeless love, retired couples in mutual support. Sad single men.

The doorway is impressive. Granite around black wood, Messrs McDonald in shiny brass. Three storeys of dependability over a basement of knowledge.

I buzz in and take the stairs. A brown carpet that's seen better days. First floor and the staircase narrows, creaking under my weight. Or is it my knees?

'Mr McDonald will see you shortly, please take a seat,' whistles a young lady with slicked back hair and slightly protruding teeth.

Barely time to clear the magazines from a seat before the man himself comes through a doorway and offers his hand. Firm and dry.

'Mr Mayes. It seems like we're old friends at this stage.'

I'm reluctant to say anything because, based on past experience, he'll charge me per word for listening.

'Come on through. Tea and biscuits please, Sinead.'

McDonald leads me into an office of indeterminate size. Boxes, files, papers everywhere. On shelves, on chairs, on the floor.

'Are you on the move?'

His pasty face cracks a smile.

'We've been here for a hundred and fifteen years, Mr Mayes. And we'll be here for another century. Well, I won't, obviously, but it's a family firm.'

About time they did some filing then.

The girl appears with a tray and McDonald gathers up papers, clearing space on his desk.

'Do you take sugar?' she asks, lifting the pot.

She's young. Willowy and pretty, just the teeth need fixing a little. She runs the tip of her tongue over them as she pours.

'No, thanks, but no.'

'Thank you very much, Sinead. That'll be all.'

McDonald's daughter. I can see the facial resemblance. And I can see he doesn't want her too near the likes of me.

'Well, Mr Mayes.'

'Ger. Please call me Ger.'

'Well, Ger.' He spreads his hands over the desk. 'A decade's work is what you see in front of you. This is everything. I want you to see what you've paid me for.'

I pick up a file about an inch thick. Bad choice. The divorce. I select another. Sale of the family home, proceeds to my ex-wife. McDonald's desk is littered with the detritus of my disasters.

'You see, Ger, men who've been inside, they don't always appreciate the work we've put in, the amount of to-ing and fro-ing, proposals and counter proposals.'

'Yes, I see.'

His industry has to be admired. And that of his legal correspondents.

'You've had bills from me, periodically. I've summarised everything here in one document for clarity.'

He hands me a stapled sheaf of papers. Top of the list is the bill from my original solicitor, Duggan the Double-crossing Bastard. Then fees from McDonald. Services of a barrister at the central criminal court when the judge declined my legal aid application. That protracted law suit against Aunt Mary's life insurance company. The wrangle over Renée's estate. It goes on.

Bottom line: one hundred and forty-seven thousand euro and twenty-seven cents. You would have thought he could afford braces for his daughter.

I have to pay. Really I've already paid. McDonald has had control of all my money.

'And here's the closing statement.' He hands me a single sheet.

It's straightforward. Renee's life insurance paid out, I've bought a small house in absentia, McDonald and the legal system in general have fleeced me and there's not as much left as I had hoped.

'These are the papers for number 32 Maudlin Street. Sign here.' He scratches a cross with his ink pen. 'Here, and here.'

I think again of Renée, standing on the parapet. Her wave and last smile. She jumped into the river, taking her cancer with her and a child that could never be born.

'It may not be my place to say it, but you were very fortunate to have been the beneficiary of Miss Martin's estate.'

'You're quite right. It's not your place.'

'Ahem … right, here's your debit card. You won't be able to get a credit card for some time but I don't think that will be a problem. You'll see that this amount has been placed in your new current account.' He reaches across and scratches an ink mark against a number on my sheet. 'And the rest is in an interest bearing account here.'

'Thank you.'

'Everything has been cleared with the bank. The paper trail for the money has been signed off. As I said in my letter, everyone has to prove the source of any substantial

funds these days. It's not because of your incarceration.'
He makes it sound like I was kidnapped.

Looking at that piece of paper I see what Ger Mayes
has become. I can do the sums. An early retiree in an old
woman's cottage with enough money to last me for the
second half of my life if I eat porridge for every meal,
abstain from alcohol and don't turn on the heating. No
wine, no women but I can sing to myself in the cold
shower.

'Is that everything?' I ask.

'Almost. We'll exchange contracts this afternoon and
complete on Monday. You should be able to collect the
keys here, let's say Tuesday.'

'Right. Good. All done and I'll see you Tuesday.'

'There is one more thing.'

McDonald wrings his hands and licks his lips. I know it
kills him for people to walk away with money still in their
pockets, or bank accounts.

'Do you have any plans for the money, Ger?'

'Yes. I plan to get it all out in cash and roll around
naked in it.'

'In Rita Slaney's guest rooms?'

Of course he knows where I'm staying. The whole
town knows by now.

'Figuratively speaking.'

He looks at me like I'm mad.

'Ha! Very good, yes. No, I mean, have you considered
any business investment opportunities? A quarter of a
million is a good sum of money but it won't last forever.
There are ways and means to grow your money.'

Groucho Marx springs to mind. I refuse to invest with
someone who would have me as a client. But I'm curious
to know what McDonald recommends for the likes of me.

'Go on.'

He opens a drawer of his desk, takes out a file and opens it on top of my scattered papers.

'Well, there are a number of retail opportunities. Electrical goods. A camera shop.'

Just the sort of family businesses that have been driven out of town by big chain stores on the retail park. I shake my head.

'There's a chipper that's up for sale. Very high cash flow in the takeaway food business.' He rubs his palms together.

I wouldn't mind being a fish and chips magnate, and I could eat some right now. Not a good idea to go investing on an empty stomach. Also McDonald's appetite for cash flow has me wondering what I'd be getting into.

'Let me think it over. I'm just out today, give me a chance to get on my feet.'

'Sure. Of course. We'll be seeing each other on Tuesday. Think it over between now and then.' He gathers the papers together and puts his file back in the drawer, locking it.

I'll bet more people than just McDonald know about my little nest egg.

We shake hands to conclude.

~

Langton's at six o'clock on a Friday night. I'm showered, fragrant and dressed to the nines in a new outfit from River Island up at the MacDonagh shopping centre. There are six of us in the big u-shaped bar and I'm the only one not wearing a barman's uniform.

'You okay?' one of them asks.

'Smithwick's.' I raise my nearly empty glass and grimace. 'Is it always this busy?'

'You're just a bit early, is all,' he says, placing my second pint on a fresh beer mat and holding out a hand for payment.

I feel quite pissed, despite the fish and chips I ate in my room at Slaney's. Ten years of abstinence, the night will end in disaster. I hope.

'Well,' says a voice in my ear and a ruddy faced, stocky guy hops onto the stool beside me.

I raise and tilt my glass.

'End of a busy week,' the fella says. 'How about yerself?'

'Eventful, you could say.'

'Two Guinness,' he says to the barman.

Another man comes walking up from the direction of the toilets. Sandy hair, an outdoor look about him. These two have to be brothers.

'Liam,' the new arrival says, shaking my hand.

'I'm Shane,' says the first. 'We've been up at Goffs, sold a few horses. We always stop in on our way back to Cork. Haven't seen you here before.'

'Ger,' I say.

Their handshakes are energetic.

'That's good, boy!' Liam puts his empty glass on the bar top. 'We made forty grand this week. Thoroughbreds. Good bloodstock.'

Shane signals the barman with three fingers. The pints are lined up and we're off. The brothers are in a race to make their millions and they drink at the same pace.

Liam and Shane's enthusiasm is infectious. I'm investing in horses. Bloodstock is your only man. The lads can treble my money in a year, they just need working capital.

'Them Arabs are in every week, paying top euro on instinct, and we've some fine fillies,' says Shane.

'Fine fillies,' Liam says, looking across the bar to where the bunny-eared hen party has staked out their hunting ground.

We get another pint. I try to pay but they're having none of it.

'Thanks, lads. I appreciate the company.'

'Nice to meet someone new like yerself, someone who's interested,' Liam says.

'Yeah, you see, I'm just today out…'

'Ger, we have to love ye and leave ye,' Shane says, thrusting his hand out. His other hand clasps over the top of mine.

'Here.' Liam takes a card from his shirt pocket and slips it into mine. 'I know we've all drink taken but if you're seriously interested in the business then give us a call.'

My new best friends exit stage left and I'm alone again, this time in a crowded room. Not for long.

'Hey. Have yer fellas left ya all alone?' A blonde with a short tight haircut laughs and slips onto Liam's barstool.

'Don't mind her. She won't wear her ears.' Shane's stool is taken by another blonde with longer hair in a bob. She has her pink ears on. They're from the hen party.

'What is it you're doing here then?' the girl with the short hair asks.

They look more pissed than I feel.

'Considering some local business.'

'Local business is it?' she asks.

'Like I said, don't mind her,' the one with the bob says. 'She works for the revenue. Be careful what you tell her or she'll be investigating your arse. My name's Susan, by the way. Sue.'

Sue gives me her hand. I shake it gently and turn her palm upwards. Trace the lifeline. Then turn it over and run a fingertip down a finger to the manicured nail.

'Beautician,' I say. 'You have your own salon, up in Dublin.'

'Spot on, Sherlock. And all tax declared!' She puts a slender arm across my shoulders and signals the barman for a round.

'I'm Denise,' the tax inspector says, offering her hand. She's substantially less drunk and has a strong grip.

'Den's a karate expert,' Sue says. 'A ball-breaker by day and a ball-breaker by night, she is. We're sisters, you know.'

Denise grins and feels my collar.

'Nice shirt. Did you buy it today?'

I look down at the front of my shirt and notice the packet folds in the material for the first time.

'Yep, up at the shopping centre. My luggage was lost on the flight in from Zurich, had to buy some clothes and stuff.'

'Zurich?' Sue says, wide eyed. 'What sort of car do you drive then? Mercedes or BMW?'

'No, I'd say he's a Saab man. Isn't that right?' Denise says.

'Spot on. Saab 9-5 Aero.'

I don't even own a bicycle.

'Sweet Jesus! You could take me any way you want me in that car,' Sue says.

'She means it,' Denise adds. 'Very materialistic, my sister.'

'What're you both drinking?'

'Mine's a Margarita,' Sue says.

'And mine's a Long Slow Comfortable Screw against the Wall,' Denise says with a determined straight face.

I signal to the barman and he starts on another round of drinks.

'So, what did you say your name was? And what's it you do in Zurich that buys such a flash motor?' Sue asks.

'Phil. My name is Phil.' I'm really on the blag now. 'I'm a clinician.'

'Like a physiotherapist or something? Me back is killing me. You could fix that, couldn't ya?' Sue squirms on her stool.

'Get a room, you two,' Denise says. 'Don't mind her, Phil. She won't still love you in the morning.'

'Plastics. I'm a plastic surgeon. Cosmetic improvements. That's where the money is.'

Denise narrows her eyes. She handles drink well, unlike her sister.

'How about this?' I say. 'When a woman walks into my clinic I can tell what she's come for within thirty seconds, just by looking at her.'

'Get lost,' Sue says. She smoothes her hands down her tight black dress. I scrutinise.

Denise laughs at her sister's drunken discomfort.

'It's me belly, isn't it? I'd be looking to have a tummy tuck,' Sue says.

She's a string bean, straight up and down, unlike Denise who is athletically built. Funny how skinny women are obsessed with fat tummies.

I shake my head.

'What then? Oh no, you don't mean…'

I look at the vague moustache on her upper lip. It's dark, unlike Denise's, which is natural blonde.

'Are you really satisfied with your boobs?'

A split second of silence that feels like an hour, then Sue lets out a scream. Denise coughs her cocktail all over her sister's dress. I grab the bar mat and wipe Sue down.

'You're right, of course,' Sue says, grabbing my hand and pressing it against her chest. 'I'm in need of, what do they call it? Augmentation.'

She gives a hiccup, goes to sit down and slides off the stool onto the floor.

I help Denise lift her sister back up.

'I'll take you to our room for a little nap,' Denise says to Sue.

'Bring him. Doctor Phil. We can have a threesome.'

She's barely able to stand.

'See you around, Phil. We're here all weekend.' Denise puts an arm around her sister's waist and leads her away. She looks around as they go through the door to the hotel reception and grins back at me.

Day 2 – I did

Her back is pale and freckled. I run a fingertip down the groove of her spine. She grunts and it fades into a whimper. That seems to have stopped the snoring.

My head feels like a gorilla has it in a wrestling hold. The same gorilla has thrown my clothes and money around the room and done something unpleasant in my mouth. On the bedside cabinet there's a half-eaten doner kebab sitting in a scrunch of tin foil wrapping from Abrakebabra. I vaguely remember staggering in there after Langton's.

Noise from the street comes in through the window, a cleansing truck moving a few metres, scrubbing, moving on. Early morning sun lights up the pine clad ceiling and walls of my room.

I look at my bed-mate again. It's Rita. She rolls onto her back and takes a deep breath. A good looking woman, for her age. I could do worse. But I know I'm just a curiosity, a notch on her bed post of notoriety.

That hair under her chin is the only blemish. I could just pluck it. Then I'll share my morning glory with her.

'Feck!'

Her eyes flick open and a hand comes to where the obstinate hair still remains. She frowns at me and turns to look at the old red LED clock on the bedside table.

'I'd better be getting the breakfast going.'

It's a one woman show here at Slaney's. I remember, through the haze, Rita told me her old man is banged up in Mountjoy for tax evasion. He's left her short financially and she likes to keep a very tight rein on things.

She swings her legs out from under the covers and hops into the bathroom. A flush of the toilet and she's back, wearing the bathrobe from behind the door.

'I'll do you a full Irish,' she says, gathering up her scattered clothes from around the floor.'

'I think you already did last night.'

Rita grins and then she's gone. It's just sex.

~

'Where would I buy some furniture,' I ask her as she places the promised breakfast before me.

Rita looks at the other two people in the bar – a young couple whose attention is solely on each other. Then she bends her head closer to mine. 'Is it all a bit too much for ye?'

'Oh, I think I can handle it.'

She smoothes a palm across her collarbone, bites her bottom lip and heads back to the kitchen.

The food is great. My head's still fuzzy with drink but I have a hell of an appetite.

Rita returns with tea and toast.

'Depends what you're looking for. There's a place up on the Hebron does all kinds, not too expensive. But I would have thought Meubles, out the Waterford Road, would be more your style. Money being no object and all.'

Did I tell her about the money last night? I don't think so.

'And where would I get a computer? A laptop.'

She puts her hands on her hips.

'What would the likes of you be wanting with a computer?'

'Bloody cheek. I wasn't pounding rocks in Portlaoise, you know. They have computers.'

Her pencil thin eyebrows arch unevenly, then she shrugs.

'The fella across the road has some offers. He's closing down, you might get a deal.'

'Right. Thanks.'

I continue with my breakfast.

Rita gives me sly smiles as she serves the young couple. Maybe I shouldn't be in such a hurry to move on.

~

Back to bed, alone, for an hour and then a long, hot shower. Because I can.

Rita gives me a lift in her old Mercedes to the furniture showroom up on the Hebron industrial estate. I've no idea what I need for 32 Maudlin Street. The pictures on the estate agent's website were difficult to judge, but it's only a terraced cottage so no point in buying a pile of stuff that won't fit. There has to be room for a double bed.

Money in my pocket and not used to spending it, I pick out a reclining swivel chair in black leather. Always wanted one of those. And a king-sized bed with a top of the range mattress. The salesman tells me they'll deliver everything the middle of next week.

The walk back into town goes on for ever. I feel like an old man. A tired and thirsty old man.

Saturday late morning and John Street is bustling. The pub doors are open, beckoning me in. Day two and I'm looking for drink again. This is what the pre-release counselling warned about. Posters in the TV shop window tell me *All Stock Must GO, Closing Down SALE*. I'll get a couple of things sorted and then run, jump into a weekend of debauchery.

A bell tinkles as I open the door. No one visible inside but sounds come through from the back of things being moved around.

The shop product displays are lacklustre. Although everything looks modern enough, I have the feeling they're all last year's models. Nothing is shiny.

'With you in a minute,' a reedy voice calls.

TVs, DVD players, radios, laptop computers and lots of other gadgets I don't recognise. What do I need here? There's a TV bigger than the one in the prison common room.

'This. I need this one,' I say to the old man who emerges from the rear of the shop.

'It's been a very popular model,' he says. 'Seven-fifty list price.'

'I'll take it.'

'The last one I have, display model. Yours for six hundred.'

'I'll still take it.'

'You can have the unit it's sitting on too. No use to me anymore.'

'Okay, thanks.'

'Full HD. One hundred Hertz. You'll need an HDMI cable, I'll throw one in. What's your signal?' The old man sure knows his stuff. I don't.

'Um, TV?'

'DVD, home theatre, cable or satellite? UPC or Sky?'

'Thanks, no. Just the TV.'

His eyes narrow.

'Been away for a while?'

'You could say, yeah. Out of town, like.'

'Right. I'll have the lad drop it round and set everything up. He'll be able to advise you how to get the best out of it.' He gives me a big grin full of grey and yellow teeth.

'Great. Thanks.'

That mega-TV will probably block the sun in Maudlin Street. And it's not even what I came for. I rub my chin.

'Anything else you're looking for?' he asks, unpeeling a red sold sticker from a roll and placing it on the TV.

'A computer.'

My favourite salesman sweeps his hand around the walls of the shop, lined with shelves of the things. The choice is bewildering. I feel my brain beginning to thump with the pulse of a hangover.

'What do you plan to use it for?'

Looking at porn, tracking down my ex-wife and kid, trying to catch up with what's happened in the world while I've been rotting away in Portlaoise.

'The usual. Just normal stuff.'

He gives a chuckle.

'We get a few bachelor farmers coming in, looking for internet dating.'

'Yeah, that sort of thing.'

In a few minutes we have a pile of boxes containing everything I need, including broadband, whatever that is, and a mobile phone.

'Do you have something to do for a couple of hours? I'll get all this set up for you.'

My thirst is growing and I don't want to come back to the shop pissed.

'I'll come by Monday, if that's okay.'

'You're staying at Slaney's, I believe.'

The guy had me made as soon as I stepped through the doorway.

'That's right.'

'I'll drop this lot over to Rita when it's ready. Okay for you?'

'Yeah. Thanks.'

My debit card gets a good pasting for the second time today. This spending money business is easy.

~

33

Maudlin Street is just down from the TV shop and left before Langton's.

It's a curious quarter, the narrow old street snaking between Maudlin Tower, St John's graveyard and rows of tiny shoemakers' cottages; from a time when people were smaller and made their own little shoes.

The wooden front door of number 32 is painted a solid black and the whole front of the house is duck egg blue. A single window downstairs with a thick net curtain across, the glass so dirty I can't see in. Upstairs the window is wider with a low roofline. I don't like the idea of passersby walking right outside my sitting room window; maybe I'll use the back room for living.

That granite tower is a curious thing, intact but it looks like a remnant of something bigger. I try the tower door but it's locked. A small sign gives me a potted history. I've managed to buy a house in a street that was home to the local leper hospital. Sounds about right.

All this sightseeing is thirsty work.

Maudlin Street takes me back to the thoroughfare of John Street. The back of Langton's is busy with noisy young people in groups, down for the weekend. That's not the sort of establishment I'm looking for. What I want is a bar where I can sink a pint or several without the likes of them making me feel inadequate.

I cross the street and wander back towards Slaney's.

'Well,' a guy says to me, walking out of a doorway, a cigarette hanging from his lip. He looks familiar. Or rather, his look is familiar. The prison look.

'Well,' I say and look at the sign over the doorway. It's the fabled Edge of the World, a bar I've never been in before but heard plenty about. From the street it looks decidedly dodgy. Just what I need.

The doorway leads into a tiled corridor, seems more like a place for a haircut than a pint. I'm up for it either way.

Inside disappoints. I was expecting a hard man's bar, something out of Port Glasgow where I was dragged up, but the place is comfortable looking. There's even a bit of a beer garden out the back.

'Smithwick's, love,' I say to the girl behind the pumps. To her credit she doesn't ask glass or pint. She can see the thirst on me.

'Tayto?' I add when she places the pint on the mat.

She shakes her head.

'All out. Had a run on them, we did. Nuts?'

I take the nuts and wash them down with the Smithwick's. One or two other men come and go, ordering drinks further down the bar, too far away for me to have to interact.

'Another?' She's back and taking care of me.

My cardigan comes off and onto the back of the chair. Settling in.

'You're staying up at Rita's?' the bar girl asks.

I frown but nod at her.

'Small town,' she says and leans across to me. Up close she's not as young as I thought. 'Just a word of advice, Ger. You wanna be careful.'

'Thanks.' I don't know if she's warning me about Rita, someone else or life in general.

She walks to the other end of the bar, picks up a newspaper and brings it to me. It's open on page seven and her finger points out an item before she moves away.

Notorious Drug Smuggler Released on Remission.

The piece goes on to say Gerard Mayes served his time as a model prisoner and is believed to have bought a house in Kilkenny city. There's a colour picture of a slimmer yours truly being led down the steps of the central criminal court by two meaty guards, nine years ago. Gotta be that reporter, Roisín McGuire. It doesn't mention her name but she's the only one I told about Kilkenny.

Sure, what does it matter? I'm hardly going incognito.

'Well, how are ye?' It's the wiry smoker from outside the front door.

He offers me his hand. The skin is brown like an old shoe, from tobacco or sun.

I shake, because not to shake is to offend and I'm going to be living here.

'John-Jo's the name. So you're Ger Mayes.'

'I am.'

'Well, fair play to ye.' His smile is truly horrible, but nothing a Hungarian dentist with a sledgehammer and a pair of pliers couldn't fix.

Difficult to tell if he's the local low-life or a man in the know. After all, my name and picture is there on the bar in front of us. I'm sure he's an old lag. Not a sex offender. I'd say burglar.

'Heineken?' I ask him.

'Too right. Don't know how you drink that stuff,' he says, disrespecting my Smithwick's.

The bar girl already has a pint glass in her hand at the Heineken pump and starts to fill it at my signal. She pours another Smithwick's and brings them to us.

'Good man yerself,' John-Jo says, raising his pint to mine.

He takes a huge mouthful of beer as if he's eating it and his hand holding the glass trembles.

'I remember ye, when ye first came in.'

'Not an impressive feat of memory. It was less than an hour ago.'

'Not here, yer eejit, up in Portlaoise. Ye were green as grass, a lamb to the slaughter.'

'Thanks. I remember being naïve. Sorry, I don't remember you.'

John-Jo shrugs. 'I'm hardly Mr Big. Make it me business to fade into the background, so to speak. But I watch people. Inside the Port I watched you and you turned out good. A survivor.'

He's after another pint. I raise my hand to the bar girl but he pushes it down.

'I'm not after free beer. I'm not after all that money you have. But there's folks that will be, is all I'm saying.'

Two more pints arrive and the girl smiles at John-Jo.

'See, Ger, there's trust here. In this pub, this community. Only there's some aren't a part of the community.'

'We look after our own, like?' I say.

He winks but then his look turns dark and he picks up his pint, walking away.

I don't know if I've just failed the test or what. I look down into my glass and get a strange odour. The beer must be bad, but I didn't notice before. It smells sour, like fear.

A hand claps me on the shoulder, tattooed knuckles. Oh fuck. The smell. It's the Gimp's halitosis.

'Mayes. Fucking hell, you ol' bastard.' Raymond McGivney slides onto the stool John-Jo has just vacated. His breath could fell a moose at twenty paces but I try not to show it.

Me and McGivney have history. McGivney the Gimp. He's the ugliest man I've ever met and the fella voted most likely to murder Ger Mayes when we were both inside. I'm not exactly innocent in the relationship. One of my few hobbies was to subtly torment him on a daily basis. It mostly went over his head until some smart arse decided to translate my sarcasm for him and then he wrecked my arm. Pulled right out of the socket and broken in two places. It would have been a lot worse if Officer O'Mahoney hadn't stepped in. So my life outside prison is going to be short.

'Double whiskey,' I call to the bar girl. May as well numb myself.

'Make that two, Mary,' the Gimp shouts loud enough for everyone in the neighbourhood to hear. 'My good friend Ger is treating his old pal.'

Mary, now I know her name, looks worried but I squeeze out a brave smile.

'You're one lucky man,' the Gimp says and throws the whiskey down his throat.

'How so?'

He waves his empty glass at Mary.

'A little bird told me you've got a stash. A fairly big stash.'

Crap. How can he know about the money?

'And a house, just over yonder. Pretty little place, like.'

I shake my head. What the hell?

'See, I have a proposition for you, Ger. A business proposition.'

McDonald. It has to be McDonald. He has all the scumbag clients.

'Does this proposition involve my brains or your good looks?'

The Gimp twitches on his stool and I'm bracing for a thump but he just exhales his paint stripper breath. I think my eyebrows have burnt off.

'You always cracked me up, yer bastard. I hated yer smart mouth, but always had a laugh when I was back in me cell. Remember when you said I had arms like a chimpanzee and you bet my hands reached my knees?'

I nod and smile, but I don't remember.

He stands up and lets his arms dangle. The original missing link. Gotta laugh at that. He gives me a playful swipe on the back of the head from an improbable distance.

'You could've been a contender,' I say.

'Nah! I was always a big slow lump. You're handy enough yerself. Seen ye sparring in the gym.'

The Gimp is my new best friend.

Pints and shorts. Shorts and pints. He starts to share the big idea.

'See, Ger, a man's needs are infinite. An auld fella of seventy can still get it up.'

'Uh-huh?'

I look at the Gimp blankly. Is he going to make this new friendship physical?

'You know yerself, just out of prison, a man has to do what he has to do.'

I nod. Rita's obstinate chin hair springs to mind. I'm going to pluck her later.

'Well, you're up at Mrs Slaney's, that's common knowledge. But when that's done and dusted, what're ye gonna do? Who are ye gonna do?'

I bite my top lip with my bottom teeth.

'I dunno.'

'C'mon, man, Rita rides every half decent lag who steps through her door, especially since her old man went away. But, when she's done with ye, do ye think some young one is gonna give ye a go? C'mon, get real.'

'Maybe I'm not looking for a relationship.'

'Fuck relationships.'

Two truer words never spoken. The Gimp is a philosopher.

'The most beautiful women ye can think of are waiting, just around the corner. Seriously, Ger. Just around the corner.'

'What're you saying? Are you a pimp?'

He laughs hard. His halitosis is almost masked by the whiskey.

'There's no pimps anymore. It's all internet these days. You wouldn't believe it.'

I'm no slouch when it comes to computers and internet. After all, I spent most of my pre-convict civil servant days surfing or cruising or whatever it's called these days. But we weren't exactly allowed to go looking for web tarts in Portlaoise.

'Porno sites? They're all a rip-off, aren't they? Or full of viruses?'

'No, no, no.' He shakes his head like I'm a beginner. 'Irish escorts and stuff like that. They advertise themselves online, you choose and you collect. Or some even deliver.'

'Not in Kilkenny, for sure. You're joking me. I'm no prude but it wouldn't be allowed, not in Holy Catholic Ireland. You always were a spoofer, McGivney. Things can't have changed that much since I went away.'

The Gimp laughs and waves to the bar girl for another round.

'Take a look on the internet if you don't believe me. It's one big knocking shop. Here, Waterford, Wexford, all over.'

He's so excited he's forgotten it's my round and paid the girl.

We sup our pints, the Gimp grinning and laughing to himself. My head's beginning to get a bit thick with it all.

'Smoke?' he says.

I'm not a regular smoker but I know what's needed for camaraderie.

We stand out on the street like veterans. Young ones wobble by in their high-heeled finery, oblivious to our existence. Lads eye us warily and pass by with a wide berth.

The hen party from Langton's puts in an appearance.

'Hi,' I say to the sisters, racking my brain for their names. Sue and Den, that's it.

'If it isn't Doctor Fucking Phil,' says Sue. She's well on the way again already.

Denise, the ever sober ninja, gives me a once over and pulls a face.

'Er, plastic surgeon? You looked better last night, whatever yer name is.' She grins over her shoulder at me as the party moves on down the street.

'What the fuck was all that about?' the Gimp asks.

I shrug, toss the stub of my cigarette in the gutter and turn back towards the Edge of the World.

Our stools are still unoccupied, my Dunnes Store's cardigan draped over one of them. Reserved for Grandad.

Although I know it's got to be a bad idea, I can't help my curiosity about the Gimp's tart obsession and have to return to it.

'Okay, okay. So kerb crawling has gone cyber. What's that got to do with a business proposition?'

'Obvious. You've just bought a house, smack in the middle of town. Perfect location, people coming and going all the time. Get some of these girls in. They move around every week or two. Put your place on their list and you'll be raking it in.'

'That's it? Your big idea is to use my cottage as a brothel?'

He grins from ear to ear.

'I have contacts, Ger. Made it my business to know all these girls.'

I'll bet he has.

'Some of them will come over to us. Defectors, like. Get another couple of flats or houses with that money of yours, cram in the girls and we'll be laughing.'

'And what about the people these women are working for right now?'

'Yeah, I'll take care of that side of things. You just provide the premises. Easy money, Ger. Easy money.'

We swap convict stories about beatings and failed attempts to smuggle contraband into prison. People come and go around us, all of them giving the Gimp a nod or a word of acknowledgement. I make trips to the toilet with increasing frequency as the pints work through my system, leaning with one hand against the tiled wall by the urinal.

Mary brings out platters of deep fried snacks, sausages and chicken wings, and distributes them amongst the clientele. It's the closest thing to a meal I've had all day. The clock behind the bar twirls its way through the hours.

'There's a few screws on the streets here,' he says. 'Ye'll recognise them, don't let it be a shock to ye. And don't go for them. The guards will have your number, being new out and all.'

I take in what he's saying like a partner in crime. In truth there's not a prison officer I'd have a problem with, but I'd prefer to put it all behind me. And with that in mind, I really don't want the Gimp as my business partner.

The business proposition gets a breather when John-Jo reappears at the Gimp's side and has a few urgent words in his ear.

'Feck off, John-Jo. Feck off.'

'No, seriously, man. Have it on good authority.'

John-Jo looks up at me but I can't read the expression on his face. He walks away without ordering a drink.

'Right, Ger. Time to strike while the iron is hot. Our competition is just after being raided by the guards. They're out of business for a while and their ladies will be looking for new digs. Let's go take a look at this house of yours.'

The Gimp takes me by the arm and we're heading out the door before I can object.

'My top. Has my keys in it.'

A bit unsteady on my feet back down the corridor to the bar, I try to pull the door open and remember it pushes. Mary is waiting behind the bar, holding my cardigan up in one hand.

'Take it easy, Ger,' she says.

I reach to take the thing and my hand closes around hers.

'Watch McGivney, he's a real head case.' She looks into my eyes. I could get lost in hers.

I fight the urge to stay in the bar and have a crack at Mary. Her figure looks tidy and I know she likes me, but I also know it's the drink thinking.

'See ya, Mary. Thanks.'

I find the Gimp puffing away on a cigarette outside the door, in conversation with a couple of meat-head security men in black jackets. They walk away when they see me coming.

'Maudlin Street, right?' he says.

'Right.'

'Used to be a fucking leper hospital.'

'Yeah, I know.'

'Wouldn't put me off, though.' He gives a rattling laugh that turns into a smoker's cough.

Two youths in hoodies walk a bit too close to us.

'What're ye at, lads?' the Gimp says, but they don't reply.

By the time we stagger up to the cottage we've an arm across each other's shoulders. It's easier to stand that way, although once or twice we've lumbered into the stone walls of houses that butt right up to the narrow pavement.

'This'll be nice, Ger. Very nice. I can see meself living here.'

'What?'

'I'll be needing somewhere to stay and all. The contract is up on my place. Well, I'm being thrown out, due to a few *incidents*. Just you and me, Ger, and a couple of tarts. What d'ye say? Then you buy a couple of flats, we fill 'em with girls and we're away.'

'No fucking way!'

Living off the immoral earnings of a hard-working harem, no problem. Sharing my house with the malodorous Gimp, big problem.

'Aw, c'mon, Ger. Don't look a gift horse in the mouth.'

He's leaning on me, breathing right in my face. I'm going to have to puke.

I shake him off and walk up the street, turning into St John's graveyard where I decorate an old grave with vomit.

'Ye dirty old bastard,' he laughs, collapsing against the side of a crypt.

I wipe my mouth with the back of my hand.

'Listen, you've no choice in the matter. I've been told to set up the knocking shop and you're paying. End of story.'

No dinner. I should have eaten something. Feel a bit better now, though.

'Feck off, McGivney. No way I'm moving in with you. Just forget about it. That money's mine, and the house, Gimp.'

'Who are ye calling a gimp!' he shouts and he's at me.

It's a drunken tussle. He tries to grab me but only manages to rake his fingernails across my face. The Gimp isn't a man to tangle with. His other hand grabs my hair and I feel a tearing as I wrench myself free. He swipes at my head and knuckles drag across my face.

'Come back, ye bollox,' he roars.

The ground is uneven and I trip over a broken stone, but regain my footing and break into a run through the graveyard towards Dublin Road. The Gimp lumbers after but he has no chance of catching up.

'I'll be seeing ye, Mayes. I know where to find ye. Tell Rita I said hello.'

At the top gate I turn and look down at my would-be housemate and business partner. A Dickensian escaped convict in the moonlight.

Behind him, at the Maudlin street gate to the graveyard, two hooded youths stand like latter-day lepers. Let the Gimp take out his frustrations on them.

Day 3 – A day of rest

St John's church bells crash through my sleeping mind, the hurt tangible. It feels like I've slept on my hair the wrong way. I put a hand to my head and the scalp is rough and sore. Dried blood.

'You look like shit,' Rita says.

'I look how I feel, then.'

'Who did this to ye?' Through my squinted, bleary eyes I see concern on her face.

'McGivney. He says hello.'

I don't know why I said it. A sense of obligation or something.

Rita sits up and slaps me across the face. What the fuck is all that about? Before I can ask she's gone.

It was quite a smack she gave me. I feel my cheek and then remember the Gimp clobbering me there as I wrestled with him in the graveyard.

~

Downstairs at breakfast I get the silent treatment from Mrs Slaney. The plateful of food is thrown together, pudding and sausages stuck to an egg with yolk like a pebble. Toast burnt, tea like tar.

'That was lovely,' the love-struck young couple say when Rita collects their plates.

It must take some skill to cook two totally different standards of the same meal. I force it all down to spite her.

The couple leave. I can hear clattering and banging somewhere out the back where the kitchen must be. Eventually Rita emerges and picks up my empty plate.

'So, you were drinking with Raymond McGivney last night.'

I have a sudden fear I've married this woman during a drunken binge and can't remember it.

'I was.'

'And?'

'Well, he knew I was staying here, and the rest.'

She puts the plate back down on the table.

'The rest.'

'He implied you were in the habit of giving comfort to newly released criminals.'

I'm ready to duck another slap but her hand goes to her mouth. I look her in the eye and realise she's been crying.

'McGivney is a lying bastard,' she says

'Yeah, I know that.'

'He stayed here when he came out last time.'

I don't like the thought that I've followed in the Gimp's tracks.

'He raped me. That big ugly bastard raped me.'

My hands go through what's left of my hair. Then I stand up and take the woman in my arms. She folds into me and sobs for a moment, then steps away.

'I don't want your pity, Ger.'

Oh Christ! Think, think what to do.

'I just want that fucker dead.' She picks up my dirty plate and throws it to the floor. It bounces off the carpet and shatters on the metal edge of the lino around the bar. 'Two years ago, it happened. Every time I see him around town with that leer on his face. Fucking rapist scumbag!'

'I'll fix him, Rita. Just leave it to me.'

Protectiveness is a strong male instinct, even if it makes little sense.

'No, Ger. It's my problem and I'll handle it my way. I've managed so far. Don't you go getting into any trouble over him.'

She picks up my cutlery, cup and saucer from the table, then fetches a dustpan and brush for the broken plate.

'Old Mr Delaney was here yesterday. There's a package in your room. You probably didn't see it, what with your hangover and all.'

She's back to business as usual.

'Thanks.' I put a hand on her arm. 'Rita?'

'I'm fine, Ger. I'm fine.'

~

Delaney has delivered me the key to the wondrous world of the internet. Fifteen minutes and I have my new hardware connected up on the rickety desk by the window. A bit of frigging around with passwords and stuff, but the old man has kindly written everything down in his spidery scrawl on a lined sheet of paper.

Username: Houdini

Password: Templemore

I have to give it to Delaney, he has a sense of humour. The Romanians' theft of Ireland's entire national store of hard drugs from An Garda Síochána's police training centre in Templemore was pretty much my fault. I didn't manage a Houdini-style escape from the situation, however.

After just half an hour or so of shouting and swearing the broadband is working and I'm online. Now to find a woman. Not just any woman.

Josephine Mayes, Jo to her friends. The mother of my child.

Things haven't changed so much from the days when I used to arse around all day on the computer at the Railway Procurement Agency in Dublin. I know Jo uses facebook.

If only it was so easy. Nine years away from the online world and none of my stuff is working. Either I have passwords wrong, my user name is incorrect or my accounts have been deleted. Ger Mayes has to be reinvented online. One hour later and I'm still struggling. The head is thumping and I'm looking at two options – lying down on the bed for an hour or hair of the dog.

The pint goes down well. Rita is nowhere around and some young lad named Tim is behind the bar. My blood alcohol level starts to recover its equilibrium and I feel ready to get back to work. Then I realise I can have my cake and eat it.

'Tim, another one in there. I'll be back in a minute.'

He gives me the nod and I go get my laptop from the bedroom. On the way back downstairs I see Rita stick her head out of her bedroom door but she retreats back in again.

'You'll not get any reception with that thing in here, you know,' Tim says when I pick up my pint from the bar. 'Them dongle things are useless, very patchy coverage here, but we have Wi-Fi. Network name Slaney, password Rita. Anyone can get in there with that.'

'Right,' I say, not really understanding and wondering if it's a slur on Rita.

The booth in the corner looks private enough. I can sit with my back to the wall and my laptop on the table. Right enough, my internet connection has flaked out. A bit of jiggery pokery, another pint and a reminder of the details from Tim, and I'm back online. There are a couple of people coming up on Google for Josephine Mayes but facebook tells me I have to become a member to see their pages.

Not one to miss the chance of anonymity I choose the name Peter Piper, of picked a peck of pickled pepper fame. The rigmarole involves providing my mobile phone number to get some code or other. Mobile phone upstairs and still in the box. I fetch it and find it needs to charge for eight hours before use. Finding my ex will have to wait until tomorrow.

So, with three pints in me, and the internet at my disposal, I'm looking at naked women before I even know it.

'See anything that takes your fancy?'

I slam the lid of the laptop closed and the few people in the pub look over. Rita leans on my table. Her face is sad and I can smell strong spirits on her breath.

I reach a hand to her arm and run my fingers across her skin.

'I do.'

She sits down opposite me, a glass of vodka in her hand.

'You're not a bad man, Ger. I'm sorry for this morning. It's not your fault.'

'It's me who should be sorry. But I had no idea, honest.'

The vodka is downed and a hand waved at Tim.

'It's time I stood up to McGivney,' she says. 'But I'm gonna need some support.'

Half an hour later and I'm lurching Rita's old Merc out of Slaney's car park. I'm not sure if my licence is somehow forfeit for Offences Against the State, but it should be, the way I'm driving. Better me on four or whatever pints than Rita in the state she's in.

'Lintown,' she says. 'On up past Nowlan Park. I have the address on a piece of paper here somewhere.'

We nudge around Lintown estate, trying to find McGivney's apartment. Sunday afternoon and the place is busy with parked cars, everyone having their lunch. The houses are okay but the duplexes have a downbeat feel, mostly rented to non-nationals.

McGivney's digs are up a flight of concrete steps on the side of a house. Loud, thumping music is coming from the flat below, which makes me think he isn't home. I can't imagine he'd tolerate the noise and it's a rare man who would defy the Gimp.

I turn off the Merc's engine.

'You go see if the bastard is in there,' Rita says.

'And if he is?'

I don't know what we're doing here. It made sense in the pub when she was upset but I don't see myself holding a counselling session for the pair of them.

'Just go, will you, Ger?'

The steps are grubby and strewn with bits of rubbish. It looks like the Gimp has spilled his guts on the doorstep. I look for the doorbell but it's just a shattered wreck and, by the look of it, the door itself has been kicked in on a previous occasion.

Knocking on the small glass pane in the middle of the door doesn't get an answer.

'Don't think he's in,' I shout down to Rita.

'Keep knocking,' she calls back.

A good hard thump on the wood of the door and it swings inwards a few inches. I take the doorknob in my hand; there's all muck on it. The door sticks in the frame as I push it wider.

It opens straight onto a sitting room with a beige carpet. The Gimp has left a brown trail of size twelve footprints across it.

'McGivney?' I call out. 'It's Ger. Ger Mayes.'

I'm expecting an earful of abuse or worse but still no response.

The small kitchenette is neat and tidy except for a few dishes lying broken on the tiled floor. Smears on the stainless steel sink look like blood.

'Raymond? Are you okay?'

More blood on the laminate wood floor leading to the bedrooms and bathroom. Brown hand stains on the painted walls. I slip in the blood and land on one knee, my hand flat in a puddle of red.

He's in the bathroom.

I've seen things before, in Portlaoise prison. Men cut by homemade knives fashioned from a sharp sliver embedded in a toothbrush. The Gimp looks far worse. He's sat on the tiled bathroom floor, slumped against the side of the bath, hands trying to hold his insides together.

I nudge his shoe with the toe of mine. No reaction. I poke his shoulder with my knuckles. Stiff and unyielding. His eyes gaze dully across the floor.

On my knees, in a pool of Raymond McGivney's life blood, I throw up my pints into the toilet. It's a combination of finding him like this and the thought of what a fucking mess I've walked into.

'Ger? What's going on? Where are you?' Rita's voice comes from the hallway.

'Don't come in here!' I shout in a voice made gruff by vomit.

Of course she does, and screams.

'He's dead, Rita. Must have happened last night.'

She collapses against the door frame, sobbing.

'Don't come in the room. Let's keep you out of this.'

Her reaction has sobered me up. I take her out to the kitchen where I wash my hands and face with cold water in the kitchen sink.

'Let's get out of here, Ger. You can't afford to be mixed up in this. Oh my God! Oh my God!'

I take her by the shoulders.

'My fingerprints are all over this place now, in blood. An Gardai Síochána would recognise my fingerprints at fifty paces. I have to call them. But you should go. You don't have to be part of this mess.'

There must be a phone around here somewhere. Mine is back in my room above the pub.

'You're right. Here.' Rita hands me her mobile.

I press 999 but hold my thumb above the call button, staring at the phone as if it's going to speak and give me advice. There's nothing else for it. I press call and ask for the Gardai.

'An Garda Síochána, Kilkenny.'

'Can I speak to Andy McAuliffe, please?'

I don't know if he's alive or dead. Maybe he's retired? I don't know why I'm asking for my nemesis, the man who sent me to prison for nine years. Yes I do. McAuliffe can be trusted to get to the truth.

'Who's calling?'

'It's Ger Mayes.'

'Hold please, Mr Mayes. Detective Inspector McAuliffe won't keep you long.'

No promotion for McAuliffe in nine years. I'm not surprised, I fairly ruined his career. And sad bastard he is, working Sundays.

'Andy McAuliffe.' My man is on the line within seconds, like he's been expecting me.

'Andy, it's Ger. Ger Mayes. Someone's after murdering the Gimp.'

Day 4 – Smile for the camera

'It's never happened to me before.'

Rita lifts the unwilling lad with a finger and lets him fall. He's vaguely interested, but not enough to serve the purpose.

'Should I take it personally?' she says.

'No, no. It's just blood. All I see when I close my eyes is blood.' I daren't mention the Gimp's name in bed with her. Just because he's dead doesn't mean her hurt is healed.

'Stress. Stress at seeing the mutilated, dead body of a rapist bastard. That's probably the problem,' she says.

I know she's right. I do fancy her; even her chin hair is growing on me. Hopefully the Gimp hasn't left me with a permanent legacy of limpness.

It's mid-afternoon on Monday. Rita and I spent the whole of Sunday evening and this morning being interrogated in Kilkenny Garda station. They have a nice new extension to the original 1940s brick building, much smarter than where I was grilled during my drug smuggling days. But the coffee is still crap

~

McAuliffe didn't waste much time getting out to the house in Lintown. We were sat together on the sofa when he arrived, the front door still wide open. I could smell the cigarettes on him.

'Where's McGivney?' he asked, without preamble. Not a mention of me dying for three minutes on the floor of the interview room last time we met.

'Bathroom,' I said, pointing to the short hallway off the kitchenette.

'Okay. Don't go anywhere. I have men on the door.'

I turned and saw a guard standing in the entrance doorway. A big meaty fella with an expression that said he wanted to punch my head off, just needed half an excuse.

McAuliffe's muffled voice came from the bedroom, phoning the cavalry to come photograph, swab, clean up with a mop and bucket or whatever the hell they do.

'Ger!' he called to me.

I stood up and McAuliffe came back out through the hallway.

'Your hand and footprints?' he asked, pointing at the floors and wall.

'Yep.'

'And are some of them yours, Rita?' he said more softly.

She just nodded. Jesus, I thought, is there anyone in town she hasn't shagged?

'He's dead, in there,' McAuliffe said.

'No kidding,' I said.

'I'm talking to my colleague, you idiot.'

The guard at the door turned to someone outside and there was a crackle from a mobile radio. McAuliffe walked to the door and had a cigarette out on the steps. Then he came back in with the guard who towered over him.

'Gerard Mayes and Rita Slaney, I'm arresting you both on suspicion of the murder of Raymond McGivney. You are not obliged to say anything unless you wish to do so, but whatever you say will be taken down in writing and may be given in evidence.'

The Gimp would have pissed himself laughing.

By this time a good crowd had gathered out in the street and we had an audience for our hand-cuffed exit.

'At least the press aren't here,' I said to Rita.

A female guard helped her into a marked car with flashing blue lights.

'Give them time,' McAuliffe said. 'It'll not be long before they smell blood.'

Mine or McGivney's, I wondered.

'Just like old times, Ger,' McAuliffe said as we bounced around the old city streets and over Green's bridge.

Sunday afternoon drivers pulled over, if they could, when we hit the siren at every stoppage. It was all show. An Gardai Síochána had Ger Mayes back in custody and wanted everyone to know it.

'You can take them off now, Eamonn,' McAuliffe said to the big guard and he removed Rita's handcuffs, not mine.

I recognised Eamonn from previous encounters, despite the uniform. He and another plain clothes detective once arrested me on a train. At the time I thought they were Mormons.

Eamonn took me by the handcuffs and frog-marched me in through the back door of the station, behind Rita.

We were checked in at the desk.

'Don't worry, Rita,' I called out as she was led away to her own interview room. 'Just tell it like it is.'

Eamonn wrenched back on my cuffs and nearly took me off my feet.

'In here, Mayes.' He turned me in the opposite direction.

I had to sit on the edge of the plywood chair until McAuliffe unlocked my cuffs.

'Tea?' he asked.

'Sure. Thanks.'

'Do you want legal representation?'

'No. Just tea will be fine.'

'Still the fucking smart-arse.'

'Apparently.'

It felt very different to a decade ago. This time I was older, wiser and, most importantly, innocent.

'I know you did this one, Ger.'

I slurped my tea and said nothing.

'McGivney was a bastard, nasty piece of work. A lot of people wouldn't blame you. Rita, for example, would be very grateful.' McAuliffe looked at me over the rim of his tea mug.

'Why Rita?'

'Ger, it's a well known secret, what McGivney did to Rita. He boasted about it all over town. I tried to get her to press charges. McGivney off the streets would have been a plus, but she wouldn't.'

'She should have,' I said. 'But McGivney would probably still be dead all the same.'

'Meaning what?'

'Meaning his murder has nothing to do with Rita.'

He put the tea aside and made a steeple of his fingers.

'Look, Ger, we know where you've been since you arrived in Kilkenny.'

'Following me? Then you'll know I was drinking with him.'

'And more. You left the Edge of the World together. Had a disagreement, probably about all that money you have. He bashed you up a bit and you stabbed him.'

I rubbed the stubble on my chin.

'Do you think I'm stupid?' I said.

'Hanging around, heavy drinking with the likes of McGivney is pretty stupid, Ger. And you were stupid with drink, that much I know. Look at the state of you.'

I squinted at McAuliffe and it hurt my face.

'McGivney gave me a few slaps, right enough.'

'I'd say we'll find traces of you on him. What did you do with the murder weapon?'

'What murder weapon? I mean, of course there must be a murder weapon, but I didn't do it.'

McAuliffe stood up and left the room. He came back almost immediately with another guard in plain clothes, a broad shouldered fella with a deadpan look.

'This is Detective Sergeant Cian Purcell,' McAuliffe said. 'You've waived your right to legal representation and we'll now conduct the interview.'

Purcell pressed the button on a smart new recorder and we went through the formalities, recounting our informal chat.

'So, where's the lovely Detective Sergeant Faloone?' I asked.

'Detective Superintendant, these days,' McAuliffe said. His tone wasn't envious, it just said I'd fucked his career a decade ago, but not hers.

'Look, Andy. You know somebody's trying to fit me up here. Just out of prison, I walk into a bar, pick a fight with a known head-case and stab him to death in his flat?'

'So you're admitting to the stabbing,' Purcell said.

McAuliffe couldn't help raising his eyes to heaven.

'Come on,' I said. 'If I did it then why would I go back there the next day and call you guys?'

'I don't know,' McAuliffe said. 'A lot of things you do make little sense, Ger.'

Purcell laughed, eerie with his lack of facial expression. McAuliffe frowned at him, eyeing the recorder.

'You'll find he died while I wasn't there.'

'Where were you, then,' Purcell asked.

'With Rita Slaney.'

'Hardly an alibi, under the circumstances.'

McAuliffe looked like he needed a cigarette.

I leaned back in my chair. He'd hardly changed, a bit more haggard, still a good head of straggly hair. His green brown suit might even have been the same one from back in the day. Unless he had a wardrobe full of the things.

'Why did you go to Raymond McGivney's flat?' Purcell asked.

'Because Rita wanted to take him to task.'

'Meaning what, exactly?' McAuliffe said.

I spelt it out slowly for them.

'McGivney gave me a message for her. I passed it on. She got upset, then she got drunk. She wanted to confront him with it and get it all over with.'

'With what?' Purcell asked.

'The rape. The bloody rape! What d'you think?'

'DS Purcell is new to the station,' McAuliffe explained. 'So, you both went to his flat and had a row?'

'No, the row was the night before, in the graveyard.'

'So the stabbing occurred in the graveyard,' Purcell said.

'No. Yes. I don't know. Maybe.'

'Try and remember, Ger,' McAuliffe coaxed. 'Try and remember what happened.'

I could feel my pulse thumping through the foreign heart in my chest and that wasn't a good thing. I ran my hands over my head and took a deep breath.

'Right. We left the pub and walked up Maudlin Street to look at my new house.'

'What time was that?' Purcell said.

'I don't know. It was dark. Not a lot of people on the streets. No idea, we were drinking all afternoon.'

'Then what?' McAuliffe asked.

'We cut through St John's graveyard. I threw up on a gravestone, I remember that.'

'Charming,' Purcell said and McAuliffe frowned again.

'Then we had an argument about my money. I called him the Gimp, he got mad and we had a bit of rough and tumble.'

'What then, Ger? Tell us exactly what next,' McAuliffe said.

It was a blur. I remembered another fight, another place and time. There was a dead body that time and an iron bar in my hands. Maybe this was divine retribution.

'I don't know, Andy. I don't remember.'

McAuliffe terminated the interview and switched off the recorder.

'You'd better feckin remember, Ger. Otherwise this is looking like more than nine years. And McGivney had some serious friends. They'll be wanting to get even.'

I knew he was wrong there. The Gimp had no friends.

At that point I expected someone to bring in a bloodstained knife with the Gimp's DNA and my fingerprints all over it. Sure enough, there was a knock on the door.

Eamonn walked up to McAuliffe, bent down and whispered in his ear. Purcell leaned in to them.

McAuliffe's face was fixed in a frown by that point.

'You're free to go, without charge, and so is Rita,' he said. 'We're following a different line of enquiry.'

'What? How? Why do you suddenly believe me?'

Things had reached the point where I'd nearly stopped believing myself.

'I'm not the only thing that's new in town,' Purcell said. 'We've CCTV at key points across the city.'

'You're in the clear, Ger. For now. Off you go,' McAuliffe said.

Purcell led me out to reception where Rita was waiting with Garda Sergeant Eamonn.

'The Detective Inspector has asked me to run you home,' Eamonn said, obviously unimpressed.

Rita was silent in the car on the way back. My mind was trying to picture the two hooded youths in Maudlin Street. There had been something odd about them.

The removal

'They wore their trousers strange. Can't quite put my finger on it, but I'd say the Gimp was killed by foreigners.'

'Don't call him the Gimp, Ger. The man is dead.'

This is too weird. My naked, hairy-chinned landlady is telling me to show some respect for her dead rapist. No wonder I'm having an attack of impotence.

'Well, nothing going on here.' She gives my todger one last tug and rolls out of the bed, reaching for her dressing gown.

'Rita.'

'What?'

'I'll be moving out, you know.'

'I know.'

'I get the house keys tomorrow and I've furniture ordered.'

She pauses at the door, her hand on that knob.

'I know, Ger. Don't be a stranger.' And she's gone.

My body aches more in the shower than it did yesterday. Gimp wrestling and ten hours of interrogation. I'm just not up to it anymore. The water soothes my back and legs but my head aches like I've slept in a draught. I rub my scalp, trying to tell if the hurt is on the outside or inside.

This might be the last decent shower I get, not sure what 32 Maudlin Street will have to offer. There's no rush. It's not prison. I can drop the soap with impunity.

After a good while the water begins to lose its heat and the shower tray is filling up, something blocking the drain.

I rub the hole with my foot and it moves a mat of hair, helping a little. I don't like to look too close in case it's all my hair. Better if it's someone else's, I can't spare it.

I have one change of new clothes left from my shopping foray of Friday. It seems like a lifetime ago. The pants have an awkward label in them that will irritate my waist, so I go fish an old prison pair out of my holdall. I'm rummaging around in there when my hand touches something unfamiliar.

Out comes a cardboard Bewley's coffee cup, heavy with contents; a short, stubby knife which now has my fingerprints on it. Blood, doubtlessly Gimp blood, lies dried in the groove of the evil serrated blade. The cup still rattles and I know what else is in there: a five cent coin.

~

I once confessed to murder. Two people heard my confession and they're both dead. I killed a man. Not McGivney the Gimp, but another man, a long time ago.

It's not something I'm proud of; beating a crippled beggar to death with an iron bar. No way to put a positive spin on that. Tom was my buddy and he helped me through it. Renée loved me in spite of it. Now they're both gone and there's no absolution for my crime.

McAuliffe doesn't know the story. Portlaoise Prison's happy campers are oblivious to it. The only people who know are the beggar's gang, the Romanians. Those lads with the funny trousers.

I lie down on the bed with the murder weapon in one hand and my old prison pants in the other. For how long I don't know. Until I'm cold.

'Are you coming down for breakfast or what?' Rita bangs on my door.

'Yeah, I'll be right down.'

Altogether too domestic. She'll have me putting out the rubbish next.

Rita's breakfast has recovered from the previous day's effort.

'Not hungry? After me making a special effort and all.'

She's standing with hands on hips. I shake my head. She slides in next to me on the bench seat.

'It's all over, Ger. McGivney is gone for good and I've you to thank for that. Not that I think you did it, I mean...'

She pushes up against me and the contents of my trouser pocket.

'Ouch! What's that?'

'Just my new phone.'

'Right. You still have one more night here, don't you?'

'I do.'

'Then let's make it one to remember.' She smoothes her palm along the inside of my thigh. 'We'll get your appetite back on track.'

I make a perfunctory attempt at a sausage but still can't face breakfast. Tea is all I can manage.

Rita mingles with a couple of other single breakfasters, both men. She's probably setting up her supply of rides for when I'm gone. I feel the knife through the material of my trousers. This is my priority for the day.

The black and white pudding mock me. The fried egg's single eye is that of the Gimp and the rasher of bacon his ugly mouth, laughing at my predicament. In my pocket the jagged edge threatens to cut its way through the toilet paper wrapping, slit the fabric and slice open my leg to the bone. Is this a gift or a setup?

I have no car. Maybe I could borrow Rita's but, if I did, it could easily be followed. Maybe they're even allowed to put a tracking device on a suspect's car. No, on foot is the best thing. An idea forms in my mind.

The morning air is cool on my face as I step out of Slaney's front door. I look right and left, expecting Eamonn and pals to be waiting for me.

No uniforms on John Street. A hooded youth across the road is looking at the few remaining items in the TV shop window. His trousers look a little odd. I lumber across between the slow moving cars.

'You looking for me?' I say, keeping my eyes on the shop display.

The youth meets my eyes in the window's reflection then turns to face me.

'Are ya fuckin' queer, mister?' he barks in a nasal Dublin accent. 'Do I look like a fuckin' rent boy? Fuck off before I burst ya!'

My hand is in the pocket, around the knife.

'Sorry, my mistake. Thought you were someone else.'

'Yeah? Well fuck off and find yer little bum chum, ya shirt lifting bastard, ya!'

I reckon this blade is sharp enough to break right through and stick him in the stomach before he knows what's happened.

'Jesus! Get yer hand outta yer bleedin' pocket! Pervert.'

The youth looks at my wriggling trousers and turns, trotting off up towards the train station.

'Dirty aul bastard!' he adds for good measure, just in case anyone has missed our little spat.

I look around the street. It's a jumble of old and new signs, ticket machines, lampposts. The Gardai CCTV cameras could be anywhere, or nowhere. If they're watching then I probably only have a few minutes before I'm dragged off for being a general arse, so I'd better get about my business.

A butcher selling pork. Nothing else, just pork. The joints and cuts in the window look fresh. They have a deal on pork fillet and I'm tempted. Then there's a tray of offal and I think of McGivney slumped against the bath, his hands trying to hold himself together.

A few shops down I find a bakery and wander in. One wall is lined with shelves of bread in all shapes and sizes. Any of those would do the job I have in mind. I pick up a small white bloomer and feel the warmth still in it. Warmer than McGivney was.

'One ninety,' a cheery woman behind the counter says. 'Will that be all?'

'Um, two cans of drink from the fridge back there. I'll pick them up on my way out. And, let's see…'

Hunger starts to get a grip on me. The glass covered display is full of cakes and buns but my sweet tooth is long gone.

'Something savoury?' she says, sensing my interest and moving around to the other counter.

Sausage rolls look good. Pies. Fancy little continental things.

'I'll take a pie. Minced beef and onion.'

'Just for yourself? Or a family one?'

I'd love to have a family to share a pie with.

'Medium. That one there.'

The nice lady takes my money and gives me my picnic in a white plastic carrier bag. I feel like a normal person.

Back in my room I hatch the cunning plan. Everything is laid out on the bed. Bread, drinks, pie, and the knife in my hand. The toilet paper goes down the toilet after I've wiped the knife as clean as I can, then I pick up the loaf. It seems a pity to desecrate it with the murder weapon, I'd rather eat the bread. The pie, on the other hand, isn't going to be easy to eat. An impulse purchase driven by hunger, it's not really picnic food.

The sharp point of the knife slides easily around the golden pastry lid of the pie. I lift one end and push the knife inside. It just fits, the point of the knife starting to make itself shown against the foil tray at the far end. Now I've cleverly concealed the murder weapon in a minced beef and onion pie my troubles are nearly over.

Backpack loaded with picnic, laptop and my new phone, I lock my room and head back downstairs. Rita's face appears with a grin from behind her bedroom door and I give her a smile in passing.

MacDonagh Junction train station is busy with pensioners making use of their free train travel. The queue for tickets is long and I join it, surrounded by elderly ladies chirping to each other through their dentures. Another day's prison pay buys me a return ticket to Waterford.

Out on the platform a bunch of young men in sports gear smoke cigarettes and laugh too loud. One of them points at me and the others turn. It's the hooded youth I propositioned outside the TV shop. They start to shuffle over and I swing the backpack off my shoulder, wishing the knife wasn't in that pie.

'The train now arriving on platform three is the 11:43 to Dublin,' a recorded voice says over the public address system.

My would-be assailants turn, pick up their holdalls and clatter over the metal bridge to the other platform, just as the train pulls in. I stop holding my breath and slump onto a metal bench.

A hammering sound draws my attention to the train carriage opposite where I'm sitting. The hooded youth and a couple of pals making wanker signs at me through the window. My knife hand comes out and I give them the middle finger with a slow nod of the head. That's right, lads. Up your hole with a big jam roll. It incenses them and they're jumping around in there like chimps. I'm very brave when I'm safe. I stick out my thumb and draw it across my neck in a cut-throat action, just as the ticket collector calms them and looks out the window at me with a frown.

My timing isn't great. The Waterford train is nearly an hour coming. This platform is a trap, the only way out back through the station building, still thronging with wrinklies. If the authorities want to get me then I'm cornered. I just have to tough it out.

So I play with my new mobile phone. It looks very high-tech and I'm just working my way around it when the thing buzzes in my hand and starts to play the Irish national anthem. Several of the old folk on the platform instinctively stand to attention.

It's a local number I recognise but can't put a name to. My finger hovers over the answer button but I fumble the phone to the ground and the ringing stops.

'You dropped your phone,' a female voice says.

'Thanks,' I say, gathering my phone, battery and cover from the tiny hands of a small boy next to a woman.

'He's the man in the paper, Ma,' the boy says.

'Don't, now,' she says to the child.

The woman reminds me of Renée. Pale, slim, defenceless looking. Pretty in a starved way.

'You don't recognise me, do you, Ger?'

'Sure. It's…'

It can't be. Renée is long dead. If only she weren't.

'Ella. I'm Ella. You haven't changed a bit.'

One of my ex-wife's friends from the wine bar. She always had a soft spot for me.

'Thanks, but I've seen in the mirror. You, on the other hand. You look great! I mean, you always looked good but you're looking great.'

She laughs, a pretty, tinkling laugh. Flattery is always effective.

'Divorce. That's what did it for me. I got back my self-respect and lost a load of weight. That and I don't eat, not really.'

'Well, everyone has to eat. How about I take you to dinner sometime?'

She laughs again. Sure, an ex-con dinner invite. I'm such a catch.

'Listen, it's okay,' I say. 'Just got a bit carried away with seeing you again.'

'No. I'd love to.' She points at my phone. 'If that thing's still working then give me a call. I'm in the phone book.' She starts to walk away.

'Right.' I laugh this time.

'Under Cullen. Ella Cullen. I've gone back to my maiden name.'

That gives me an idea.

'Me too.'

'Back to your maiden name? You're so funny.'

'I mean me too, D.I.V.O.R.C.E.' I mouth.

'Divorce!' the little boy shouts.

'Yeah, I heard Jo remarried some guy up in Dublin. Houlihan. She's Josephine Houlihan now.'

'Everything moves towards its end.' Sounds kind of doom laden. 'I'll give you a call, Ella. Dinner.'

'Do that, Ger. See ya.'

She raises a hand and so does the boy, then they board the train that's just arrived.

I wouldn't mind chatting up Ella all the way to Waterford but decide to quit while I'm ahead, taking a seat in a different carriage.

Josephine Houlihan. Jo Houlihan. Or Mayes. I have my laptop all set up with the mobile broadband and everything within, what, half an hour or so. By which time we arrive at Waterford. Just saw enough to find her facebook page under Jo Houlihan. No address or phone number but about thirty friends that don't include me, of course.

The return passengers are forcing their way onto the train by the time I get all packed up and ready to go. Everyone seems annoyed that I'm there. No sign of Ella and her lad when I finally do make it onto Waterford soil. I had half a plan to tail her and find out what she's at. No harm in a bit of hobby stalking. Best to screen the dinner date beforehand and check she's not some kind of low-life nutcase.

Waterford's Rice Bridge spans the broad Suir so boringly. It's not nice for pedestrians to cross, all steel, concrete and heavy traffic; a real contrast to the quaintness of Kilkenny.

Halfway across I get nervous that there'll be a bridge lift and see myself sliding down the raised half with my picnic. So I take my backpack off quickly, pull out the plastic bag and make a show of taking a bite out of the pie, on one corner so I don't accidentally chew on the blade. Then I pull the pie from its foil tray and throw it into the river. It sinks like a stone. Six fathoms deep.

The tide is turning and the water runs fast. They bring ships up this river, I know it's deep. Some big fish is going to get a surprise when it bites down on that pie.

I'm stood there holding the foil tray, thinking about letting it go, when the phone rings again. Same Kilkenny number as before. I fumble the phone again but this time answer the call unintentionally.

'Hello?' a gruff voice says on the line.

'Hello.'

'Ger?'

'Yeah.'

'Andy McAuliffe here.'

'Hey, Andy.'

I play nonchalant but my pulse is racing. How the hell did he get my number? And does he have me on camera or something?

'I heard you left Kilkenny. Are you coming back?'

'Just a day trip. I'll be back.'

A few seconds of silence.

'Going to see your old friend Duggan?'

He knows I'm in Waterford.

'Duggan's no friend of mine, as you well know.'

A heavy lorry revs its engine behind me and hits its horn at the traffic.

'Well, Ger, don't be leaving the country.'

He hangs up before I can.

My name is

Everywhere seems to have wireless internet these days and The Granville Hotel on Waterford quay is no exception. I'm not the only diner with a laptop on the table. But I'm probably the only one creating a false identity.

Jo's list of facebook friends has some significant omissions. One is Ella Cullen, but she does have a facebook page. Jill Cormac, on the other hand, doesn't seem to be on facebook. She used to be in Jo's book club but emigrated to Australia before I went away. So my adopted online name is Jill Cormac in Brisbane, originally from Bagenalstown. I connect the facebook account to my email and send a friend request to Jo with a little reminiscence of how much *I* enjoyed the book club and wine bar sessions.

'Tea or coffee?' a thick-armed barman asks as he clears away the remains of my lunch.

'No thanks.' I raise my beer glass to show I'm taken care of.

'It's included in the price. Tea or coffee?'

'Tea then.'

Some people won't be told.

I've no idea how long it'll take for Jo to spot and respond to the friend request. I don't know if she works daytime or anything about her life these days.

The unwanted tea arrives with a clink of cup, saucer and spoon.

'Tea for one,' he says and clutters my table, tea spilling a bit too close to my computer.

'It's not bloody waterproof!'

'More's the pity,' he says.

'You forgot the biscuits.'

He nods and ambles off.

I check facebook to see if there's any reply from Jo. It must be nearly five minutes now. No response. I start to fiddle around with my phone and email account to get mobile notifications. Getting up to speed with these things now.

The waiter deposits two handfuls of individually wrapped biscuits on the remaining table space, burying my phone. Stupid bastard. If we were inside Portlaoise I'd hatch a plan of petty retribution.

Ah, those were the days. Playing *Torment the Gimp*, kiss chase with Delaney, run to mummy with O'Mahoney. Every day had a purpose, to be one day closer to release. And now here I am, free, with all the biscuits I can eat.

What was it the Gimp said? Irish escorts. Google search brings up a page of links and I hesitate to click on one. Then I do.

Page blocked by the network. I'm trying to look up tarts on the Granville Wi-Fi. No doubt Waterford vice squad, if there is such a thing, will be down upon me in seconds.

The waiter appears again out of nowhere and I slam the lid of the laptop down in a panic. The smirk on his face tells me he knows what I'm at. My flat smile tells him his tip is the leftover biscuits.

I pack away my gadgets and walk out onto the quay. A small riverboat chugs slowly upstream against the current.

What are the Romanians at? The knife and coin in the coffee cup was a message, not a plant. They took care of the Gimp, that's clear. He would have been a pain in the arse for me, with his cohabitation pimping plans, but gutting the old bastard seems a bit harsh. I could have just moved on somewhere else.

The boat on the river looks tired and makes slow headway, its old engine chanting a strained drone.

My mind turns to Duggan. His offices aren't that far away, if he still has a practice. I should feel angry with him, even after all this time. Duggan caused me a lot of trouble and stress when he was supposed to be helping me. All he did was push me towards a near fatal heart attack. But I don't feel anger. I feel stupid. Stupid for not taking his advice, stupid for not realising he was in with the Romanians.

On the water things are changing. The current stops its downstream flow and begins to swirl as the tide changes. The boat's engine noise deepens and it makes good headway towards the bridge and beyond.

Duggan will know what the Romanians are at. Whether he'll tell me is another matter. I can but ask.

The brass plaque with his name is still on the wall of the decrepit looking three storey townhouse. I push the black door inwards and mount the creaking staircase. On the landing is the same glass paned door marked Duggan Solicitors. It looks more like a seedy private detective's office than the high-powered legal representative of drug smugglers, organised crime gangs and violent murderers. If Duggan is rich from his spoils he hides it well.

'Yes?' a stern middle-aged woman says from behind her desk as I enter the reception. 'Do you have an appointment?'

'Is Jim Duggan in?' I counter.

'Who wants to know?'

'Ger Mayes.' Stick that in your pipe and smoke it, you old bat.

Her eyes widen and she arches her neck, as if she's an alien about to emerge from the frumpy clerk disguise. She gives me the once over then breaks into a smile.

'Please take a seat, Mr Mayes. I'll just let Mr Duggan know you're visiting.'

I've barely parked my backside when the man himself emerges from a door, walks straight up to me and offers his hand. Last time I tangled with Duggan it cost me nine years in prison. I shake his hand.

'Ger Mayes. Well, well.'

He doesn't let go of my hand. His is small and cool, and I suspect there's a secret handshake going on that I can't interpret.

'Come on inside. Brigette, would you organise some refreshments?'

'Certainly, my pleasure.'

We're all such jolly friends. I let him shepherd me into his office.

Duggan waves towards a studded leather captain's chair at the window and takes a seat on the other side of a small round table. His huge desk sits formidable in the corner, covered with paperwork.

Brigitte enters with a tea tray and lays it on the table.

'Thank you, Brigitte.'

The cups and saucers are fine bone china. Duggan pours for both of us.

We take sips of the scalding hot brew then he puts his down on the table.

'Is this a social visit then, Ger?'

I'd forgotten all the things Duggan knows about me. He knows I murdered Alin Petulengro ten years ago behind Heuston Station, although I've never told him about it. He knows the late Tom McMenemy and I bought six kilos of pure cocaine from the Dutchman and had a short-lived attempt to start our own distribution. Very short-lived, as far as poor Tom was concerned. Duggan knows everything because he's in league with the dark side. So no point mincing words with him.

'No, Jim. It's not a social visit. You'll have heard about Raymond McGivney.'

He sucks in his cheeks and nods.

'I had a calling card.'

'Seems like someone did you a favour, Ger.'

'How do you come to that conclusion?'

Duggan looks out the window. I see how lined his face has become. He turns back to me and his hazel eyes are warm, deceptive.

'People in this business have long memories. You played your part and paid the price for your mistakes. It's not for the likes of McGivney to come muscling in on you.'

Christ! Am I under protection by the mob or something?

'And the calling card?'

Duggan takes another drink of tea before answering.

'For avoidance of doubt.'

'And the knife?'

For my own avoidance of doubt.

'To see what you're made of,' he says, his voice tightening. 'What have you done with it?'

'I put the knife in a meat pie and threw it in the river.'

Duggan coughs on the ginger nut biscuit he's eating. I pour more tea for him and he gulps it.

'How was prison, Ger?'

'It was a fucking laugh a minute. I was really popular. Miss all my friends. What do you think?'

When Duggan grins it's a cross between a paedophile and a cannibal who wants to have his cake and eat it.

'McDonald has you all sorted, I understand.'

'Not that it's any of your business.'

'Oh, but it is, Ger. If it wasn't for me you would never have collected the insurance money on Renée Martin. If you remember?'

'I remember.'

How Duggan and the Romanians tried to fit me up for Renée's murder when she had jumped off the bridge herself. How I had to dance to their tune to get off. Result – nine years of shifty showers and the status of national social pariah.

'So now you have your nice little house, a few euro in the bank and you're your own man. Don't fritter it away, it won't last forever. You should get a job.'

'What is it with you lawyers and career advice? And what do you have in mind? Troublesome ex-con eliminator? Murder weapon disposal expert? Internet pimp?'

Duggan's eyes narrow at the last suggestion.

'What would you say your work skills are, Ger?'

'Sewing mailbags and crushing rocks.'

He laughs and I laugh with him.

'I know of a job that's come up and they're asking me for a recommendation. Managerial – salaried. You just boss some lads around to get things done to a schedule.'

'I always knew I was management material.'

'Seriously, it would suit you down to the ground. A distribution company up on one of the industrial estates in Kilkenny. The owner's a client.'

'What's he done, then?'

Duggan bites his lip.

'Don't look a gift horse in the mouth, Ger. Not all my clients are murderers. It's a tight community down here in the south east and we do our bit to help people back onto the straight and narrow.'

I shake my head. Duggan the fucking reformer. On the other hand, no harm in checking it out.

'Okay. I'll take a look at it.'

'Good. I'll text you his details.'

He picks up a phone from the desk and his fingers fly across the screen like a spider on crack. There's a chirp and my trouser pocket vibrates.

'I don't recall telling you my number.'

Duggan gives a chuckle.

'Like I said, it's a tight community.'

~

On the walk back to the train station the skies begin to drizzle. It's like cloud meeting the ground. Maybe I should leave this goddamn country, head for a better climate and anonymity. Should have thought of that before I bought the house in Maudlin Street.

The thought of my new home cheers me up a bit and the tang of moist air grows on me. Timing is good and the train stands waiting at the station, ready for me to just walk on.

Things are on the up. I count them off in my head. Tomorrow I get the house. Jo should be spilling the beans soon to my Jill persona. The dodgy Duggan job offer. Rita's farewell shag and, on that subject, not to forget Ella Cullen's dinner invitation.

But what about that job? Duggan's right. A regular income would preserve my stash. I'm sure it's a thread of the tangled web but if you can't beat them, join them.

'Reaney Transportation and Distribution, how can I help you?' A woman's voice answers my call. First impressions – it sounds legit.

'Is Bob there?' I ask.

'Mr Reaney or Bobby?'

'Mr Reaney.'

I'm getting an image of hillbilly truck drivers.

'Who's calling?'

'Ger Mayes.'

'Putting you straight through.'

I get a ringing tone and then it's answered by the sound of wind blowing.

'Hold on a minute,' a male voice says, followed by the unmistakable sound of golf club against ball.

'You're not getting any better,' another voice says in the background.

'Feck off! Oh, sorry. Not you. Who's that?'

'Ger. Ger Mayes.'

'Well, the famous Ger Mayes. Jim Duggan said you might call.'

Reaney's voice is a bit breathless as he walks.

'I understand you have a job going.'

'I do that. I do indeed. And we think you might be our man.'

I'm in

Find a vacuum and then fill it. The best piece of career advice I ever had.

Reaney Transportation and Distribution has a vacuum. It was caused by Ronnie, the previous manager, who had to *go away* for reasons unspecified. I can't get the full story out of Nora, the office manager. At least, not yet.

'Manage the business,' Reaney had said from the golf course. 'I bring in the business and you manage it. Simple enough. Shipment of goods arrives, we store and distribute. Lads do the heavy work, Nora does the admin, and you make sure it all happens. Fifty grand a year.'

Now, I know a sweet little number when I hear it, but what sort of business would employ somebody like me? It has to be dodgy.

Nora shows me around the place. She's an ice maiden. Tall, blonde and frosty.

'We get lorries in every weekday. At least one, sometimes a handful. Occasionally weekends. That's overtime rates for the lads. We ship out twice a day. Once first thing and once after lunch.'

The back of the warehouse has a big loading area and a high fence topped with savage looking wire.

'Whose is the beamer?' I ask, pointing to a dark green BMW M3 with chrome wheels.

'Oh, that's Bobby's. Young Mr Reaney. He's harmless.'

Boss's son works in the business. Rarely good news.

'What does Bobby do?'

'He picks orders. Nice lad.'

The warehouse is full of high racks of boxes and the air full of whining forklifts. I can smell weed.

'Bobby!' Nora shouts. 'Your dad will kill me if you're smoking in here.'

The forks of a truck come flying around the corner of a row of shelves, at head level. Sat at the wheel is a smiling boy's face on the body of a man. A big man.

'Bobby, this is Ger. He's the new manager.'

'Howatings, Ger?' Bobby says.

'Good. Nice to meet you, Bobby. Lay off the weed when you're driving that thing, okay?' I reply.

'Sure thing, boss.' He reverses away at speed, with a wave of the hand.

I turn to Nora and she smiles.

'You're gonna fit in just fine.'

She leads me through the warehouse to the office.

'We have two other lads do picking. Jamie and Ian. They're both out in the vans doing extra deliveries, happens sometimes.'

The office has windows right across the front of the building, looking out onto a parking area with two cars in it, backed up against the window. They're both the same shade of dark green as Bobby's BMW.

'This here is mirrored glass,' Nora says. 'That Golf is mine. The Audi is yours. It's a bit clapped out because it used to be Bobby's.'

'A car with the job? I've never had a company car before.'

'Just make sure you reverse it into the space, so the front faces the road. Mr Reaney likes things just so.'

'I think I can manage that.'

'I'm on my own in here. And over here,' she shows me into a separate office, 'is yours.'

It looks good enough. It looks great. I remember my crowded cubicle back at the Railway Procurement Agency in Dublin. This is a palace.

'Does Bob, um, Mr Reaney have an office?'

'No. Yours used to be his when I first came here.' Her hand reaches back to her ponytail and brings it to the front, fingers playing absently with the ends of her hair. 'Mr Reaney hardly ever visits the company these days. You'll be in charge.'

Nora's slight smile tells me who is and will remain in charge, and it ain't me.

The leather swivel chair is beige and worn, but comfortable. I lean back in it and put my hands behind my head. It's an odourless office. The previous occupant has been totally purged.

'The computer has access to all stock, accounts and everything. Passwords etcetera are under the keyboard.' She points to the desk phone. 'Dial zero for an outside line.'

I switch the computer on and pick up the phone.

'Yep?' Reaney answers on the first ring, half shouting. Sounds like he's driving on the motorway.

'Bob, it's Ger.'

'Oh yeah, right. Did Nora take care of you?'

'She did. So, all set.'

'Well, if Nora's happy, I'm happy,' Bob says. 'Starting straight away, okay?'

'Right. Wednesday maybe? I have to take over my new house tomorrow.'

'Maudlin Street, I believe. Nice little houses, them. Wednesday it is then. Welcome aboard, Ger.'

'Thanks, Bob. I just wondered…' I just wondered what else I have to do for my fifty grand a year, but he's gone.

Nora comes back in and puts a bunch of keys on the desk.

'The car and the office. I'll show you how the alarm works on Wednesday. We'll do the paperwork then. Bring all your documents. I'll need your PPS number, driving licence and P60. Try not to bash up the car before we get you on the insurance. Five o'clock now and that's more or less it for today, no more deliveries, so I'm locking up.' She stands by the door.

I pick up the keys and walk over to her. We're of a similar height. I look down at her feet and see she's wearing low heels. So she's tall and I'm not. Her eyes are dark green and they narrow as I look at them. There's no twinkle whatsoever. This is one cold woman. A challenge I can rise to.

'Til Wednesday, then,' she says. 'Don't forget your documents.'

The Audi's engine starts smooth enough. Everything is a bit worn out and loose, vague. Suits me. I trundle it down to the back of Slaney's in a bit of a daze. Maybe Duggan isn't such a bad'un after all, fixing me up with this job.

Time for a pint. Rita is behind the bar and she gives me a big grin as I walk in through the back door.

'Busy day?' she asks.

'Busy enough.'

I sit on a stool at the bar and watch her pull my pint. It's only been a few nights but I'll miss Slaney's with all it has to offer.

'Go out and get yourself some dinner, but don't go on the beer. I don't want you too drunk tonight,' she says, plenty of twinkle in her eye.

I smile and take my pint off into the corner. The chat can wait for later.

The mobile phone makes a weird chirping noise in my pocket. I'd forgotten I had the thing. There are two messages. One tells me Jo has accepted my undercover friend request on facebook. The other is her message to Jill

Cormac with a life story update on how happy she is with her new husband.

Rita looks over, finishes serving a customer, and then joins me in the corner booth.

'Bad news?'

'Huh?' I'm still staring at Jo's message.

'You have a face like you're sucking a lime. What's the matter?'

I feel odd, like we're a couple preparing for a night out and I don't want to spoil the mood.

'Oh, just a blast from the past. A can of worms I probably shouldn't open.'

She nods and squeezes my thigh under the table.

'I'll take your mind off it. Later.' She goes back to the bar.

Maybe I should just leave Jo and the child alone. Sure, the kid doesn't even know me. I saw him a couple of times as a baby and that was it. Jo's new husband is effectively his dad even if I'm the biological father.

I study the old wood of the table as if the concentric circles of something once living can make sense of it all.

'Ye look like a man with the world on his shoulders.' It's John-Jo from the Edge of the World. 'Mind if I join ye?

I wave a hand at the empty bench opposite and he slides in with his pint of Heineken.

'So, ye did for McGivney.'

'Did I fuck!' I look up at his prune face. He's pulling my leg.

'I know, I know. Didn't think it was you. No loss is the general opinion, but it's never good to have murder on the streets. Makes the guards twitchy.'

I push my hands through the hair on my head, which feels thinner than ever.

'Look, John-Jo. Nothing personal but I'm not having a great day, so…'

He gives me a narrow-eyed, sideways look.

'Not having a great day? After walking into a job like that?'

'Sweet Jesus. Am I in the Truman Show or something? How the fuck do you know about that?'

'Well, do ye mean apart from the car out back and the word on the street that Bob the Fly has a new man?'

'What?'

The other few people in Slaney's all turn to look at me. Rita too.

'Ye didn't know? Holy Mother, Ger. You're more of an eejit than I had ye down for.'

The Fly. The Fly will get that for you. We can have Bob the Fly bring it in. He's your only man. Bob *the Fly* Reaney. Everyone in Portlaoise knew he was the go-to guy. I'm in at the deep end, should have sussed it out first.

'But, but … Bobby's a huge lad. The Fly, he's a fly!'

'He was a flyweight boxing champ, Ger. He's not a big fella, God knows where Bobby came from. You're working for the man now. I have to hand it to ye, no idea how ye swung it. A lot of men would kill for that job.'

'That's great to know, John-Jo. So I'm the envy of Kilkenny.'

He bares those terrible teeth and gums in what's probably meant to be a smile.

'So, Ger. When ye get the specials coming in, remember me. I'll text ye me number.'

He pulls out his mobile, presses a few keys and mine buzzes in my pocket.

'Now, nothing personal, but I'm off. Your drinking partners don't seem to live very long.' He laughs, downs the rest of his pint and raises a hand to Rita on his way out the door.

I wonder what *the specials* are.

Tim has appeared behind the bar and Rita brings me over another pint.

'I'm off for a snooze and then a nice long bath,' she says and winks at me. 'See you later.'

The bar starts to fill up with men and a few of them look at me occupying the corner booth. Tim switches on the big TV on the wall, showing a pre-match discussion. There must be some premier league soccer scheduled.

I take out my mobile and try to write a response to Jo on facebook but the touch-screen keyboard is too much of a challenge for me. Three older gentlemen gather pointedly at the edge of my table, the backs of their tweed jackets almost in my beer. A pub full of men, happy to walk away from their families and seek solace in pints, sport and male bonding. Not my cup of tea.

'Here you go, lads,' I say, easing my way out of the booth.

'Good man yerself, good man yerself.' They draw me briefly into their bond and then eyes switch back to the TV.

I feel like I own the place, walking through the *Residents Only* door and taking the shallow stairs two at a time. It occurs to me I might stay a few more nights until I have Maudlin Street all set up. But maybe the manager of Reaney Transportation and Distribution, the Fly's new right-hand man, shouldn't be living in a B&B above a pub. I'm moving up in the world, to the street of lepers.

The laptop is much easier going than my mobile. I reply to Jo's news of marital bliss.

Jo, great to hear from you after all these years. Lovely that you're happy again.

That bit makes me pull a sour face, but Jill Cormac has to sound realistic.

Things are great here but I'm making a trip home. Would love to see you again in Dublin if you're free. If it's okay then let me have your address and phone. I hope we can meet up, Josie! We could relive old times! LOL!

I've seen other people on facebook LOLing around all over the place. Three times I read the message through. She'll either go for it or she won't. Send.

I browse Jo's facebook friends. Nobody looks familiar. She's living a completely different life these days. Then I look at Ella Cullen's page again. Her profile pictures are very pretty, sexy. But there's little else shared with strangers. I could friend her as Jill. My finger hovers over the mouse pad. No, play it straight with Ella. Who knows what might happen. I reach for the phone book.

'Hello?'

'Ella.'

'Yeah. Who's this?'

'Ger. We met at the train station this morning. Remember?'

I hear a kid's voice in the background, demanding his mother's attention.

'Listen, if it's a bad time…'

'No. Here, Finn. Here's your juice.'

'I can call back.'

'Sorry, Ger. Just the lad at me, as usual. Nice to hear from you, so soon.'

Hmm. She's thinking I'm over keen. Well, I am.

'Yeah, strike while the iron's hot and all that. I mean, you know.'

'So, am I getting a dinner invitation or what?'

I get a shiver. The first for a long time.

'Sure, yeah. That's why I'm calling. What do you prefer? I mean, Italian or Asian or what?'

'Well, there's a place just round the corner from you.'

So, she knows where I'm staying.

'Ah, Foodworks, is it?' I know where she's going with this and my suspicions are raised.

'No, although that's nice as well. It's Campagne I'm thinking of. You said your treat, right?' She laughs.

The most expensive restaurant in Kilkenny. Best restaurant in Leinster. Yep, she knows I'm loaded. Well, why not.

'Sounds great. French, right? I love French food.' Ex-cons love any food.

I'm ready to take her out for a good time. This money is for spending and Renée would have approved. Campagne was always her favourite restaurant.

'That'd be lovely, Ger,' she says, as if it's my idea. 'So when shall we go?'

'I suppose tonight's out of the question?' I bite my lip. Don't look for refusal.

'Monday night, silly. All decent restaurants close on a Monday.'

Portlaoise prison canteen is open every day. What am I thinking? I didn't say it.

'Um, right. What's best for you?'

'This weekend is good. It's Finn's weekend with his dad.'

That could mean all sorts. If things go well. On the other hand, easy does it.

'Saturday, then. How about Saturday?'

'Sure, that'd be grand. Gives me time to find something to wear.'

'You and me both. But do you think we'll get a table there at this short notice?'

She laughs again. Like dry ice crackling under single malt Scotch.

'Leave it to me, Ger, leave it to me. Sure, my dad owns the building.'

Ella Cullen. Of course, Eddie Cullen, the Kilkenny property magnate.

'Great. I'll pick you up, so. What, about eight at yours? My new house is in town, we can leave my car there.'

'Sure. I'm out on the Kells road. About three miles, on the right. It's signed *An Cloigín Gorm.* You can't miss it.'

'Great! Saturday at eight, I'll see you then.'

'Looking forward to it, Ger.'

'Me too, Ella, me too. Bye.'

'Goodnight.'

I listen to the dial tone and then look at my phone. Five days to get Maudlin Street into shape. Ger Mayes is back in the game.

I'm out

Don't drink too much, Rita said. I'm kind of nervous about being on a promise; it's very domesticated. Spontaneous is always better.

I take a shower before going out for food, to purify me for whatever Rita has in store later.

Then I can't decide where to eat. A lot of places are open, despite it being Monday. They must be desperate for business.

Wandering up and down the streets looking in restaurant windows is great when you're a couple or in a group, but I feel very self-conscious. People seem to be staring out the windows at me.

One Italian restaurant looks very inviting. Well, the head waitress looks inviting. She doesn't look Italian though. Most of the ethnic restaurants in town are a bit fake.

Eventually I settle on a place that looks distinctly unpopular. The windows are steamy with condensation. Peering in, I don't see anybody at any of the tables. A waitress carries a huge pizza up some stairs at the side of the main room.

Inside the place is warm and dominated by a pizza oven. The chef looks like he's from a TV advertisement for Italian food and he beckons me over, holding out a small plate of olive oil with pieces of plain pizza bread on it.

'Try, try! Is traditional from my hometown,' he says in an accent suggesting his hometown is somewhere between Rome and Manchester.

The bread is delicious and the taste, with the oil, transports me away from dreary Ireland and into the hot and sweaty south of Italy. That's probably what's steaming up the windows and scaring away the punters; authenticity.

'This oven, it's wood-fired. Gives the flavour, cooks traditionally, the old way. Not gas. No fast food here.'

The waitress comes back downstairs.

'Table for one?' Her accent is Irish.

He runs a restaurant just the way he used to in Italy. Somehow she persuaded him to come live in her rainy country. The Roman business model doesn't really work here but he's too stubborn to change. They'll never get rich from it but she's happy to accept the compromise.

I'm not a psychic; she tells me all this piecemeal with taking my order, serving and generally being desperate for someone to talk to. I'm left to mull over each snippet of information with the different courses and a bottle of Chianti. They've had some trials and tribulations, Ciara and Giuseppe. Her chat is a welcome distraction to what could have been a very self-conscious meal alone.

At the end she's even drinking a glass herself; the few other customers have left and her husband is fiddling around with his pizza oven like a boy playing with a bonfire. He eventually comes up the stairs with a bottle of Grappa and three glasses. They latch onto me as their new best friend. Clearly they've no idea who I am.

The bill is laughably small. I bid them goodnight and resolve to give them more than a fair share of my future custom. Except for next Saturday.

It's only half past nine. Too early to head back to Rita. Could go to the Edge of the World and see what kind of reception I get, but I don't really feel like further hobnobbing with the crime fraternity today.

Maudlin Street calls to me and I wander up to sample its ambience. Quite a few cars leap across John Street and thunder on up, past my house. It looks like I've bought into a rat run.

The bottom of the Maudlin Tower flares out its ancient stone base like a hippy's trousers. A small but unassailable fortress. More the style of dwelling I should have gone for.

The cycle repair man is closing up late and he gives me a cautious nod as I pass. I should buy a bike, keep fit. With this heart, not mine, I'm supposed to keep up a regular, moderate exercise regime. Since my release the regime has consisted of shagging Rita. Moderate enough.

A lane turns off right and I follow it down, towards the river. The light is fading and I'm half-surprised by a big yellow dog, its tongue hanging out, all slobbery. The thick tail wags as if I'm an old friend.

'Evening,' I say to the dog's owner, who is bending to pick up a handful of warm dog turd in a plastic bag. Another habit that's grown in popularity since I went away.

'It is that,' says a male voice from the hooded figure.

The river moves like made of solid, no swirls or eddies. Dark and green, full and deep. They have an annual swim race in the river, but not down here by the weir. The water pours briefly over the long stone edge like a natural fault line and resumes its relentless one-piece motion.

This is the last place I saw Renée, her limp body tumbling in a more turbulent flow that day. They said I pushed my pregnant lover off the bridge. I remember her falling backwards into the river like Sigourney Weaver throwing herself into the lava with her alien progeny.

If only you were here now, Renée. We would have been a nuclear family. Except for your cancer.

'You okay, mister?' a young boy on a bike asks.

I'm sat on a bench, head in hands.

'C'mon, Tony. Leave him alone,' another kid says, shooting past.

They're riding bikes that look too small, like they belong to somebody else.

'Don't do it, mister!' shouts the first. 'Not unless you're a feckin' good swimmer!'

He laughs and takes off after his friend. Little Joe would be about their age now.

The path leads me up a flight of brick steps and around the back of the ruined woollen mill. Another relic of times when people actually produced something tangible instead of health insurance and investment fund management.

An incongruous wooden walkway stretches ahead over the marshy riverbank, looking like it might float away in high water. The heels of my shoes drum a steady beat as I march along. The structure ends abruptly in a muddy patch beneath the concrete flyover of the ring road. A sign says *Nore Valley walk – Bennettsbridge 11km*. My burning thighs say *no*.

The Office of Public Works, according to another placard, has built this concrete staircase up from the river mud to the flyover; those kind of steps with an awkward depth somewhere between one and two strides.

Halfway up I turn and look at Kilkenny's cityscape. The castle stands sentinel over the river and both cathedral towers catch the last light. It's breathtaking. That's what I tell myself, because I can't catch my breath. Sweat runs down my temple and I have to lean on the wooden handrail, just for a minute. I sit down on the cool concrete.

It's not the first time I've felt my mortality. When McAuliffe and Faloone sprung their trap ten years ago the original Mayes heart couldn't stay the course. There was furore in the media when I had the transplant. At that time

I was just happy to be alive but, when I read about people who wished me dead, I emerged from the ordeal at war with the world. Now, a decade later, the docs tell me I've as good a life expectancy as the next man. Let's hope the next man wasn't the Gimp.

At the top of the steps is a car parked on the flyover. It reminds me I have wheels, although they're back at Slaney's. Could do with them now. A waft of tobacco smoke blows down past me.

'Well, Ger. Out for an evening constitutional? You want to mind yourself. There are some unsavoury characters on the loose.' McAuliffe sucks on the cigarette, his cheeks going in like a deflated balloon. 'Want a lift?'

I look for the sneer on his face but there isn't one. His body language is saying *friend – you can trust me*.

'Why not? Thanks.'

He holds the passenger door open and I step in.

He takes another puff and drops the cigarette butt into a drain cover before getting in the car. I wait for him to start the engine, but he doesn't.

'So, you're the Fly's new boy.'

'What do you want, Andy? I'm allowed to earn a crust, aren't I?'

'That you are. So you are. Just be careful, Ger. I don't have you down as a career criminal.'

McAuliffe my guardian angel. Crumpled brown suit for wings. I don't know what his angle is on Reaney Transportation and Distribution. Maybe he had an arrangement with the previous guy.

'Reaney's seems legit to me.'

He laughs, degenerating into the start of a smoker's cough. 'Birds of a feather, Ger. Birds of a feather.'

I narrow my eyes but his face remains amiable.

'Did you find who did for the Gimp?' I say, trying to change the subject.

'We're still working on it. DS Purcell has some *theories.*'

The Romanians are long gone. Their trail will be as cold as McGivney's ugly corpse.

McAuliffe starts the engine and checks his rear view mirror. He moves off and, pulling too slowly onto the carriageway, earns a blast of the horn from another vehicle. A huge dark green Mercedes swerves around us and pulls parallel, the muscle-head driver pausing to eyeball us before disappearing at high speed. McAuliffe gives a little chuckle to himself.

The mile back into town takes no time. McAuliffe casually runs a couple of red lights in the old style as there's no traffic. He pulls up outside St John's, the church with the headless tower.

I expect him to say keep your nose clean, turn over a new leaf and stick to the straight and narrow. And sorry for busting your heart all those years ago.

'Be seeing you, Ger. Good luck with the new house. Be seeing you.'

And he's gone.

Rita's not behind the bar at Slaney's. I go up to my room with the intention of checking the computer. Her room at the far end of the corridor is emitting a mixture of strong scents. She's probably in the bath, surrounded by candles.

The laptop is already open and switched on in my room. I don't recall if I shut it down or not. Jo has responded to my Jill persona again.

I'd love to see you, Jilly. Ciaran is dying to meet you, he's heard so much about you, and Little Joe is asking if you're bringing your boys.

We're up in Baldoyle, next to the sea. It's really handy for the airport and we've loads of room if you'd like to stay for a couple of days. Would be lovely if you did. We

*could go in town, walk on the beach, show you around. Of
course, I don't know your plans.*

That's right, Jo, you don't.

She gives her address and a phone number. I tap the
info into my mobile for safekeeping. The name Ciaran
rings a bell but I can't quite put a finger on it. Anger and
trepidation swirl in my head. It's not like I'm looking for
Jo to take me back after all this time. Or am I?

Tim serves me a pint and I take it back up. My room is
immediately above the booth where I normally sit in the
bar but it somehow feels a rip off to pay pub prices for
beer I'm consuming in privacy. I could have bought a few
cans for the same money. Good to know my frugal
Scottish genes are alive and well.

The alcohol soothes and a Jo plan begins to form in my
head. It involves me and Little Joe meeting on the beach
outside his house. I put the address into Google and look at
the map, then the camera view. The house looks nice
enough, and the camera angle scans around to face the sea.
With the tide out, the sun is shining down on miles of
sand. This is where my boy is growing up, with someone
else for his dad. Maybe it's best left alone.

I try a few other searches in Google on a different topic
altogether. How did the Gimp describe it? All I get are
media articles and dating sites, nothing like he described.
Call girls, prostitutes? And then I hit it. Escorts. A link
takes me to an adult advisory warning. Doesn't look like
the pub broadband has any restrictions on it. Should be
safe, unless Rita is sitting in the Slaney's command centre
and monitoring my movements. So in I go.

Holy mother! Women of all shapes, ages and sizes, in
underwear or naked.

A knock on the door. I jump like a teenager caught
misbehaving in his bedroom. My pint sloshes beer on the
carpet and the laptop nearly falls from the table.

'Ger. It's Rita. Can I come in?'

The door handle turns without her waiting for my answer. I slam the lid of the laptop down but then open it again and stare at the woman on the screen.

Somebody that I used to know. Melody, currently working in Dublin. When I knew her she went by the name of Krystal.

Day 5 – Old flames

I have to give Rita credit. She pulled out all the stops, even pulled out that hair under her chin. It was fragrant candles, perfumed oils, hard liquor and tantric sex.

'Don't be a stranger,' she said to me, her hand resting on mine before she cleared away my breakfast plate in the bar.

In these few days Slaney's has felt like my first real home of the last decade. I'll miss the slightly crummy pine décor, breakfast and beer and landlady on tap, and discovering dead bodies together.

I pack up my stuff, put my bag in the boot of the Audi and walk downhill to my ten o'clock appointment. A steady, drenching drizzle has everyone on the street with shoulders hunched and collars up. A town full of shifty characters.

McDonald's daughter greets me at her father's offices with a toothy grin. The man himself doesn't keep me waiting.

'Ger! An eventful weekend, I understand.' McDonald gives me his firm, dry handshake. I have the impression he could throw me over his shoulder with that grip. 'Tea?'

'Thanks.'

He takes a seat behind his desk, waves a hand at the chair on my side and shuffles some papers.

'Let me see, 32 Maudlin Street, 32 Maudlin Street. Ah yes, here we are.' He holds out an envelope to me but doesn't release it when I take hold.

'Thanks.'

'Drunken fist-fighting in the streets, arrested for murdering one of my clients, my favourite landlady also arrested, associating with a known crooked lawyer, going on the payroll with Bob the Fly. Yes, a busy weekend, Ger.' McDonald lets go of the envelope.

He missed out disposal of murder weapon in a meat pie, but I'm not going to correct him.

Young Miss McDonald brings in the tea and pours, standing just a little too close to my chair. I can see the strap of her bra inside the open neck of her blouse. She's pale, a creature kept hidden away from sunlight.

'Thank you, Sinead.' McDonald dismisses her.

'How am I set for utilities and stuff at the house?'

'Electric, gas, cable TV. All connected. You know it's unfurnished? I have a contact for good second-hand furniture, here.' He opens a drawer, pulls out a business card and slides it across the desk.

Parraig's House Clearances. Probably the guy McDonald sold the old furniture to, so I can buy it back.

'Thanks. I have some new bits and pieces being delivered.'

'Right. Just a word of advice. Don't be flashing your money around too much. I know you didn't come in on the banana boat, but the vultures are circling.'

'They certainly are.' I open the envelope and take out a bunch of keys. 'Are these the only set?'

McDonald's eyes narrow. 'Hold on, let me just check.'

He opens another draw, rummages around and shakes his head. I'm thinking that's another task on my list, to change the locks of my new home.

McDonald slides various papers across his desk for me to sign, relating to completion of the house purchase.

'I'll archive the deeds with the rest of your files, unless you want to take them?'

'No, that's fine.' Although I only trust McDonald marginally more than a dead Gimp there's no reason to cut ties. 'I'm sure we'll do further business together.'

He stands and gives me his Aikido handshake again.

'And a pleasure it is, Ger. All the best in your new home.'

'Thanks, Ronald.'

I'm not sure that's his name but he doesn't flinch.

'Goodbye, Mr Mayes,' Sinead whistles through those teeth as I exit the reception area.

And so, from the cut and thrust of legal and illegal dealings to the mundane task of waiting in for my furniture and electronics to be delivered.

The key sticks in the lock of 32 Maudlin Street. It won't turn. Then it does turn and the glossy black door scrapes inwards, but the key won't come out of the lock.

I take a deep breath and force my shoulders to relax. This could be a very long day. If I sink my expectations into the gutter then things can only get better.

My new house has potential, as the auctioneers would say. Especially the kitchen. Potential to be totally gutted and have a fortune spent on it.

The stainless steel sink sits forlornly on top of its unit, one of the cupboard doors below hanging open. Inside is a motley collection of cleaning stuff with brands I'm sure are no longer on the market. Across the room a double cupboard is stuck crookedly to the wall and the standalone electric cooker in the corner has a ring missing.

I'm lost in a domestic dream of granite worktops and soft-closing storage units when I hear the front door grind open.

'Hello?' I call.

Light footsteps pad down the hallway.

I step to the side of the doorway, looking around for something to use as a weapon. Maybe a rusting can of brass polish from under the sink? But that's too far away. I bunch my fist and swing a punch at head level as the intruder enters the kitchen.

A hand grabs my elbow and a very small man walks under my fist.

'Now, that's no way to greet the boss, Ger.'

He lets go and stands back. Titchy but perfectly formed, except for the abnormally large hands, one of which he offers to me.

'Bob Reaney.'

He must be around sixty but the Fly looks ready to go. It's like finding myself in a cage with a dangerous animal. I shake his hand and feel the wiry strength.

'You shouldn't be leaving your door open. Anyone could walk in.'

I'm pretty sure I closed it, but I'm not going to argue with my gift horse.

'Nice to meet you. I'd offer you tea or something but…'

We both look around the kitchen.

'Yeah,' he says. 'It's a bit of a hole. Sure, we'll have you sorted in no time. I'll get one of the lads to fix this up for you.'

Did I sell myself to this guy? I'm wondering.

'Oh, you'll have to pay for it. But just materials. Nothing too fancy, just normal. Let's say a grand. I'll take it out of your wages, before tax.'

Yep, I'm sold.

'Let's have a look at the rest of it, then.' He leads me around my house, making a few suggestions and promises.

The place is bare, except for a dark old wardrobe in the front bedroom.

'The Gimp was wrong,' he says. 'This place is too small for what he had in mind.'

Pieces click into and out of place in my head.

'Plus Old McKinsey lived here,' he says, looking at the wardrobe as if the deceased former owner might be inside it. 'That's why it was on the market for so long. No punter in their right mind would want to do business in this house. Right, well, I'd better be going.'

He turns on his miniature heel and patters down the stairs.

'Leave a set of keys with Nora tomorrow, so the lads can get in to do the kitchen and those other jobs.'

'Will do.' And then I'll change the locks after.

He pulls the door open with a scrape.

'I'll tell them to fix that as well.'

He doesn't shake my hand again. We're done with that.

From the bedroom window I can see a dark green car parked directly outside. It's longer than my house is wide. The passenger door opens and the Fly gets in. I get a glimpse of the driver; it's the same muscle-head who eyeballed me in McAuliffe's car last night.

~

By evening I'm fully installed, sat on my black leather swivel chair watching cable TV in the front room. Takeaway chicken chow mein on a plate I found in the kitchen, originally white but greyed with scratches and cracks in the glaze. The fork is the only one that didn't have dried stuff welded to the tines and it's as crooked as snaggled teeth.

Upstairs the new bed awaits, swathed with Dunnes' best bed linen, which isn't very good.

One of my spare sheets is draped over the sitting room window, hanging off the remnants of a curtain rail. It lets me forget that strangers might pass by outside just six feet away.

This Chinese takeaway is great, a dream come true. How many nights have I imagined sitting in my own place, milling through a chicken chow mein and slurping a cold can? Nine times three hundred and sixty-five.

Then something on the TV grabs my attention. A covert camera shows four women getting out of a large Audi in an underground car park. A shaven-headed, burly man opens the boot of the car and the women take out suitcases. They're dressed as if for a party. The sort of party I'd like to go to.

'Excuse me, I'd like to talk to you about the apartments upstairs,' the reporter says in a weedy voice, camera shot shaky as he walks towards the car.

Before he can reach the man and four women they've disappeared through an access-controlled stairwell door and the reporter is unable to follow.

A voiceover says the women are believed to stay at each location for around two weeks before being transported to the next town. They advertise individually on a website purported to be a marketplace for independent escorts.

The screen shows a man collecting two women who had been fined at the Four Courts in Dublin in connection with the operation of a brothel in the north city centre. It's two different women but the same baldy-headed man getting into the Audi. He must do a lot of mileage.

Then they show another location. This time baldy is making a collection in a Midlands town. Another four women and there she is, somebody that I used to know. Krystal a.k.a. Melody. She looks older than I remember, but then so do I.

My noodles have gone cold.

Upstairs and my new bed is incongruous in the front bedroom. What did the Fly mean about McKinsey? I imagine the ghost of McKinsey, whoever he was, sitting quietly in the dark wooden wardrobe and I daren't open it to check the contents, not in the witching hour.

I've found Krystal on the escort website. There are four photos of her in some sexy lingerie. Something about women looking bored does it for me. I first met her up in The Gentlemen's Club in Dublin, where Tom took me for relaxation during the cocaine smuggling debacle, God bless his soul. She used to play the major tease. No touching, just titillation. When I was in the money I endured it for hours, torturing myself. I had it bad for Krystal. Now it seems she's gone from *if you have to ask you can't afford it* to budget bonking shop.

Each girl's page has a menu of the services they offer. A lot of the terms are lost on me and I have to resort to the glossary conveniently provided on the home page. Then I have to internet search the terms because I can't quite believe what I'm reading. These girls are no more social escort than I am.

Prices are per half hour and hour. Some do out-calls and even overnight. It's all very orderly, too easy to be true. Perhaps it's a scam. Maybe she's not Krystal at all, just some tart who looks like the short Romanian I used to waste the mortgage money on.

Then I find the review section. This is where it gets nasty. Actual punters with online names like Big Bad Wolf and Captain Shagnasty have left their judgement of value for money, whether the promised services were provided satisfactorily and if they would recommend the girl. I'm repelled and fascinated at the same time.

The few reviews on the page for Melody don't paint the girl in a good light. *Looked much older than her photos … Answered the door in scruffy sportswear … Didn't provide most of the services on her menu.* One guy, under the name Donkey, has given her one star out of five and said he didn't pay as she refused him. There's an icon for comments and I click to find Melody has replied.

I know you, Donkey. You are guy who show up late, say no to shower and smell like a farm.

I check her other reviews and they're all bad, all with stinging comments. This girl is in the wrong line of work.

None of the other girls answer their reviewers back. None of them are as pretty as Melody. The old fixation is starting again. Melody, Krystal, whoever you are these days, I have to see you.

Day 6 – Eat in or takeaway?

My eyes feel like I've borrowed them from an old person. The laptop lies open next to me on the bed, screen blank and battery dead. Morning sun burns through the window onto my pillow.

A nearly empty can of beer falls to the floor as I reach for my phone. Nine-thirty. First day in the new job. I stand at the bedroom window wearing the bath robe I stole from Rita's and watch the cars take their morning short cut up my street.

'Oi!' I open the window and shout. 'What do you think you're doing?'

A traffic warden is pasting a parking ticket on the windscreen of the Audi.

'You have to pay in this zone from seven a.m.' He smiles up at me. 'That's forty euro.'

'But I'm a resident!'

'So you are, so you are. Go down the council and get a permit, so.'

The bastard tips the peak of his cap and walks on, without removing the fine from my car.

Some people like to sing in the shower. I'm shouting in mine. The four needle thin jets of water are barely lukewarm and it's taking forever to wash the shampoo out of what little hair I have. The shower head is all clogged with lime scale but unscrewing it and holding the hose over my head doesn't improve things much. Having your own home isn't all it's cracked up to be.

My new towel makes up for things a bit, all soft and absorbent. I feel a hair on my unshaven face and rub with my palm. It comes away covered in dark blue lint from the towel. I should have washed it before use, but 32 Mauldin Street doesn't have a washing machine. My tongue feels furry too with a bit of a hangover.

In the bedroom my clothes selection is wanting. The flash new gear I bought last weekend is soiled, crumpled and anyway too casual. I have a white shirt but Nora will expect more than that. Without thinking, I unlock the wardrobe and open it. There he is, Old McKinsey. Well, his suit is, wrapped in the dry cleaner's cellophane.

1980s, I would say. Dark green with a bit of a thin brown check pattern. I pull off the plastic and lay the suit on the bed. It doesn't look too worn, probably kept for best. I figure what the hell. It's clean, it's in the house and the place belongs to me.

The inside of the wardrobe door has a full length mirror and a hook with a brown leather belt on it. The jacket is a good enough fit, sleeves a touch on the long side, but the trousers give me second thoughts. They're at least a size too big. I put on the belt and tighten it to the last hole to cinch the waist. The finishing touch is a green and yellow silk tie from a shelf in the wardrobe. Not bad at all.

Nothing in the kitchen that looks like breakfast. I did keep the remnants of my chicken chow mein but, when I open the fridge door, a cheesy smell wafts out to greet me. I slam the door shut and the thing shudders into life. No kettle, no cooked breakfast, no Rita.

My favourite bakery is just around the corner. I'll buy a couple of sausage rolls and eat them at work. No need for a pie, I haven't any murder weapons to dispose of today.

The bell rings with my opening of the shop door. A couple of old ladies hover in front of the cake counter, trying to work out which delicacies won't sabotage their dentures. I turn right to the savouries. Maybe a pie would be good after all.

A woman backs in through the door from the kitchen, carrying a tray of cup cakes.

'Oh my God!' The cup cakes levitate and tumble to the floor.

She's staring at me as if I'm an escaped convict or something.

I put my hands in the trouser pockets to pull out the coins I'd picked up off the bedside table. Nothing. My fingers scrabble around and find the pockets are bottomless for easy access.

The cake thrower's eyes drop to my trousers as I fumble.

'What do you want!' she shrieks at me.

'Two sausage rolls, please.' I nod to the savoury counter.

'Who are you?'

'ID required for a sausage roll seems a bit extreme.'

'Why are you wearing that suit? The tie as well!' she says.

I begin to wonder what terrible deeds Old McKinsey perpetrated in the bakery.

'It's not him,' one of the old dears whistles through her false teeth. 'It's that Ger Mayes.'

'Take them and go,' the baker woman says, throwing two sausage rolls into a paper bag and tossing them on the counter. 'Just go.'

Free stuff. I'll have to wear the McKinsey every time I come here.

~

'Good morning.' Nora's smile is wide but doesn't reach her eyes.

In fairness to her it is a bit late. I had to stop by the council offices and get my vehicle permit sorted.

'You'll be wanting to make a copy of these,' I say, dangling my house keys. 'Any tea on the go?'

She takes the keys. 'I'll get one of the lads to go down to Brett's and get some cut. Nice suit. What's in the bag?'

'Sausage rolls. One of my guilty pleasures. Want one.' My eyes drop to her neat waist and back up to her steely grin.

'Thanks but no thanks. There's some coffee in the pot over there.'

I know they've no need to cut keys, it's all a charade. The Fly has my spares in his pocket, but we have to keep up appearances.

'Here you go,' Nora says as I tear open the bakery bag on my desk. 'White, one sugar. I reckon that's how you take it. What's that blue stuff on your face?'

'Towelling.' I take a swig and smile. It won't take long to have her eating out of my hand.

'We have a special delivery coming around two,' she says. 'We all share. Just take a wander down the back.'

'Thanks.'

'You're welcome. By the way, Ger…'

'Yeah?'

'You might want to get a new suit. That's the one McKinsey was wearing when he did what he did.'

~

Norman McKinsey. Many things passed me by while I was inside Portlaoise but the internet tells everything I never wanted to know about the former owner occupier of 32 Maudlin Street. A local pervert known for his signature green suit and yellow silk tie. Committed suicide on remand while awaiting trial for child abduction. A smiling face in an old photograph shows some similarity to my own. Small wonder the bakery lady dropped her cup cakes.

That house must have stood empty for five years or more. By the time I've researched Old McKinsey, and thought over how to get my revenge on McDonald for reinforcing my status as a social leper, it's two o'clock.

Nora sticks her head in my office. 'Time to go check out the specials. I think you'll be interested.'

'I'll be right down.'

First I have to close down Jo's facebook page and the escorts website on my browser.

Laughter fills the warehouse from the loading bay.

'It's a coffee maker,' Nora says as one of the lads holds up what looks like a metal space rocket. 'Designer. Italian.'

'What's this?' he says, reading from a box. 'Toaster with bum warmer?'

'Bun warmer, you eejit,' Nora says but she's laughing.

The lorry is backed right up to the bay and stacked to the roof with kitchen accessories. It's all Alessi, the stuff Jo used to be mad about. We could only afford a corkscrew and a kid's egg-cup and spoon, bought for the baby.

'How much is it?' I ask the guy in the truck. He's not one of ours.

'A fiver all small items, tenner the medium and twenty the electrical appliances.' He picks up a clipboard and a pen.

'Just take whatever you want,' Nora says to me. 'It'll be deducted from your wages.'

Here we go again. Sixteen tons and what do you get, another day older and deeper in debt.

'I'll take one of everything,' I say, thinking of my new kitchen in the making. Then I remember John-Jo; he was asking after the specials. I think he's a good man to have on my side. 'Make it two of everything. No, three.' What the hell, in for a penny, in for a pound.

The guy in the truck scribbles away on his board.

'Lads, put the stuff in Ger's car. It's up front,' Nora says. 'You'll get the keys from me.'

I touch her shoulder in acknowledgment and she doesn't flinch. With a nod all round I leave them to it. Bobby isn't anywhere to be seen.

The internet gives me the retail prices of what I've just bought. Even the simple espresso can is over two hundred euro. That's several thousand worth of Alessi I've just bought for a couple of hundred. I imagine some mafia heist outside Milan and the truck being driven across Europe to Kilkenny. More likely a break-in at some warehouse in Dublin or a misplaced container on a sea shipment. Those coffee pots are hot.

By half-four Nora is urging me out of the office.

'No more shipments today, Ger. You may as well go home and play with your new toys.'

She hands me back my house keys.

The inside of the Audi is stacked to the roof with boxes, barely room for me to drive. I open the back to try and put some of the stuff in there but it's full. What was I thinking?

Slowly I drive out of the car park and try to check the traffic but my view left is obscured by a very stylish blender. There's a squeal of wheels and Bobby's angry face looks at me from behind the wheel of his BMW as he swerves to avoid my car. His four lady passengers look alarmed. I lower my window and raise a hand of acknowledgment before pulling away.

The top of John Street is snarled with traffic. This is the closest Kilkenny gets to rush hour. Two big buses are inching past each other, too wide for the medieval street. A car drives out of a side turn in front of the upcoming bus and stops alongside me, window down. McAuliffe. A half-smoked cigarette hangs from his hand

'Well, Ger,' he says and his eyes take in my load.

'Well, Andy,' I say and then, 'just a few things for the new place.'

'Always good to have a few spare toasters.'

He looks like a man who would enjoy a good espresso machine; maybe I'll surprise him for Christmas. He drives on.

A knock on the passenger window. I clear some boxes on that side to see who it is. John-Jo. He reaches to open the door but thinks better of it, so I open the window and he takes out a box to study it. I may as well set up a stall here, in the traffic jam, selling Alessi.

'Thanks, Ger,' John-Jo says. 'I'll be round later, take some off your hands.'

Those buses manage to muscle past each other and I nose the car down to my turn. There's just one way in to Maudlin Street and this is it. I'd better learn to avoid the bus times. At least I manage to get parked right outside my house.

The front door is no less annoying than yesterday, even more difficult to open with a cardboard box containing a kettle under one arm. I'm looking forward to a nice cuppa using the tea bags and milk I filched from the office.

Elbowing in through the door I switch on the light and there it is; my new kitchen. With the kettle clutched to my chest I do a full circle. Amazing. In just a few hours the Fly's lads have shoehorned a kitchen intended for a much larger house into my little home. All antique pine, ornate mouldings and black iron handles. There's hardly any floor space left, just a narrow gangway. A couple's culinary battleground.

My Alessi kettle looks incongruous; Italian art in an Irish granny's dream. By the time I've brought a few of the other boxes in from my car the kettle is bubbling away nicely. Me and my appliances are going to get on just fine.

The front room is fairly crowded with all the stuff. I'm thinking about sorting it all out into three sets; one for me, one for John-Jo and one for who else? Jo, maybe. I should get on and make that cup of tea. The doorbell rings.

A peephole to check out my visitors would be a handy thing. The door groans when I pull it open.

First I get the perfume. A whiff of freedom. Then an eyeful of wispy blonde hair. Roisín McGuire the reporter.

Underworld

'Ger!' she says as if the surprise is all hers.

'Roisín.' I give her a simpleton's smile.

Before I can debate the wisdom of it she's in and I'm shutting the door behind her.

'Let me take your coat,' I say and she turns so I can lift it from her shoulders. Then I look around for somewhere to put it but there's no coat stand or hooks. It goes over the bottom of the stair banister.

'Nice place,' she says and sticks her head in the door of the front room. 'Alessi, huh? Nice. I like Alessi.'

'It's a full set of everything.' I feel the sudden urge to sell my stolen goods to this crime reporter.

'You don't do things by halves. I'll give you that.' She turns and walks across the hall to the kitchen.

'Tea? Would you like some tea?'

She nods and I go in search of the old grey mugs McKinsey left behind. The cupboard doors are stiff with newness and some of them reveal a dishwasher, fridge and some sort of storage racks.

'Are you sure this is your house?' Roisín says, placing a box on the worktop. It's a set of two cups and saucers from my collection in the front room. She opens the box and takes out the cups, rinsing them under the tap. 'Here you go.'

I flick the kettle back on and pull a couple of teabags out of the inside pocket of McKinsey's jacket.

'Nice,' she says. 'Did they belong to the previous owner as well?' She looks at the cinched waist of my trousers.

'No, I got them from Reaney's. They're just out of the box today.'

'Reaney's? You're working for the Fly? And tell me that's not McKinsey's suit, Ger.'

I feel like a child caught with his hand somewhere it shouldn't be. Somehow I manage to make the tea without a spoon.

'Sugar?' I hope she says no because I have none.

She smiles a sparkly white grin and shakes her head.

'I'd invite you into the front room but there's not really anywhere for us to sit,' I say. 'I've just moved in.'

'Here is fine,' she says and sits up on the kitchen worktop. Her skirt is just long enough for decency. She has very slim ankles.

I sit opposite. The kitchen is so narrow we could reach out and touch.

'So?' I say.

'So, here we are. Here you are, Ger. Working for the main man, living in a child murderer's house and wearing his clothes.'

'Will that be your headline?'

She raises one eyebrow. 'Why did you let me in if you don't trust me?'

'Because I'm a sucker for a pretty face.'

Some white yellow strands of hair are loose and she brushes them back behind her ear, just like she did the first time I met her on my release. Unlike that day her face isn't orange.

'Does that mean I can twist you around my little finger?'

'Probably.'

We sip on our tea.

'I'm investigating the death of Raymond McGivney.'

'I thought that was the job of An Garda Síochána?'

'You know what I mean. He was part of the local underworld here.'

I cough on my tea. 'Underworld? This is Kilkenny, there's no underworld here.'

'Again, you know what I mean. It's not all petty crime down country.' She throws a thumb back in the direction of my Italian collection.

'Nothing petty about that lot,' I say. 'It's the genuine article.'

'I'm sure it is. Are you the genuine article, Ger?' She fixes me with her steely blues.

I don't really know what she means. I fumble a slightly crushed packet of ginger nuts from my jacket. 'Would you like a biscuit?'

She takes the packet from me but puts it on the worktop beside her.

'Money laundering. Human trafficking. Smuggling.' She nods at my kettle. 'I wouldn't be surprised if drugs are involved somewhere.'

'Well, that would be right up my street then.'

'Have you any idea what you've got yourself into here?' She waves her empty cup in the air. 'I know you're a nice guy, underneath the smart talk. Will you help me with this?'

'Tell me why I should. I have no idea what you're talking about. If all that is going on and I'm sat in the middle of it like some kind of eejit then talking to you will earn us both an express ticket to the bottom of the river.'

As soon as the words are out I regret them. Her hair reminds me of Renée and she has the same pale skin. An underfed look of vulnerability. I move to her and brush the backs of my fingers against her cheek. She doesn't flinch.

'People get hurt around me, Roisín.'

She puts her hand up and pulls mine down.

'Are you getting soft on me, Ger? You don't even know me. You don't know me at all. I'm not some lost little girl who can't look after herself.'

Her words are harsh but she's at the limit of her bravado.

A bang on the door makes us both jump.

'Ger?' a man's voice shouts. 'Ger, it's John-Jo.'

'You'd better go upstairs,' I tell Roisín. 'I don't want you seen here.'

She takes a deep breath, nods and runs up the stairs.

John-Jo bangs on the door again. He's not a fan of door bells.

'Well, John-Jo. Come in, come in.'

He walks into the kitchen and sees the two teacups on the worktop. 'Not disturbing you, am I?'

'Not at all. Just a bit of company, like. You know.' I give him a wink.

'Ye old dog. Only here five minutes and working your way through the fillies. Fair play to ye.'

'Here,' I say, switching on the front room light and beckoning him in.

'Fancy,' he says, picking up one box after another and looking at the colourful illustrations on them. 'Very fancy. I don't really recognise most of these things. Sure, if the missus doesn't want them I can always sell on.'

'There's a complete set if you want.'

'Not sure I can afford it. Looks expensive. Italian, right?'

'Right. You can have it at cost. Just a few hundred. I'll let you know exactly how much when I get the bill but you take it in the meantime. As a little thank you from me.'

'Thanks, Ger. Good man yerself. I have the van outside.'

We ferry the boxes out to his Hi-Ace after a fair bit of fumbling around to make sure he has one and only one of everything.

'Listen, I'll be getting on,' he says and motions with his head up the stairs. 'Leave you to your business.'

I shake his hand and push the door shut behind him.

'The local fillies?' Roisín says laughing from the top of the stairs and then walks on to inspect the rest of the first floor.

'What's so funny?' I call after her. 'A man has to live.'

I find her in the back bedroom. It's just bare floorboards and a cold open fireplace.

'You have some work to do on this place if you're going to entertain lady friends. Not that anyone local will want to set foot in Old McKinsey's house.'

We walk into the front bedroom. My room.

'Nice bed. Nasty cheap linen but nice bed. That,' she points at the child murderer's wardrobe, 'has to go.'

I'm nodding at her suggestions.

'And that.' She points at the suit I'm wearing. 'Dump it. Get rid.'

Off comes the jacket and I start to un-belt the trousers. I'm no slouch when a lady tells me to undress.

'No, I mean give it to charity. Better still, burn it. Why the hell did you buy this house anyway? Of all the places you had to choose this.'

'McDonald,' I mutter. 'Look, I'm not asking you to move in or anything.'

She laughs with her eyes all screwed up. It's kind of weird but nice.

'Maybe you could give me a bit of home furnishing advice?' I ask.

'I can that. And I can give you a bit of self-image advice as well.' She reaches to the old wooden chair in the corner and pulls a couple of my recent but soiled clothes purchases from it. 'Wash these and wear them. If you have to wear a suit then go to Next and buy one. Clear every speck of McKinsey out of here. A complete cosmetic makeover. Repaint the front of the house, the door too.'

'Right. Will do.' I put the jacket on its hanger in the wardrobe. 'I'll get some of the lads to throw this out.'

'I'll help you, Ger, but I need you to help me.'

She bites her lip and I move closer but she sidesteps me.

'I'm going to uncover the goings on in this town. You can help or you can be part of the story. It's your choice. Think it over and give me a call.'

She hands me another of her cards and walks out of the room.

'Thanks for the tea,' she calls as she trots down the stairs and the front door bangs shut.

Well, had the first woman visitor in my bedroom and almost got my trousers off. Not bad.

Appetite

I have a hunger. Roisín McGuire's fault, she tickled my taste buds.

Rita stands behind the bar at Slaney's together with Tim, then she's working the room and comes over to me.

'Hey, stranger. I was wondering when you'd show your face again.'

She's not the spring chicken Roisín is, but after a couple of pints Rita is looking good and I'm getting the buzz. That lone hair under her chin is nowhere to be seen. I can claim some positive influence.

'Any more from the guards?' she asks, sliding in on the bench next to me.

It seems a long time since we found the Gimp in a pool of his own blood.

'Not a dicky bird. I think we're safely off the hook.' I take a big swig of my pint.

'How's the job shaping up?'

'Yeah, good. A nice little number.'

'And 32 Maudlin Street?' She raises an eyebrow.

'I could kill McDonald. So much for keeping a low profile.'

'It was on the market for years, that place. You probably got it for a song.'

'He well and truly stuffed me on the price. I really had no idea.'

'Not to worry, it will all work out. I'll have to come over sometime, if I get an invite.' She squeezes my thigh and heads back behind the bar.

After another pint I notice a guy in the corner getting a bit of Rita's attention and I'm no longer Johnny Come-lately. She didn't pluck that hair for my benefit. Slaney's isn't the easy option I was hoping for and my appetite is becoming more than a rumble.

Outside a drizzle has descended on the town and there's no one abroad. Wednesdays are quiet anyway. What I have in mind doesn't require a crowded bar and an evening of mating dances. I hurry home to my internet connection.

At first I can't find the escort website on my laptop. Maybe it's been shut down, I wouldn't be surprised. Then I find it. The girls have made their move and there are new names in Kilkenny, six of them, including the tantalising Melody.

Do they all live in the same apartment or is it really a freelance operation? Maybe it's already too late to call. It's probably not Krystal after all.

'Hello?' a voice calls down the phone. I don't remember actually dialling the number. 'Yes?'

I look at the phone and look at the half-naked picture of Melody on the screen.

'Hello,' I answer but they've hung up. I hit redial.

'Listen, if this is a joke I've heard them all so save your credit,' a female voice says. Even angry she sounds sexy.

'Sorry, no, it's not a joke. Can I speak to Krystal, please?'

'We don't have anyone called Krystal here. Who do you want?'

'Oh, I mean Melody.'

I hear her sigh and a hand goes over the phone. She shouts something in a foreign tongue that I can't make out but it sounds slightly French.

'Hello?' It's Melody and her voice is small, husky. 'You want to come see me? Have you seen me before? What's your name?'

'Sure. No. Yes, I mean. My name is … Peter.'

'Okay, Peter. Tonight? You can come tonight. What do you want?'

'How do you mean?'

'What services do you want? From the menu. You're looking at the website, right?'

I look at her picture on the screen and scroll down to the list of services. I can't bring myself to say any of the words written there. 'Everything. I'll have some of everything. Surprise me.'

'That could take some time. How long do you want?'

'An hour, let's say.' I'm thinking three minutes is more likely.

'Okay. That will be two hundred euro, Peter. You can come straight over.'

She gives me directions. It's only just round the corner from Slaney's. I hang up.

What the hell am I doing? The stubble on my chin has grown, my rubbing palm notices. Not once in my life have I paid for sex. This is sordid. But I am fascinated to know if it really is the dancing girl I used to know as Krystal. Only one way to find out.

Those pints are still coursing through my veins. Out on John Street a Garda car rolls past and I look at the pavement, walking on up the hill to where I can do absolutely whatever I want.

At the cash point on the corner I withdraw the Melody money. I can't help but look shifty; it feels like I have a huge neon sign hanging over my head. The money burns a hole in McKinsey's jacket pocket. Maybe that's what happened to his trousers.

I have the directions in my head and find the address just off Gas Works Lane. The flats are newish but already feel seedy, as if no one lives there but just uses the place. I press a button marked 'The Agency' but before there's any response a fella comes down the stairs in a hurry, opens the door and walks past me. Probably running home to write a review on the website.

I'm in. The second floor stairwell door opens onto a carpeted corridor where a tall girl stands in a long silky top and not much else.

'I saw you on the camera,' she says.

It's not her.

'Right, yeah.'

She raises a finely trimmed eyebrow. Everything about her is calculated to catch the eye.

'Peter. I called, spoke to, um, Melody.'

She smiles, her lips shiny, and takes me by the hand.

'Come on, then. Don't be shy.' We walk through a door at the end of the corridor, into a flat, and pause outside another closed door.

'If you're not happy with Melody then ask for me next time,' she whispers, her lips touching my ear. 'My name is Sonya.'

I hear a raised female voice from inside the room. Sonya knocks on the door.

'Melody? I have Peter here for you.' She waits until the door starts to open and then walks away. 'Sonya,' she mouths to me as she goes, all legs.

'Peter,' a husky voice says and there she is.

Her face looks older, of course, but she's still beautiful. Between the first two fingers of her left hand is a smoking cigarette and the right holds a phone to her ear. She's shorter than I remember, but then I was usually sitting down while she danced. I don't think much of the tracksuit she's wearing.

She stands aside to let me enter. A few more words in what I assume is Romanian and she puts the phone down on a bedside table.

'There's a shower in there.' She points to a door. 'Shower gel, towel and everything. Take as long as you like but the clock starts now. Put the money here on the table. One hour is two hundred euro.'

Wow. Maybe Sonya next time.

'I'm not sure I need a shower.'

She looks McKinsey's suit up and down.

'You take a shower,' she says, puffs on the cigarette and slips off one of her runners with the heel of the other foot.

It's not optional. In the bathroom I take off the dead man's clothes and let the hot water blast away at my body. What the hell am I doing?

The world's grumpiest, worst dressed tart calls into the bathroom. 'Listen, you can spend the whole hour in there if you like. It's all the same to me.'

I try to remember if any of the items on the menu included this sort of service. Maybe it's some kind of role play.

The bathroom mirror is mercifully misted up, obscuring my pasty complexion, sagging physique and a back that has more hair on it than my head, which isn't difficult. A bath robe sits folded on the toilet seat and I put it on.

'Lie on the bed,' she says from a chair in the corner when I come out of the bathroom.

There's a big cluster of pillows and I half sit, looking over. She's changed her clothes and done something with her hair, pulled tight back from her face and giving her almond eyes a Slavic slant.

'What do you want?' She sounds like an interrogator but there's a touch of a smile on her mouth.

'What's on offer?'

'Everything. Anything. Except for one thing.'

I want it.

'Which is?'

Her lips go thin.

'G.F.E. I don't do G.F.E. Everything else.'

I rack my brain, trying to recall the online tarts' glossary. Good for everything? Gross foot-job effort?

'No kissing, no cuddling. No romance. No G.F.E. – girlfriend experience. You know nothing about this, do you?'

I shake my head. Nearly twenty years older than her but I feel like a kid.

She walks over and sits on the side of the bed.

'It's just fucking. Fucking, fucking, fucking. Any way you want. You pay me and I let you fuck me.'

Her eyes are dark brown. She runs a pink tongue over the tip of her top lip. I know this tease. I really want to kiss her mouth.

'Do you have some music?' I ask.

'Sure.' She gets up and walks over to a music system. 'What would you like.'

'Whatever you like.'

A press of some buttons and a heavy rhythm starts to come from the speakers. I roll off the bed and stand by the chair.

'You want me to lie on the bed?' she asks.

I shake my head and sit down in the chair.

'You want to watch me do something to myself? Is that it? I can do that.'

Would be nice. But I just smile at her.

'What? What is it you want me to do?' She looks at me crossly and glances at the phone on the bedside table.

'Come over here,' I say to her.

She walks over and stands in front of me. I smile again. Her leg is moving to the rhythm of the music and she starts to twist her hips. A look of recognition passes over her face.

'I remember you. Yes. A long time ago.'

She lets the music move her, hands above her head. I relax and enjoy. Her slim body is lithe beneath the transparent negligee. She closes her eyes and does a few quirky moves to loops in the music.

'I like this one.' She leans over me and drapes her long brown hair over my head, her eyes open now and sparkling.

I have the urge to touch and reach up but she leaps back before I can, all in time to the rhythm.

'You used to spend a lot of money, up in Dublin. Your name wasn't Peter...'

'And your name wasn't Melody.'

She spins around and the negligee comes flying off, thrown to one side.

'Yes. You are the guy who used to sit and watch. Ger.'

Her underwear is patterned with flowers, expensive looking. She's petite, small-chested but perfect.

'Will I take it off?' she asks, smoothing her hands down her chest and over her bra.

I nod. My pulse is audible in my ears. The donor's heart is being exercised.

The room is warm and her naked skin builds a sheen. I remember Krystal once told me she had dance training in Romania as a teenager. The beat builds to a climax and then the music stops. A buzzer sounds on the bedside table.

'Your hour is up, *Peter*. You can get dressed.'

'I'll pay for another hour.'

She laughs. 'This isn't the Gentlemen's Club. My next client will be knocking on the door in five minutes. You have to go.'

In five minutes some punter is going to be fucking her nasty. My passion is piqued. I go to the bathroom and get McKinsey's suit back on in haste.

'It's okay, Ger,' she says and touches my arm as I reach for the door. 'I enjoyed you being here. I like to dance.'

'I like to watch you dance.'

Her eyes are a warm brown, pulling me in. She stands on her toes and kisses my cheek.

'Come back and see me again.'

A knock on the door, so I open it. Sonya is standing there, her eyebrows raised. She steps aside to let me pass, a guy who looks like he just came in from the fields standing behind her.

'My name is Sonya,' she whispers in the farmer's ear and ushers him in to Krystal.

I don't even make it to the front door before Sonya is making her pitch.

'Did you enjoy your first visit, Peter? Everything to your satisfaction?'

She runs one hand down my arm and the other across her collar bone and down her cleavage. Nice skin tone, tall, leggy and attractive in a scary way, but she's like the last Christmas turkey. Everyone in the shop has already manhandled this bird.

'I had a great time, thanks.'

Her mouth drops open and she takes a couple of seconds to recover.

'Great. We'll see you again then?'

'For sure.'

Cat and mouse

I can feel the blood coursing around my body like an athlete. *I had a great time* she said.

'Well,' a voice says as I step out onto the street. A waft of tobacco rolls out of Andy McAuliffe's open car window. 'Get in, Ger. We're going for a little drive.'

'I don't think so.'

'Just get in. I want to talk to you about Roisín McGuire.'

After looking up and down the street I walk around, get in the passenger side and slide deep into the seat.

'We'll have to stop meeting like this,' I say as he takes us across the lights, past the Bucket of Blood and on towards the stadium.

'I understand, Ger. You're working for Reaney. I understand. But you have to understand that your predecessor and I had a close working relationship.'

It seems I'm destined to wear dead man's shoes, one way or another.

'Ronnie? He was your snitch?'

'I'm not saying that. I'm saying he played his part in maintaining the equilibrium around here.'

We pass worryingly close to Reaney's offices and then we're on the long link road to the motorway. This is all new since I went away.

'What happened to Ronnie?' I ask.

McAuliffe puts his foot down on the gas and the car surges forward.

'Let's just say he's gone away. He had a difference of opinion with Mr Reaney on a business matter.'

'What business matter?'

McAuliffe shakes his head at me. 'You really don't know what you've got into, do you, Ger?'

I want to say a detective inspector's slightly smelly car, but I don't.

'Where are we going?'

'Just for a drive. I need you to listen for a few minutes to what I have to say.'

'Well, I'm all yours.'

McAuliffe's police radio crackles and he turns the volume down.

'First of all, what were you doing in there?'

I laugh. 'You wouldn't believe me if I told you.'

'That's not what I mean. Were you checking out the opposition? Don't you realise that's probably how McGivney got himself killed?'

McGivney was killed by the Romanians. I know that because of the knife in the pie situation. So that means they're running the girls. My head's in a spin.

'How's that going, by the way?' I ask, trying to turn the conversation.

'McGivney? Let's just say we're pursuing several different lines of enquiry.'

'So you have nothing.'

'I can't say. So, what were you doing in there?'

I look at the speedometer. We're well over the limit, like we're in a rush to get somewhere with this.

'I was just seeing a girl. That's not against the law, is it?'

He turns and looks at me for a worrying length of time, considering we're hurtling towards the rear of a car in front of us.

'Not in Ireland, no.' He flicks a switch, a flash of blue light and the car in front pulls onto the hard shoulder to let us pass. 'If that's really why you were there then it's your choice. I would suggest you keep away.'

Well, that's not going to happen. Not after tonight's experience.

'Thanks for your concern, but I can look after myself.'

'The record suggests otherwise. As for Roisín McGuire, be very careful there.'

We come to the end of the link road and take the turn south onto the motorway proper. I bite my tongue, waiting to hear more.

'She's a very ambitious young lady,' McAuliffe eventually says. 'Investigative work should be left in the hands of An Garda Síochána. Steer well clear. I can't imagine any scenario where it's to your benefit to be involved with Roisín McGuire.'

'I can, but I take your point.'

'Try and think with something other than your dick for a change.'

'You sound like my wife. My ex-wife.'

We move into the overtaking lane and the engine roars. Involuntarily I grab hold of the door armrest.

'You're out of your depth, Ger. I know what happened ten years ago.'

He doesn't know the half of it.

'You're not a career criminal. These people will eat you for breakfast. You're a lone wildebeest surrounded by hyenas.'

I nod. That image is hitting home.

'Do you want my suggestion, Ger?'

I shake my head but say, 'Go on.'

'Leave. Never mind about the house, just up and off. Spain, somewhere warm. Make a new start.'

'Get the hell out of Dodge, you mean?'

'If you want to put it like that, yes.'

He puts on the indicator and we pull off the motorway at the Stoneyford exit.

I let myself have a chuckle. 'I'm being run out of town by the local sheriff.'

'For your own good. You were lucky to come out of it in one piece last time.'

'Lucky? A heart transplant and ten years in Portlaoise is an odd sort of luck.'

McAuliffe's mouth tightens as he sucks his teeth. This is about his guilt. Fair enough. His ruthless interrogation methods led to me having a stranger's heart beating inside my chest.

'You're alive, Ger. My advice – get out. This organised prostitution is an ugly business. New people are involved, not from around here. They don't respect the status quo. And as for Roisín McGuire, if she goes stirring things up it'll make all our lives very difficult.'

'Perhaps she'll go away.'

'How well do you know her?'

'She's going to give me some advice on home furnishings.'

'Jesus.'

We both laugh this time.

'Seriously,' he says, 'I've dealt with her before. She's like a dog with a bone. She's going to be sticking her nose into everything, unless something bigger comes up elsewhere.'

'There's nothing I can do about that.'

We hurtle through the darkness, past Danesfort and back into the outskirts of Kilkenny.

'I'll drop you in behind The Village,' he says.

The drive-through car park behind the pub is half empty.

'I'll think about what you said.' I open the car door.

'Good man,' he says and he's gone.

First stop The Village, as I'm here. Then it's across to Christy's, and after on down to the Blue Bar where I stay for several. By the time I stagger downhill over the bridge and home, I've figured out a plan. How to have my cake and eat it.

Day 7 – The Fly

The phone buzzes and rings, buzzes and rings.

'Well, Ger.' It's the boss.

'Uhh,' I manage to say. 'Bob?'

'Yep. You sound like you're still in bed. Are you still in bed?'

'Yeah. What time is it?' I hold the phone away from me and try to focus. Ten o'clock. Crap.

'Time you ran a little errand for me. How's the kitchen?'

'Yeah, it's good, thanks. The lads did well.'

'Pleased to hear it. I'm giving you the opportunity to pay it all back with one little job.'

'What price a new kitchen? Do I have to whack someone or whatever they call it?'

'Funny. You're a real comedian, did anyone ever tell you?'

'Yeah. Andy McAuliffe.'

The line goes quiet.

'He keeps at me. The fecker won't leave me alone.'

'Keep him sweet, Ger. No point in upsetting McAuliffe. As for that journalist, has she been on to you?'

I have to think quickly but my brain is porridge.

'The blonde?'

'Yeah. Just how many female journalists do you have sniffing around?'

'Well you know, Bob, when you're as big and famous an eejit as I am they're always on the lookout.'

His breath comes faster down the phone and I wonder what he's doing.

'Don't be cute. If I thought you were really an eejit I wouldn't have taken you on.'

He gives a cough and I hear the sound of hands slapping skin. He's having a massage.

'Listen, I have to go. Get yourself up to Dublin. Marks and Spencers at Liffey Valley for two this afternoon. You'll get a text with instructions. Bye.'

'Right. Bye,' I say but he's already gone.

I kind of like the guy but his trust is misplaced.

Liffey Valley. Very handy for a bit of clothes shopping but also in the right direction for dealing with another open issue. I imagine a small boy walking along the beach, throwing a stick for his dog while his mum laughs and the wind blows her curtain of hair across her pretty face.

A blink of an eye and it's half eleven. I must have dropped off again. Quick shower, casual clothes, no time for breakfast. I'll grab an all-day breakfast roll at the garage en route to the motorway. I quickly check Jo's facebook page again and write down the address. I don't have a printer for the Google map but it's pretty straightforward. There's just one coast road north out of Dublin.

I feel on the road to freedom, heading up the long motorway link road that McAuliffe introduced me to last night. A day off work, some nefarious deeds and a surprise for my ex. The boxes I put in the boot slide around as I take the slip onto the main motorway a bit too fast, one hand feeding me the breakfast roll, the other holding the coffee, my elbow guiding the wheel.

The thought crosses my mind that the Fly might be setting me up for something but I shake it out of my head like a flea in a dog's ear. He's investing in me; the job, this car, my new kitchen. There's no reason he would stitch me up – not yet, anyway. My strategy, as usual, is to rely upon my spider-senses.

At around 130 kph the old Audi settles into a rhythmic pattern of vibration that builds and climaxes in a huge shudder. One convulsion coincides with passing under a bridge and the sound resonates like a car ferry.

I can see the new road stretching out into the distance across the farmland, underpasses and bridges built for farmers to move their livestock and tractors. After a few attempts I manage to get the Audi to do its shuddering thing under another bridge. It takes a bit of slowing down and speeding up, not much of a problem with almost no other cars on the road.

The next bridge has a string of cows ambling across it and I have to boot the accelerator to time it right. I'm laughing at the rear view image of cattle running scared across the bridge when a car pulls up level in the overtaking lane. Two uniformed guards.

My speedo says 160 and that's a trip before the judge in these parts. The guards look impassively over and I let the car drift back down to the 120 limit. They keep level until I get there and then they boot it off into the distance. Whatever the Fly's errand is, now I've been spotted I'm going to have to take the scenic route home.

The road empties out before me and I have no idea where I am, even which county I'm in. They've done a great job of removing the character of the country. All those annoying little doglegs in one horse towns were part of the patchwork quilt of quaintness everyone loved to hate. This long haul, without even a service station, gives too much time to think.

What am I going to say to Jo? I could just turn up unannounced or call ahead; I have her number. She might want to let the kid know his dad is going to visit. On the other hand that gives her a chance to blow me out. In truth I don't want to see her but I do want to see my son.

The smooth surface of the road is interrupted only by the Audi's intermittent shuddering. Then the road noise increases and I'm on an old stretch I recognise near Naas. My phone jigs about in the cup holder and the screen flashes a picture. Looks like some sort of sports bag. On the edge of Dublin, at the Newland's Cross traffic lights, I get a good look at it.

Go into M&S at 2pm sharp and buy a bag exactly like this one. Then go to Costa Coffee and wait until someone drops a do-nut.

Maybe *drop a do-nut* is some sort of Dublin criminal slang. Only one way to find out.

The M50 feels completely different to when I was last here. Traffic moves uniformly at 100 kph and vehicles peel off and slip on seamlessly. I miss the Liffey Valley turn and have to cross the toll bridge but the pay booths have disappeared. Dublin traffic looks like a well-oiled machine instead of the twentieth century disaster I remember.

Liffey Valley, on the other hand, hasn't changed and, once I've managed to work my way back down to the right exit, I find M&S just where it always was.

The clock on the car dashboard says half one; time to spare. The trip was quicker than I expected.

Marks and Spencer remains the bastion of menswear. A suit jacket and two pairs of trousers, a pile of work shirts and several pairs of socks. I have quite a little shopping spree under my belt when I remember to check the time and see it's nearly two and I haven't yet bought the sports bag in the picture.

At two minutes to the hour I'm at the pay point with all my purchases and almost throwing my money at the woman on the till.

'Will I put your things in the bag?' she asks.

'Thanks,' I say, feeling the perspiration breaking out on my back. 'I'll do it.'

After paying I grab the sports bag, all my stuff inside, and run out of M&S into the mall. Of course the alarm goes off so I spin on my heel and sprint back to the pay point where the woman removes a security tag from the new suit.

It's five past two when I get to Costa Coffee. No free tables. I hover until an old lady vacates her pitch.

'You have to go to the counter to get served,' says a lad in a uniform as he clears off the table.

I sit myself down and put my bag next to the chair.

'I'll give you a tenner if you bring me a latte,' I reply.

'Okay,' he says, takes my tenner and turns straight into the path of an old man carrying a plate of pastries which fall to the floor, the plate breaking.

'Sorry, sorry!' the lad says, picking up the pastries. 'I'll get you some more of those.'

The old man grumbles, bends, hoists his sports bag over a shoulder, and follows the lad back to the counter.

Eventually my latte turns up. I sip on it and people-watch. Mostly pensioners walking painfully slowly and teenage girls with fake tan. I'm twitching to check the bag at my feet. No sign of that old man.

At half-two I decide to go. The sports bag feels heavy but I resist the urge to open it until I've placed it in the boot of the car.

Cash. A lot of it. British sterling, Northern Bank notes. I know what kind of a mess this is. Over £26 million stolen in a robbery in 2004, most of it never recovered. I'd say there's a good million of it here. I'm one of the bad guys now, for sure.

I zip up the bag, close the boot and get in the driver's seat. My first thoughts are to drive to the ferry and get off the island. But that's pointless. Even now Europol probably have an alert for large numbers of these notes turning up anywhere. Not to mention what the Fly and his associates would do when they caught up with me, which they surely would. I look around the car park. There's probably someone watching to make sure I play it straight.

That bag is a one way ticket to a long stretch back in Portlaoise prison. Next time I'll ask more questions before running errands.

The Audi's steering wheel feels clammy under my hands. My palms are sweating. The M50 roundabout. I look at the signs for south and take the turn for north. A bag full of bank heist cash from a suspected terrorist raid isn't going to keep me from seeing my son after ten years.

~

The sea looks cold out at Baldoyle. I know Jo's house is on the strand and I roll the Audi up and down the seafront until I'm sure which one is hers. Brick built, semi-detached. A good solid house from the middle of the last century. There's a nearly new Alfa Romeo hatchback on the driveway. Jo always wanted one of those.

I park a good bit up and take a stroll along the beach. Sun breaks through the clouds and blinks off the shallow water. This would be a great place to bring up a kid, out every day for walks along the sand.

The sun dips back behind its grey blanket and a cold wind buffets my ears, a reminder of what seaside really means in Ireland.

Traffic begins to get busy on the strand road and I check my watch. It's nearly four and the kids will be coming out of school. The Alfa pulls out of Jo's drive but I'm too far away to see if she's behind the wheel. It drives up past my car.

Back in the Audi, out of the cold breeze, I have to come up with a game plan. What am I here for? A boy I've never met and an ex-wife who doesn't want to know me. Or does she? Of course it made perfect sense for her to have full custody of the lad with me locked away for the duration.

No contact for years. Jo will know I'm out, though. If no one has told her then she'll surely have seen or heard it on the news. The infamous criminal bungler Ger Mayes, back on the loose. She must be half expecting me.

The Alfa comes whizzing by my window and I catch a glimpse of Jo, I'd recognise her profile anywhere, and the top of a tussled, sandy coloured head in the back. They pull onto their driveway and get out. I'm a good way off but I see the boy run to the front door and then Jo sends him back to the car for his schoolbag.

Can I just walk up to the door and into his life? Presumably I'm not breaking any laws by approaching them. I should have had McDonald check that. If Jo calls the guards there's the small matter of those banknotes in the boot of my car to consider.

Let them settle in for a few minutes and do whatever they do.

Inside the boot, next to the Fly's money, are my offerings for Jo. Three items from my Italian kitchenware collection. She always loved Alessi, I can't go wrong with that. What should it be? Kettle, hand blender or kitchen timer? I don't have a present for the boy. A pit forms in my stomach.

It's an excuse not to go to the door. I don't need a present for him. No, Jo would expect me to turn up empty-handed. I always got things like that wrong.

Compromising on the hand blender, I go to the boot, take out the box and start walking towards the house. Then I stop and lean against the sea wall. Perhaps the boy will come out on his own and I can talk to him. No, not a good idea.

I turn the box over in my hands. Jo has remarried. Jo has a hot temper. It would be better to call her and arrange a meet. But then she might say no.

My intuition continues to fail me as the door of the house opens and the boy comes running out. He looks just like I did at that age. Smiling, round face full of freckles. A little chubby.

Jo walks out behind the lad, a hand raised. I begin to raise mine until I see a black Saab pull into the driveway. The driver's door opens and out steps a man I vaguely recognise. What I do very clearly recognise is that the boy is a miniature facsimile of the man. The child doesn't really look like me at all.

The blender in its box drops to the ground. Jo looks over with a hand shielding her brow from the sun which has broken through again. I turn my back and march up the strand to my car.

Bastards

She gyrates to the music, her fragrance swirling around the room. This is how I want her to be.

'You're not allowed to touch,' Krystal says, her naked body tantalisingly close.

She sits lightly on my lap and I brush her shoulder with my lips. I can taste her scent.

'No touch,' she says and whirls away again.

~

It was a long drive back from Dublin; a nine year journey.

Ciaran is the father's name, I remembered. Jo's former Pilates instructor.

Those concrete pillars holding up each bridge over the M50 looked increasingly attractive. My speed was up to 120 and rising, just needed to twitch the steering wheel at the right moment and it would all be over. Me, the Audi and its engine in a mash of rusting regret.

She did nothing to make me believe I wasn't the father. Taken for an eejit, I was.

I turned the wheel in towards the central reservation, aiming for the supporting pillar of the next bridge, and then pulled it away again.

It wasn't melodrama; I'd seen enough of that inside prison. Who would give a shit? Rita? I'd be just another dead ex-con bed partner. Krystal? Loss of a new client. Jo? Ex-husband lying dead in a cloud of stolen banknotes and designer Italian kitchenware. I didn't want to die an eejit.

The car slowed down to the speed limit and slipped over into the middle lane. I pulled down the sun visor and offended eyes looked back at me from the mirror. Getting even would be so much better than getting dead.

The twisting, bendy roads on the country route home suited my mood. Jo and Ciaran had done well out of the divorce settlement. A range of punishments wandered across my imagination as the day darkened and the Audi hurtled along the Wicklow lanes. Financially swindled, emotionally water-tortured and, worst of all, cuckolded. All deserved payment in kind.

In an old fashioned way he needed a beating. That's not really my department so I would have to call in a few favours. By the time I got through Blessington and on to Baltinglass I was burying him in a shallow forest grave and Jo underneath a new shed in my garden. That left the boy and I wished him no harm. He could go live with her sister who had always been on my fantasy list.

With that suggestion revenge segued on to something more subtle. I would look up the sister and move into her life. Plans for Jo and her fella matured from straightforward body disposal to financial ruin. That's what led me to stash a handful of Northern Bank bills in my trouser pocket before I stowed the sports bag with the rest of it under the sink in my new kitchen.

With my plan carefully formed my focus switched to getting drunk, getting teased and, sooner or later, getting shagged.

~

It's the allure of the belly dancer.

'Would you come to my house?' My voice sounds breathless.

'I don't do outcalls,' she says, her lips touching my ear and then she's spinning across the room to the beat. She freezes, arches an eyebrow and continues to dance.

The hour is done. This time her lips are soft on mine as I leave; her shoulder moist from perspiration under my hand. If it's hers or mine I don't know.

No sign of McAuliffe, thank God. I can do without the fathering routine tonight.

No visit to Slaney's, Rita can't slake this thirst. Nevertheless, a brief pang of conscience causes me to hesitate at the entrance to her pub. It's less than a week since we were wallowing in the Gimp's blood and sharing the cross of suspicion. But sure, she knows where to find me if she needs me.

The conversation hushes when I walk into the Edge of the World.

'Smithwick's, Ger?' Mary asks, like I'm a regular.

I nod and smile.

'My wife was fucking another man,' I say to her, six pints later.

She leans in, her voice low. 'My man was fucking another wife.'

Her hard smile weakens at one corner.

'Treachery is lurking everywhere,' I say in my best Shakespearean. 'Fucking treachery, fucking bastards.'

A rancid odour wafts from behind me and, in a moment of drunken confusion, I think the Gimp has come back for me. It's John-Jo.

'She doesn't like Eye-talian,' he says. 'She never liked pasta or pizza or any of that. And she doesn't like the Eye-talian kitchen design.'

I give my best ironic grin but it feels like I've lost my teeth.

'She says this is Kilkenny, not Milan. She doesn't want her kitchen appliances looking like a child designed them.

She wants a kettle, a toaster and a can opener. No names, nothing fancy. *None of that shite.*'

My Smithwick's glass clinks with his whiskey tumbler.

'I know a fella will take the lot off me, though, for a coupla grand.' John-Jo downs his Jameson. 'One of them big houses out the Kells road.'

Kells road, Kells road. Something flickers in my dulled mind. Ella on Saturday, my date. Maybe a job lot of Alessi coming her way?

'What's the name?' I ask John-Jo.

'Cullen. Eddie Cullen. For his daughter, she lives out there.'

Bingo.

'What's he like, Eddie Cullen?'

John-Jo drains his whiskey and raises his empty glass to Mary. I shake my head as he looks at my pint, still half full.

'Old money. Well connected. One of the local names.'

'And the daughter?'

Mary brings John-Jo his whiskey with a pint of Heineken.

'Steer well clear is my advice.' He throws back the Jameson's and takes a gulp of the lager.

'She's trouble then?'

His eyes narrow and he shakes his head. I may as well post details of my upcoming date with Ella on the pub notice board.

'No, not her. The ex-husband. Headcase. She has an injunction against him.' He takes a packet of cigarettes from his jacket and flips open the lid.

'Why doesn't the father have him sorted?'

'This isn't fecking Limerick, Ger. Anyhow, the husband is a guard.'

I cover my eyes with one hand and squeeze my temples.

'It's not for me to say, Ger, but I'd leave it well alone. Going for a smoke. Join me?'

'You sure? You know what happened to the last guy.'

John-Jo barks a laugh, shows those devastated teeth of his and gives my shoulder a slap with his hand. It's like being hit with a baton.

Drunken smoking is becoming a bad habit for me.

I'm not sure of the time or even the day. The few passersby keep their distance as we lean against the steel shutters of the shop front by the bar's entrance.

'How come the ex is still a guard?' I ask in between puffs. 'If she's got an injunction then it must be pretty bad.'

John-Jo looks at the ground then up at me.

'Sergeant Eamonn Murphy is good at the balancing act, is what. She won't prosecute and the guards look after their own.'

'Eamonn Murphy?' I say.

'Yep. He's a fucker.'

I recall Sergeant Eamonn's manhandling during my recent trip to the Garda station when the Gimp was found.

'He's a fucker all right.'

'So steer well clear, Ger. A bit of friendly advice.'

I nod. Of course I won't.

John-Jo flicks the butt of his cigarette into the gutter and turns. I have to go before I start to blurt out all my troubles. Need to keep some cards up my sleeve.

'Gotta go. Good luck with the kitchenware.'

For a second his look says I have nothing to go to, then the judgement drops from his face.

'Yeah, thanks. See ya, Ger.' He gives me a brother handshake and heads back inside.

I feel conspicuous and drunk, alone on the street. The idea of food crosses my mind but it's not that late and I can't be rolling drunk into a chipper or somewhere at this time and making a show of myself, so I cross the road and head for the house.

The air is cool and I feel tired. At the Maudlin Tower I falter and next thing I know the ground has risen to meet me. That's the knee out of Old McKinsey's suit trousers. I laugh and then swear out loud. Some money-laundering, Northern bastard has my new suit in the switched sports bag, together with a nice selection of socks and pants. Health to wear them, as my granny used to say.

The key doesn't want to work the front door lock. I look up the street and see someone watching me from a parked car. Then the lock turns, the door yields begrudgingly and I fall inside. Barely have I turned on the light when there's a tap on the door. Not again. Won't the bastards leave me alone?

'Ger. We need to finish that conversation from last night.'

'Roisín. What a pleasant surprise.'

I let her in and push the door closed. She walks into the kitchen and turns on the light, which seems very bright to me.

'You're drunk,' she says.

'I must be. When did we get married?'

'Funny.'

She looks at the McKinsey suit, the bloody hole in the knee, and shakes her head.

'Have you eaten today? No, I didn't think so. Go sit down and I'll be back in ten minutes.'

I hear a bang on the front door and open my eyes. I'm in the leather chair in the sitting room, must have dozed off. My knee hurts when I stand up to get the door.

'I didn't think you were going to let me back in,' Roisín says, carrying a brown paper bag into the kitchen.

The smell of vinegar on hot battered fish and chips gets my taste buds watering. She finds two greyish plates and serves up the food.

We stand in the kitchen and eat with our fingers. The kettle boils and she makes tea.

'You'd make someone a lovely wife,' I say through a mouthful of fish and chips.

'You'd make someone a terrible husband.'

'I already have.'

I lick my lips and wash down the food with tea.

'So, to what do I owe the pleasure of your visit?' My words are a bit slurred.

She wraps up her chip paper and looks at me.

'Are you going to help me, Ger? I know the Fly is up to something and I'm not talking about your little Alessi collection in there.' She nods her head towards the front room in a gesture that doesn't seem to belong to her.

My eyes are fixed on hers with all the intensity I can muster. Don't look at the cupboard under the sink. Don't look at the cupboard under the sink.

'What do you think he's up to?'

'Drugs, human trafficking, organised prostitution and money laundering,' she says.

I shake my head.

'You're wrong. He's just a Mr Fixit.'

'Come on. You must have seen and heard something by now. There's a war starting over organised internet prostitution. That's why Raymond McGivney was murdered, I'm sure of it.'

'That's as maybe. I wouldn't know anything about that sort of thing. I'm not the sort of guy needs to pay for sex.'

Roisín laughs. 'You're just out of prison, Ger. I wouldn't put anything past you.'

'Want a drink?' I ask, walking to the fridge. The kitchen seems to be a bit unsteady.

'You should lay off the booze a bit and get in shape. A storm is coming, Ger, whether you admit it or not. You'll need your wits about you,' she says, but takes a can of beer from my hand regardless.

And that's about the last thing I remember.

Day 8 – Friends

A bee buzzes right in my ear and I flick a hand at it. The noise recedes up the road. It wasn't a bee but some boy racer in his souped-up Honda Civic. I'll track the bastards down and cement their exhaust pipes.

Roisín has a point; this has to stop. Week two of freedom starts today and I've woken up mouldy from drink every morning, just like the prison counsellor said I would. I turn to thank her for setting me straight, and for the great sex last night.

She's not there. Not only that, I still have my underpants and shirt on. How I got to bed I don't know. There's a plaster on my knee where I ripped McKinsey's trousers last night. I remember doing that and eating a fish supper.

The money! Holy Jesus! I leap out of bed.

The knee is seized up when I try to run downstairs, like a schoolboy's football injury.

It's open an inch, the cupboard door under the sink. I almost rip it off the hinges and sink to the ground. Empty. No holdall, no million pounds of bank robbery cash.

The steel sink is cold under my palms as I puke. Dead. I'm dead.

Upstairs I cram the few clothes piled on the old wooden chair into a backpack and then go to the bathroom. The knee gives way and I have to lean on the cistern. Then the cold sweat starts on my neck, moves down my back, and the other leg gives way. I've had this before. Nothing else to do except curl into a ball on the floor and let it pass.

The shirt is cold and wet on my chest. After a few minutes I'm able to roll on my back and enjoy the coolness of it. The heart feels fine; it's some other kind of attack. Booze, anxiety, I don't know. Then I'm too cold.

I crawl into the shower, reach up and let the miserable flow of water warm up on my back. The shirt and pants are difficult to peel off and I lose it again, on my knees under the water. The waste bin under the sink is just at eye level and something red catches my eye; a tissue with lipstick on it. A glimmer of hope sparks through the haze of last night.

Covered in soapy shower gel and leaving sodden footprints in the crushed old carpet, I stagger back into the bedroom and pull open McKinsey's wardrobe door. The holdall full of money smiles back at me. I vaguely remember now, stashing it there while Roisín was in the bathroom. I knew, of all places, she wouldn't look in McKinsey's wardrobe.

So I will live to give the Fly his money. Except for the few notes I've swiped for my own purposes which must be in the torn suit trousers.

A wave of embarrassment warms me as I find the trousers on the floor and start to realise Roisín must have put me to bed like a drunken father. The pockets are empty, of course, because they're bottomless, which I forgot when I stuffed the notes in. So somewhere between the car, the sink, the street, Krystal's boudoir and the pub, there are a half dozen hot sterling banknotes blowing about. Brilliant.

The door bell rings. If it's the Fly he'll just let himself in. If it's the guards they'll kick it in. If it's the Provos they'll shoot their way in. I grab a hand towel, try to wrap it round my waist and peek around the top of the stairs. The bell rings again. I tiptoe back into the bedroom, pull back the curtain and look down through the closed window.

Apart from that bastard traffic warden who looks up from his malicious ticketing and gives me a wave, all I can see is the top of a woman's head and long blonde hair. Down I go.

'Morning.'

It's Mary from the Edge of the World. She looks at my too small towel and laughs. That worldly wise face turns into a young girl when she grins. I feel immediate chemistry. She brings a hand from behind her back and waves a fistful of notes at me.

'I think these are yours.'

I try to grip the towel together with one hand and hold the door open with the other.

'Come in, come in.'

When the door is shut I just grab her in a big hug.

'You've saved my life!' I'm almost crying on her shoulder.

Her hair feels soft on my face and smells heavenly. She's taller than I realised, almost my height.

Mary takes a half step away, the towel in her hand.

'Your towel.'

We both look down at the towel and my passion.

'Nice, Ger.'

She lets her hand brush the lad as I take the towel and wrap it back around my waist. Her other hand waves the notes again.

'I used to work in a bank. If I'm not mistaken…'

I take the notes and fold them into my palm.

'You're mistaken.'

She looks me up and down.

'You're all lathered up and your breath smells of beer,' she says but she's smiling. 'I'll put the kettle on and you go finish your shower.'

Under the water I think about what next. I instinctively trust Mary. Something about her. She feels like an ally.

'Here's your tea,' she says when I come back down. 'You have some nice stuff in here but I don't much like what the lads have done with the kitchen.'

'It's Alessi. If you like it I have loads more in…'

Her grin reaches from ear to ear.

'You said what *the lads* have done?' I say.

'Yeah, Dad's lads.'

Holy crap. I can see the family resemblance now between her face and young Bobby's.

'You didn't know? Ger, you can be a bit slow.' Her grin shows wide, perfect teeth.

'But, but … if you're Bob Reaney's daughter why are you working as a barmaid?'

'Excuse me, it's my pub.' She moves a bit closer. 'So, are you going to tell me why you filched those notes?'

Her big blues are open wide in feigned innocence. I'd say she's ten years younger than me. I'm putty in her hands. Honesty is the best, no, honesty is the only policy. For a change.

I tell all.

'Ooh!' she winces when I tell her about the boy. I omit the part where I was bonking Renée, Jo's best friend. And the bit about Renée jumping pregnant off the bridge when her cancer was diagnosed as terminal.

'So I had the idea to plant the notes and stitch up Mr Bendy Pilates with a little call to the guards.'

Her eyebrows raise and she holds out a hand. I fish the notes out of my pocket and give them to her.

'Where's the rest of it?' she asks.

'Come here and I'll show you.'

Mary follows me upstairs and grimaces at McKinsey's wardrobe.

'Do you know what he did?' she asks.

'Not exactly, but I think you're going to tell me.'

'No, but I think you're a brave man to take on this house. You should gut the place, make it yours.'

'I intend to.'

She flinches when I open McKinsey's wardrobe door, as if he were going to spring out.

'You know he kept them in there?'

'Kept what?' I ask.

'His trophies.'

'Where are they now?'

She looks at me like I'm crazy. 'Where do you think they are? The guards took them all away.'

I lift the holdall full of notes out of the wardrobe, place it on the bed and lock the door forever on McKinsey.

'You'd better get this over to Dad before temptation strikes again,' she says, unzipping the bag and putting the stray notes in.

Self-assured, glamorous in a slightly tarty way. I fancy her as my gangster's moll.

She looks up at me looking at her and her eyes narrow.

'Get a haircut, fix up this place and I'll think about it.'

I add telepathy to her talents.

'You need to make a serious effort, Ger. Take a few nights off the beer and get this place properly sorted. Interior designer, that's what you need. Make it real classy, like.'

'Where would I find one of those?'

'No idea,' she says.

Her phone rings, a fast dance rhythm. She mouths sorry at me and answers it.

'Dad. What? Oh, Jesus! Is he at the hospital? No, I'm at Ger's house. Right, we'll be right there.'

'Is your dad okay?' I ask. The last thing I need is to be stuck with this bag of notes.

'You need to drive us to the warehouse. It's Bobby. He's been stabbed.'

~

On the way up to the Hebron I have just a few minutes to process what I heard of the phone call. They're not taking Bobby to the hospital. He's been stabbed. This is complicated.

'Park around the back,' Mary tells me as we pull up to Reaney's Distribution.

Sure enough, when we get to the loading bay it's a scene of devastation. Bobby is sitting on a packing crate, Nora holding a blood-soaked towel. The Fly is standing next to Bobby's BMW with one hand to his forehead. Inside the car are two very scared looking dolly birds and on the concrete floor, just inside the rollover door, is a man's body. Blood is pooled under the head, the angle of his neck looks wrong and so do his trousers.

Turf war

'He just walked straight in, came from nowhere,' Bobby says, his breath short. 'Came straight up and stuck me with the knife. I got the fucker.' He points at the body.

'You did that, son.' The Fly looks at the dead Romanian. 'You'll be okay but he's going nowhere.'

He pulls out his mobile, steps away and makes a call. I hear something about Bobby having an accident at work and the Fly arranging a game of golf for next week. Then he returns to his minions.

'Right. This is what's going to happen. Nora, you take Bobby to the Scotsman's house. You know where it is, right?'

'I do.'

'Use your own car. If the Scotsman can't fix you up, Bobby, then he'll take you to the hospital. Ger, give me the bag and then take the girls on in Bobby's beamer. You know the place?'

I shake my head.

'Bobby, give Ger directions before you go.'

I fetch the holdall from the Audi's boot and hold it out to the Fly. Mary is standing behind him, her face grim, but she gives me a slight wink before turning away.

~

The three storey townhouse over basement is in a new build on the north side of town. Unlike Krystal's place, it looks to be a very respectable neighbourhood.

I press the remote mounted on the BMW's dashboard and the underground garage door rolls slowly up.

'Where are you girls from?' I ask my passengers. They haven't uttered a word since we left the Hebron.

'I am from Catalonia,' the darker one says with some pride. 'Is in Spain.'

'So you moved here for the weather then,' I laugh. She doesn't.

'Russia,' the other girl says and looks out of the window.

'Have you been in Ireland a long time?' I ask, pulling into a parking space with the BMW's registration number painted on the floor.

'Since I was fifteen,' the Russian says. 'You ask lot of questions. Are you journalist or guard or something?'

I look at her eyes in the rear view mirror. She's not much more than a kid but there's enough hatred there for a lifetime.

'No. I'm just a regular guy.'

'Ha!' She gives a bitter bark of a laugh. 'Regular guy who runs brothel.'

'No, Anna,' the Spanish girl hisses to the Russian and then speaks to me. 'She didn't mean nothing.'

'What's your name?' I ask.

'You can call me Lupe. Means wolf,' the Spanish girl says. 'What do we call you?'

'Ger.'

'I thought your name was Pete,' Lupe says. I turn and see why she uses the wolf name; her grin is carnivorous. 'We're coming from the Romanians. That's why Constantin attacked Bobby.'

Holy crap.

'Was it Constantin who killed the Gimp?' I ask.

They both go quiet in the back. I look at their scared eyes in the mirror.

'Was it?'

'We never heard of this gimp person,' Anna says.

I get out of the car, open the boot and the girls take out their two suitcases on wheels before I can play the gentleman. The Russian is tall, the Spanish girl diminutive like Krystal. They walk easily on their heels to the stairwell. I half expect Roisín or some other reporter to jump out from behind a car and accost us. Ger the pimp, as seen on TV.

The fob on Bobby's key ring releases the door and we take the lift up to ground level. Two doors lead off the lobby and I knock on the one marked 13. One of the lads from the warehouse opens up, gives me a nod and ushers the girls in.

'Tea?' he asks me.

'Thanks, no. Things to do. See you later,' I reply.

Bobby's car is so quiet I have to rev the engine in the garage to make sure it's running. My mind is racing. I have the feeling Lupe is a career girl. The Russian has to be here illegally. They've both switched camps sometime recently and that's why the Gimp was done in. Bobby was lucky.

I'm in way over my head here.

Back at the warehouse things have been cleaned up but the air is filthy. I can hear Mary through the closed loading bay door.

'You always said you'd never get involved in something like this, Dad, and look what's happened. We're lucky Bobby isn't dead! When they find out he's killed that young lad there'll be no end to this. You've ruined everything!'

The Fly's voice is low and steady. I can't make out what he's saying but the rhythm is controlled and assertive. Silence follows for a few seconds and then the fire door next to the loading bay flies open with a bang. Mary thrusts a hand at me and I give her Bobby's keys.

'I hope you know what you've got yourself into,' she says to me as she climbs into the car. She lowers the driver's window. ' Look after yourself, Ger. And I don't just mean the haircut.'

She leaves with a scrabble of tires on the concrete.

'Mary has a temper.' The Fly has come out to stand beside me. 'Come on in, I have a little job for you.'

~

What was I thinking?

'Leave it to me,' I said to the Fly when he opened the Audi's boot in the loading bay to reveal the dead Romanian Constantin with a plastic bag over his head. I didn't flinch; I've seen my share of dead bodies, up close.

'Get rid. I want no trace. Looks like you'll be getting a new car out of it,' he said

I wanted to impress, let him know I could handle things. It seemed the right thing to do. Now I have a dead guy wrapped in a tarpaulin to dispose of. I don't even know where to get rid of my household rubbish these days. In prison we had a big bin.

Alin Petulengro went in the river and was never seen again, but I think I was just lucky with that. Renée jumped into the river at Kilkenny of her own accord. The other bodies in my pre-prison trail of disaster were stumbled upon by me and dealt with by the authorities, as was the Gimp. I have no idea what to do.

'I'll make you a coffee,' Nora says when I walk into my office.

She brings it in to me, closes the door and sits down.

'Thanks for the cuppa,' I say.

'Do you need some help?'

I nod. 'Quick, clean, he has to disappear forever.'

She bites on a thumbnail – the first time I've seen her anything other than icily cool.

'Did he come here alone?' I ask.

'Yes, as far as we can tell. He had a motorbike,' she says. 'It's already gone; one of the lads took it away on the back of a truck.'

'Any ideas? We can't take the risk of the body being found. I'm thinking they won't report him missing. They won't want the guards involved.'

'I have an idea,' she says, 'but I need to make a phone call first.'

She dials on her mobile.

'Hey, Phil, it's Nora. Are ye busy today? Durrow pigs? Sure, his business must be booming. What time's feeding? Delivery about eleven, you say?'

She gives me a thumbs up and listens for a few seconds.

'In your dreams, Phil. But there's no harming in dreaming, like. Thanks. Bye, bye, bye.'

'Pigs? You're kidding me.'

She looks at her phone. 'We don't have much time. Let's go.'

We're in the car and moving before I realise it's a team effort.

'Head direction Portlaoise,' she says, throwing two new pairs of work gloves into the passenger footwell.

Everything goes smoothly until we hit the Castlecomer road and the traffic grinds to a halt. A car is pulled to the side of the road, the driver standing talking to a uniformed guard in a high visibility vest.

'Don't worry,' Nora says, 'it's just a routine check. They're after tax and insurance, not dead bodies.'

Another guard stands in the middle of the road and checks the passing car windscreens one by one. He puts up a hand as we approach and I lower the window.

'Well,' he says, 'if it isn't the famous Mr Mayes.'

I don't recognise him.

'Well, guard,' I say, trying not to pee my pants. The foreign heart is doing a drumbeat in my chest.

He bends down to look in through the window and sees Nora.

'Well, Nora.'

'Right, Jim. I'll call you when the next specials are in.'

He smiles at her and indicates I should close my window. I guess that's what the raised middle finger means.

'We do have legitimate imports,' Nora says as I rocket the old Audi along towards Ballyragget. 'It's not all knock-off. Have to keep the local An Garda Síochána sweet.'

Her phone rings.

'Right. Can you hold them off for another half an hour? Thanks, much appreciated. Yeah, yeah. Bye, bye, bye.'

I smell the pigs before I see the farm.

'Pull up over there,' Nora says, pointing at the side of a big metal shed. 'Put these on.' She passes me a pair of the gloves.

The pigs come running out when they hear our footsteps. Huge porkers barging each other to get their snouts through the wooden fence. I open the boot.

'Not yet,' she says, pushing it shut. 'Follow me. It should be round here somewhere.'

We walk around the side of the shed to where the concrete ends in a huge expanse of rubble.

'Come on, we need to shift some of this.' She walks over to the rubble and has to jump down, into a depression in the ground.

It takes us about ten minutes to clear a man-sized hollow in the rubble. Then we go back to the car and I reverse it up to the mess. The Romanian is lighter than I expected, almost like a woman. We take one end each of the tarpaulin and schlep Constantin into his grave.

'Put rubble back on top, like this,' she says, kicking bits onto the body and placing heavier chunks with her gloved hands. 'Otherwise he'll float.'

When we're done the body is completely covered, invisible.

Five minutes out of the farmyard we pass a small fleet of concrete lorries going in the opposite direction, their huge mixers turning slowly.

'You've done this before,' I say, looking across at Nora as she files her nails.

'There used to be a lot more construction work going on,' she replies, and begins to apply nail varnish. 'Make sure you leave those gloves in the car.'

~

Two hours later I'm reliving my Marks & Spencer menswear shopping experience. This time I aim to hang on to my socks and pants.

When I come out my car has gone, according to plan.

'Goodbye Audi,' Bobby says from the window of his BMW. 'Kinda sad to see it go that way.'

'Yeah,' I say, feeling like it's my fault. He seems so artless. 'You seem to have staged a miraculous recovery from that knife attack.'

'Sure,' he says, 'I was wearing a stab vest. All I got was a flesh wound in the love handle.'

Not so artless after all then. I get in the passenger seat and we roar off.

'So you were expecting trouble?' I say.

'After what happened to the Gimp I'm not taking any chances and neither should you.' He turns to me and raises the eyebrows on that childish face. 'The girls recognised you, Ger. It's not exactly a bright idea to go visiting the other crowd. If you have to be doing that sort of thing then you should come to ours, now you know where it is.'

'Keep it in the family, like?'

'Sort of, yeah.'

'Well, I won't be going there again. Certainly not after today's little incident.'

He gives me a wide grin and a wink, and lets one hand swing the wheel around. Bobby drives fast and haphazardly on the motorway, overtaking vehicles on the inside when it suits him.

'This car goes well,' I say, hoping he might ease off a bit, but the ploy backfires.

'You ain't seen nothin' yet.'

He presses a button on the centre console and the car surges. We weave in and out of the traffic like it's standing still. In no time the M9 turn-off comes up and Bobby leaves it to the last second to take the slip road off.

'So, what sort of car is Dad going to get you, now the Audi is toast?'

He could be teasing me here. Daddy's little boy.

'I'll be more than happy with anything as long as it's not pink.'

'Come on, Ger. You must have your eye on something. Bringing the cash down and getting rid of that fecker this morning, I reckon you're in for a bonus.'

I just shrug.

'Suit yourself. What did you do with the body, by the way?'

'Weighted it down.' The way I see it, best to keep the nitty gritty knowledge to a limited audience.

'You fucked him into the river? Fair play.'

The miles roll by and then Bobby starts laughing.

'What?'

'You should have seen him, Ger. I nearly took the head right off him. Snapped like a stick, his neck did.' He laughs again and this time it gives me the chills.

Bobby proceeds to tell me about how he's had every girl who passes through the brothel. He insists they demonstrate everything advertised on their menu. I've heard men talk about women as sex objects before, especially in the seclusion of Portlaoise holiday camp, but not like this.

Prison lust drove some straight men into the arms of happy campers but Bobby talks about women like they're computers or mobile phones. He describes their features and functions with superlatives but no emotion. I'm coming to the conclusion that his huge frame and baby face are a psychopath's shell and, behind closed doors, he might emerge from his human form like a giant carnivorous insect.

'Good luck with your car,' he says as he drops me and my shopping back to Reaney's Distribution. With a squeal of wheels he heads off, probably to validate the offerings of Anna and Lupe.

'Hey, Ger,' Nora says with a tired smile that doesn't reach her eyes. 'Bob asked me to give you this.'

My very own stab vest.

Sleepover

'Hello, can I speak to Melody please?' I say in my best Dublin accent.

'Sure. Who shall I say is calling?' Sonya sounds like she'd make a good secretary. She'd probably make a good anything.

'Ciaran.' I pluck Mr Bendy's name out of the air and have to suppress a surge of anger.

'Hello.' Krystal's husky voice is a melody to my ears.

'Hi, it's Ger.'

'Sorry, I'm fully booked up today.'

I hear a hand go over the phone and muffled voices, then a door closing.

'Ger?' Krystal whispers.

'Yeah.'

'You can't come here.'

I close my eyes and have an image of me, sat in the chair at Krystal's wearing my stab vest, her dancing and bloodthirsty Romanians trying to beat down the door. For all I know Constantin is something, was something, to her. But she's still talking to me and there's no hint of outrage in her voice.

'I know. Will you come to my place?'

'I told you, I don't do outcalls.'

'I'll make it worth your while.'

She hesitates. Come on, come on. Money talks.

'One thousand euro.'

'What?'

'One thousand. I need the money.'

I can see my little nest egg evaporating rapidly at this rate. But, as George Bernard Shaw would have said, we've established what sort of a lady she is and we're just haggling over the price. I wait for her to yield.

'One thousand euro and I stay the night at your place.'

That's the kind of yielding I'm willing to pay for.

'Okay, it's a deal.'

'When do you want me to come over?' She sounds keen.

I consider negotiating on the menu but remember Bobby's boasting in the car and feel confused.

'How about nine o'clock?' I suggest.

'It's five now. I don't have any clients booked. I could come over now.'

'Um, no, I have to do a few things. Nine is good, bring your music with you. Will I pick you up?'

'This isn't a date, Ger. I'll come to your place in a taxi, or I'll walk. One thousand, in cash, in advance when I arrive. See you at nine.' She hangs up.

My hand is shaking as I look at my phone. The list of reasons why this is a bad idea flows through my mind like a TV autocue. Park all that and try to focus.

First things first and I need to get a permit for the new car before Mr Slap Happy sticks a fine on the windscreen. The old permit disappeared with the Audi but Bob did me proud with my replacement motor. Taking another look from the front room window like a kid with a new bike, I admire my Saab 9-5 Aero.

One hour later and I have a parking permit, vacuum cleaner, cleansing stuff, an iPod with docking station and some groceries. Five hundred notes lighter in the wallet. Nothing like a sense of urgency to spur things into action.

The Alessi boxes go upstairs into the spare room and I set up the iPod in my bedroom. Only then do I notice the absence of McKinsey. A handwritten note sits on the clean rectangle of carpet, edged with dust.

> *Ger,*
> *I had the lads get rid of the wardrobe. So, I figure you owe me one!*
> *Mary*
> *X*

I read it again, and again, looking for subliminal content. After a few minutes my cheeks are aching from my smile. Then the head starts to ache. At what point did I go looking for all this complexity?

Hoovering is good therapy. The tired carpets and worn floorboards look better for it and my new vacuum cleaner sucks good. Sponges, cloths, creams, polishes. The place is sparkling. Nine years inside has taught me how to clean.

The place looks Spartan but sanitised. With a well earned can of beer from the fridge, I go switch on the TV and have a relax in my leather swivel chair. The programmes are inane but ads during the breaks tempt me with home furnishings. I'll soon have this place looking good. Who needs a designer? New car outside, kitchen paid off and the dancing queen staying over. I let my eyes close.

My throat clicks with dryness when I breathe in through my mouth. An unfamiliar show is on TV with a bunch of fake tanned eejits of both sexes talking nonsense in Dublin accents. I press the info button. Shit! I've been asleep for two hours and it's five to nine. Krystal will be here soon. And there's the doorbell.

If it's her she's early. In my book early equals keen. With one hand on the latch I pause to consider.

She owes me nothing. Her bosses could be with her, poised to extract vengeance for their brother. I imagine it's a family affair, not her family though. This weekend I'm going to sort out some security measures for the house, starting with that peephole. For now I settle with lifting the letterbox cover with a finger and peeking through.

'Who is it?' I say to the bare tanned legs.

Krystal drops down and we're eye to eye.

'Are you expecting someone else?' Her eyes crinkle and my heart lurches.

I open the door and she walks in, looking every inch the call girl. Well, a short call girl. When I close the door and turn, she's standing with one hand on her hip and the other holding the strap of a leather backpack.

'You could have made an effort,' she says, looking me up and down.

Typical woman, you spend hours cleaning the place and all they see is your sweat and grime.

'What's that?' Her finger points at my stab vest lying up against the wall.

'Protection.'

'Then why aren't you wearing it?'

The price of a thousand euro seems to include being married for the day.

'Because I trust you.'

Her face looks like stone, beautiful stone. Then it breaks into a relieved smile. A face to launch a thousand ships.

'And I trust you. I don't know why, but I do. I need someone to trust. Now go take a shower.'

Her wish is my command.

Music comes from the bedroom as I shampoo the scruffy, sandy remnants on my head. I'll fix those tomorrow. The music is Radiohead or something, not the dance music Krystal normally performs to. She's brought along a part of herself.

Warm, spicy smells waft into the bathroom. I dry and slip on the stolen Slaney's bathrobe. I wonder how Rita is doing but the thought passes as quickly as it appeared when I get a glimpse of Krystal doing her thing through a gap in the door.

She's transformed the room. Incense sticks and candles, a mood light and her music. Somehow the room is warm. My clothes are off the chair and it's repositioned in the corner so I can sit and watch.

I get a feather light kiss on the lips and she leads me by the hand to the chair. She fiddles with her iPod in the docking station, legs straight, knees together and her backside teasing me. A hypnotic beat comes from the speakers and she does her staccato moves, hands in her hair. I've never seen anyone else dance like she does.

This is a golden moment. If music be the food of love, dance on, or something. She dances over and pushes my legs together, straddling me and letting her hair fall down on my face. She pulls my bathrobe apart and her hair caresses my chest, then she's off again.

The music plays on, tune after tune, but she doesn't tire. Down to just her knickers and a sheen is forming on her golden skin. When the album finishes she goes back to the iPod and I stand up.

'I'll be back in a minute,' I say and run downstairs.

The Champagne is good and cold from the fridge. I open the bottle upstairs.

'Cheers,' I say.

'Noroc,' Krystal replies.

We clink glasses and sip.

'Sit down,' she says.

I do as told and go to take another sip but her hand pushes mine down. She straddles me again, takes a mouthful from her glass and then her lips are on mine, slowly letting the cold Champagne trickle from her mouth into mine.

When it's all gone she smoothes away the trickle from my chin with her hand.

'I thought you said no girlfriend experience?' I smile at her.

'Does your girlfriend do that?' she asks.

'I don't have a girlfriend.'

~

We lie in the bed, her nestled into my shoulder. Light headed with Champagne, we cuddle. No intimate touching, compassion more than passion.

'I need the money,' she says.

'Oh, sorry. I'll get it for you.'

'No, silly. I don't need it now. I need money for when I leave.'

'In the morning, no problem.'

'No, I mean I'm leaving. I'm giving up this business.'

I tighten my arm around her. Possibilities flood my mind, insane ideas.

'What will you do? Will you stay in Ireland? In Kilkenny?'

She gets up on one elbow and looks me in the eye.

'Are you crazy?'

'I remember you telling me you had family back home.'

'That was a long time ago, Ger. My parents are dead and my sister has someone to protect her. When I first came to Ireland I was illegal.'

I don't want to ask what sort of illegal she was. Back in the day I paid a lot of money to have her dance for me. I owe her.

'But now you're free to do what you want?'

'You're joking. Nobody walks away from this business, these guys own me. If I give it up and stay in Ireland they will kill me. Or worse, turn me into a crack whore in some big city.'

'So, what are your options?'

'I can run. I can stay. Or I can pay.'

She sinks back down into my arms. This could be a sting. So sting me.

'How much?'

'A hundred,' she says in a whisper.

I give the amount a whistle of acknowledgement.

'Suppose you could pay them the hundred grand, where would you go after?'

'Somewhere warm, where it doesn't rain almost every day of the year. Somewhere with hot summers and mild winters, on the coast with the sea and beach outside my door,' she says, her voice flying with the clouds.

'Sounds good.'

'It's my dream. On bad days it's the only thing that keeps me going.'

The deal is on the table. She doesn't have to spell it out.

'What will you do, Ger?'

Go with you. Anywhere really.

'I don't know. Sort of setting roots here in Kilkenny.'

She laughs, not a pleasant one, and sits up again. 'You can't stay here. Constantin has gone missing.'

She doesn't sound too concerned about her countryman.

'Who's Constantin?' I really don't know him; he was wearing a tarpaulin and a plastic bag.

'One of the brothers. He went to bring back Lupe and the Russian. I heard them talking; sometimes they forget I'm Romanian too.'

'What did you hear?'

'That they killed the ugly one and the girls would be brought back. They own them. They know all about this Fly and his boys. I'm pretty sure they know you.'

I take a deep breath.

'The Fly will sort them out. This is his town, he knows everyone, the guards, everyone.'

Krystal shakes her head. 'Don't fool yourself. There's no *taking care* of them. Like Hydra, cut off one head and another appears. Your Fly boss should have kept out of this business.'

'We'll see.'

I think about the results of my previous dealings with the Romanians; ten years of my life gone, all my friends and family lost. At least I'm alive.

'You should leave here too,' she says and settles back down into my arms.

We lie quietly, drifting away to a world where the sun bathes our skin and waves lap the sand.

Day 9 – Tourists

The soil is heavy on the shovel but easy to shift. It's only a couple of days since the funeral. I don't recall being there.

When the blade of the shovel hits the coffin's wood I stop digging. My charge doesn't need the full length of the grave dug out but I need to place him deep.

An owl hoots and makes me jump. The gibbous moon gives a strangled light and the church tower is a vague silhouette against the damp night sky. Next to the graveyard the rugby club is deserted except for one car, its windows steamy and the suspension bouncing. The owl is joined by an occasional shriek from the car's occupants.

He would appreciate the irony of this, the Gimp. What was I thinking, moonlight grave digging in semi-public? Why didn't I fuck the body into the river like Bobby suggested or go for the acid bath?

Constantin is heavier than I remember. He's somehow absorbed moisture from the night air. I manage to roll him in his tarpaulin shroud, half into the grave, and now he's stuck at an angle. Nothing for it but to climb down into the hole.

The body should be stiff by now but it's awkwardly bendy and even feels warm. I wrestle the tarpaulin and feel movement inside it. The Fly mustn't have tied that plastic bag tight enough around the head. He's alive for sure.

But wait! Didn't Nora and I give the Romanian a concrete overcoat out at the pig farm? Who's in this package? Mr Bendy Ciaran or maybe the cheating Jo? The giant maggot starts to wriggle and falls on top of me.

Then I smell it. The unmistakable halitosis of the Gimp. His huge and hairy hand breaks through the casket like paper and pulls me down.

'I have you, Mayes. This time I have you.'

'Aaargh!' I wake with a shout, my hands balled into aching fists.

Krystal isn't in bed next to me. For a second I wonder if I've entombed her with the Gimp, then I catch the aroma of coffee from the kitchen. I throw on some clothes and wander down.

'Is a nice coffee maker,' she says, taking the jug from the Alessi and pouring two cups. I find her accent very cute, almost as cute as her negligee. 'Here. They said in the bakery this is what you like.'

She looks gorgeous, almost as gorgeous as the sausage roll she offers me.

'I can stay here today,' she says over a sip of coffee. 'I don't have any clients until this evening.'

I purse my lips involuntarily.

'Is it a problem for you?' She sounds businesslike now.

'No, no. Not at all.'

I have no idea what to do with this situation. But if it means a day being able to look at Krystal then that's a day well spent.

'I go upstairs to get ready.'

What do prostitutes, or escorts, do on their day off? I can't see us going for a country walk with her slinky outfit and heels. A wave of panic washes over me; I'm used to Krystal the erotic dancer, not Krystal the day tripper.

One thing's for sure; we have to get out of town. If I stumble across the Romanians it'll mean trouble and if we're seen together it'll be double. I don't really even know what these guys look like, except for the trousers.

A plan is formulating in my mind over another cup of coffee when there's a knock on the front door. Then I hear knuckles rapping on the front room window, which is usually a sign of familiarity, except I don't really have any familiars.

On with the stab vest, can't take any chances. I edge the door open just a little, my foot behind to kick it shut if need be.

'Ger.'

It's fucking Roisín again. She elbows her way in.

'Listen, Roisín, now is not a great time.'

'Why are you wearing a vest? Is it all kicking off?'

She looks me up and down, sticks her head in the kitchen and then looks up at the ceiling. The power shower is roaring away up there.

'You wear a stab vest while your girlfriend is in the shower?'

I shrug. 'She likes it.'

'Funny guy. You were expecting someone else to come to your door. What's going on, Ger?'

'I'm test driving some new security equipment.'

'Talk of test driving, is that your new car outside? Very tasty. You'll have to take me for a ride.' She starts to ladle out the charm. Her perfume accompanies it, as if she can somehow smell nice at will.

'I'll do that, just not today.'

I put my hand back on the front door latch and she puts hers over it, moving close.

'Look. I can see you're getting in deep. I just know it's all going on. I can smell it. Give me some time. Talk to me.'

The tip of her tongue licks her lips, whether in anticipation of a story, to tease or just from habit, I don't know.

'I've found something on the human trafficking angle,' I say, thinking on my feet. 'Come see me Monday night and I'll share it with you.'

'Why wait 'til Monday?'

'Roisín, this crime journalism thing might be your life but I have some living of my own to do.' I cast a look upstairs and adopt my best Casanova expression.

She laughs and takes her hand away from mine.

'It's a date. I want the full story on Monday night. Warts and all. Stay safe, Ger.'

I let her out and turn to see Krystal at the top of the stairs, wrapped in a towel, even though the shower is still running. Sneaky. I'm not sure what if anything she heard. She gives me a knowing nod and walks into the bathroom.

The plan is we go to Waterford. I don't know what Krystal has in mind but, if it's expensive boutique shopping, Waterford is safer than Dublin. Money is for spending but, at the end of the day, my Scottish genes play the trump card.

'Okay, where are we going today?' She breezes into the kitchen.

I look once, twice and my mouth hangs open.

'What?' she says. 'You don't like?'

She looks so, well, normal. Jeans with calf-length boots, a jumper and a knitted hat. She looks like a catalogue model for petite clothes.

'You look great!'

I grab her in a hug. I want to pick her up and carry her off. Her hands pat the back of my stab vest.

'You look terrible,' she says. 'Take off this thing.'

I slip off the vest and throw it into the hallway.

'I thought we'd go to Waterford. Walk by the river, spend some time in town, maybe get lunch out at the golf club or on the island? And there are lots of furniture stores.

You could help me choose some stuff, be my interior designer.'

'Waterford is not a good idea,' she says, shaking her head slowly.

'Why not?'

'There are girls in Waterford. You've seen the escort website. The same guys run the girls down there.'

'Right.'

'Also, what do you need furniture for? Are you going to stay? I thought…' She looks worried.

In the cold light of day I don't know what I'm doing.

'No, you're right. It makes no sense. What would you like to do?'

'I thought we could go and see the Rock.' She smiles at me, a wide mouth of sparkling, even teeth.

'The Rock?'

'Every time I get some … client … who wants to talk, they ask me how long I've been in Ireland and start to tell me all the sites I should see. Like I have spare time to go sightseeing, or would be allowed to go playing the tourist.'

'Right.' I guess we can't just park her life of prostitution.

'Rock of Cahill, they always tell me in Kilkenny. Cliffs of Moaner when I'm in Limerick.'

'Ah, the Rock of Cashel! And the Cliffs of Moher.'

'Whatever,' she says, annoyed for a second. 'Let's go to the Rock!'

Despite Krystal's objection I don the vest for the few steps out to the car. No one is on the street and I wave her out when she peeks from behind the sheet hanging over the sitting room window.

Just as she closes the door behind her there's a roar of an engine. I look down the street and see a low slung blue saloon with a huge spoiler at the rear. It crawls along and the passenger window slides down. Instinctively I duck down behind the Saab.

A wolf whistle pierces the air, followed by a blast of horn, and the car speeds off up Maudlin Street.

'Let's get out of here,' Krystal says.

The Saab's engine starts with a whirr, like a jet preparing for take-off. I've only driven it from work to home and that was in something of a daze. Maudlin Street is my runway as the turbo kicks in and we're almost airborne at the first speed hump.

'Did you say you can drive?' Krystal laughs, her doorstep trauma fading.

'Ha de ha ha.'

I blast us out of town to the ring road and then around to the Castlecomer road.

'This is a great car,' she says, wriggling in the leather seat and looking around the interior.

In five minutes we're heading into the country.

'I think something bad has happened to Constantin,' she says.

I bite my lip. 'How would you feel about that?'

'I would feel good if something bad has happened to Constantin. Very good.'

'Why?'

'You have to ask why? These guys have held me more or less a prisoner for over ten years and you have to ask why?' She shakes her head. 'There isn't one good guy in this business. They are all bastards.'

'And Constantin?'

'He's the worst of the brothers. They are all family. Constantin was the guy with the knife. If you caused trouble he would threaten to cut you. Here.' She makes a slicing gesture on the side of her face.

'Did you have any trouble with him?'

'He threatened my family, back at home. In that situation you have to do whatever they say. Anything they want.'

I look across and see that pretty mouth take on an ugly twist.

'Can you be sure they'll let you go for a hundred grand?'

'Yes, I'm sure. It's happened before. One girl met a client and he bought her out. A farmer.'

'Right. And what if you just run away?'

'Like I said last night, they catch you. Sometimes a beating, other times girls disappear. Or worse. There's nowhere safe, not in Europe anyway.'

My mind processes the options. There has to be a way to do this without spending money, my money.

'Why are you quiet now?' she says as we pick up the motorway at Urlingford. 'This is the reality. We can go for our day trip to the Rock and I can dance all night for you, whatever you want, but this is the reality.'

'I have an idea. It needs some work, but I have an idea.'

'Is this a stupid idea?' she asks.

This girl knows me so well already.

'If it works it will be a great idea,' I say.

'And if it doesn't work?'

'Then it will be a disaster.'

She looks at me like I'm crazy.

'So let's talk about something else,' I say. 'Tell me about your family.'

I remember some of what she tells me from before, when she was dancing up at the club in Dublin a decade earlier. Things haven't turned out well. Her mother died despite all the money Krystal sent home for her healthcare; sounds like that was inevitable. The abusive father moved away with another woman and also died. Her younger sister is about to marry into the mob, removing the continuous threats of harm or at least keeping them in the family, and Krystal has lost all motivation. All in all, little to show for a decade of enslavement.

I tell her she's a very kind and generous person to have given her life in an attempt to save her mother and protect her sister. I do really believe that, but Krystal is clearly embittered. I tell her she's still young; she's nearly young enough to be my daughter but neither of us says that. After ten years of debasement she has serious health problems. I tell her about my foreign heart and she says I'm still likely to outlive her.

'Do you have a boyfriend?' I ask, trying to bring things back into the fun theme for the day.

She laughs. 'Yes, I have about five boyfriends a day, sometimes twelve. The most boyfriends I had in one day – twenty. This evening I will have three.'

Oh boy. I wasn't looking to discuss her throughput.

'No, I mean, is there someone special?'

She turns and looks out of the window. The Rock of Cashel begins to appear through the haze up ahead.

'Back home, when I was fourteen, I was engaged to a boy. His name was Alexandru. It was arranged by our families.'

'Do you still hear from him?' I turn to look at her.

She pulls down the corners of her mouth. 'He died. A lot of people were sick, it was a very poor village. I left.'

'Did you love him?'

'I liked him. It was arranged by our families. I was expected to love him.'

When I think of my own childhood sweetheart and hollowing out copies of Agatha Christie novels to conceal trinkets I sent her in the post, it seems like another world. This Alexandru boy would have died not long before Krystal came to Ireland. Not long before I was throwing hundreds of euro at her to dance naked. I really had no idea. What a bastard.

'Is there someone else? Or has there been somebody else?'

Stupid, I know, but I expect her to say me.

'There was.' She takes a breath that sounds like a sniffle and then gives a disarming laugh, the laugh of a young and heartbroken girl. 'Another Alex.'

'What happened with him?' More tragedy, no doubt.

'*Her.* She married a farmer. Here, in your country.'

'It's not my country,' I murmur and slide past the exit for Cashel in my distracted condition. 'Was she, is she Greek? Alex?'

'Bulgarian,' Krystal says slowly.

'I remember her, from Dublin. Tall and blonde. Very good looking.'

Krystal looks out of the window again. What a day trip. Let's talk about your lesbian ex-lover sex slave, turned straight by an Irish farmer's stash of cash.

'Sounds like Alex,' she says finally.

I take the next exit and we come into Cashel the back way. Krystal lets out a gasp. The view is even more impressive than I remember; a fairy tale ancient fortress on a huge outcrop of rock, the town small and subservient at its feet.

'Do you want a cup of tea or something,' I ask as we roll down the high street past quaint bistros and tea rooms.

'I came to see the Rock, not to drink tea,' she says in an absent voice.

The car draws a few admiring glances. It's nothing, though, compared to the reaction Krystal gets when she steps out and we start to walk up the stone ramp of the Rock. Every man and woman does a double-take when they see her. She looks like one of those diminutive film stars travelling incognito. I get looks too, the sort that say what on earth is she doing with you? A taste of how it would be for me and Krystal.

'This is amazing!' Her head is angled up to the Rock, neck craning to try and take it all in. 'We have fantastic castles in Romania but this feels older. Much older.'

I pay the few euro at the kiosk and take two leaflets.

'Come on.' Krystal takes my hand and leads me into a cave-like room where a film about the history of the Rock is about to start.

The lights dim and she squeezes my hand. She remains rapt throughout the fifteen minute show, occasionally whispering in my ear to ask the meaning of some of the more obscure words.

Afterwards, outside, the sunshine is blinding. She looks at the leaflet and we start the self-guided tour, taking it all very seriously. Every time there is an account of a gruesome or disastrous event in the Rock's history she asks me to read out the description a second time so she can fully immerse herself in the horror and magnificence. The massacre of three thousand men, women and children by Cromwellian forces in the 17th century particularly fascinates her.

The first few times I enjoy her focusing on my every word but, after a while, it's hard for me to maintain enthusiasm. She's like a child and, for the first time, I realise she's trying to recapture those lost years.

'Here, have a read yourself.' I offer her the leaflet.

'No, I like to hear your voice,' she says, pushing it back at me.

'But if you read it for yourself it's a different experience.'

'I don't read.'

'You can't read English? Maybe they have French or German or something that would be better for you.'

'Ger.' She puts a hand over mine. 'I can't read. Anything. Or write. Okay?'

She walks out of the Grand Hall and I'm left with the pigeons. One of them lets a stream of droppings splash to the floor.

I catch up with her at the foot of the Round Tower.

'So how did you write those reviews on the website?' She looks at me. I shouldn't have mentioned it. 'I'm sorry.'

'No, it's okay. Alex helped me. She read what those bastards had written and helped me write the reply. Since she went I can't tell what's going on anymore.'

You don't want to know, I'm thinking.

'Hey, Ger, maybe you can help me? When we get back to your house?'

I'm thinking no thanks. Next she'll have me watching her on a webcam and giving marks out of ten.

'You won't need to worry about all that when you leave.'

She takes that as some sort of promise and holds my hand.

'This is like Rapunzel,' she says, looking up at the tower. 'There's no way to get in.'

She's right. The single door to the tower is at least twenty feet off the ground. Accessible only to witches and medieval window cleaners.

'You'd need to grow your hair a bit longer,' I say.

We're distracted by the whoops and shrieks of children cavorting across the burial ground. A millennium of souls groan under the fallen stones and decrepit crypts.

Around the other side of the Cathedral a vista opens out in front of us.

'This is Tipperary County, right?' Krystal asks.

'Yep. Tipp town over that way.' I point to the left of the Golden Vale.

'He was a farmer from Tipperary. She's out there, somewhere, with him.' She sits down on the warm grass and hugs her knees to her chest.

'Do you want to try and find her? Maybe when you're free?'

'What is the point? She's made her choice. She's not free.'

Across the vale I imagine two opposing armies of foot soldiers. To the south are the Romanians, dark and lithe with strange trousers. North are the clients, Dublin beer tourists with pasty faces in sports clothing and red faced farmers in wellies, normal trousers but held up with string. Krystal and I will watch the battle from the citadel and sit out any siege.

Our peace is shattered again as the children invade the grassy slope. They lie along the top edge of the incline and set themselves rolling down in a race to the bottom, squealing with delight as they tumble.

'Come on!' Krystal pulls me up by the hand.

The grass is thick and the ground soft. She reaches the bottom before me and I roll over her in a tangle. It's the most fun I've had this century with my clothes on. A few tourists stop to take photos of us. Well, of Krystal. I imagine she'll be appearing on facebook pages as an incognito celebrity behaving badly. She doesn't seem to mind.

She rolls me off, sits on my chest and sprinkles torn grass over my face. I shut my eyes and the blades tickle my lips. She blows the grass away and kisses me there, lightly. If I had a sister, and she kissed me, I imagine it would be like that.

'Let's get afternoon tea,' she says.

We walk up the hill. I turn and imagine Romanian pimp and brothel punter bodies littering the Golden Vale.

Krystal looks out and sees Alex, I guess, providing her side of the deal with that farmer.

Downtown we walk into a little tea shop and take a pot of tea.

'Will you have a sandwich or something?' I ask her.

'No, thanks. I'm not hungry.'

My breakfast sausage roll is an ancient memory but she had nothing. My thoughts must be on my face.

'I don't eat, Ger. Milkshakes and vitamins. How else do you think I stay like this?' She outlines her figure with her hands.

'I thought you … went to the gym, or something.' I'm really thinking her work is exercise enough but can't say that.

'You're joking, right? This is the first free day I've had this year. Except for when I'm sick I never get a break. Seven days a week, morning 'til night. Since I can remember. Now I don't even have a family to go home to, so they won't let me leave for a month in summer like they used to.'

Her face is like thunder. I stir my tea, even though there's no sugar in it.

'What will you do when you leave?'

'Go to Spain or somewhere, we already discussed that.'

'No, I mean, what will you *do*? With your time?'

'Just live. A normal, quiet life.'

'Will you have children? You're still young. Will you want to start a family?'

She laughs, letting the stupidity of my question sink in.

'Even if I wanted to play happy families, I can't.' She waves a stiff palm at her flat little stomach. 'Nothing is working there anymore. Nothing is there anymore.'

She raises her eyebrows at the hand I put over my mouth.

'Don't feel like it's your fault, Ger. This would have happened to me even if we had never met in the Gentlemen's Club. Don't blame yourself.'

But I do.

In the car, on the motorway back home, she puts her hand on my thigh and kisses me on the cheek.

'I had a really good time today. Thanks.'

The Saab's cruise control hurtles us along. I brush the back of my fingers against her face and she closes her eyes with a smile.

'We're going to get you out of this,' I say. 'Whatever it takes. They'll get their hundred grand and you'll get your cottage by the beach.'

Her face doesn't change as she lets out a deep breath. The sleep of the innocent.

An Cloigín Gorm

Ella Cullen's house on the Kells Road is a fortress. Seven foot iron gates in stone clad walls that look like a bulldozer would bounce off them.

I lower the Saab's window and press the intercom button, smiling at the camera.

'Hello, Ger,' Ella says through the speaker. 'New motor? Very nice. Come on in.'

The gates slide back with a rumble. Flashback to Portlaoise maximum security prison. I don't like this at all.

A winding tarmac road takes me up between trees that must have already been pretty big when they were planted. It all looks fairly new and well kept. The house at the top of the hill can only be described as a mansion. Eddie Cullen is building a dynasty.

'Hello, stranger.' Ella stands at the top of the stone steps and looks down at me as I step out of the car. She's bag in hand, ready to go.

'Quite a place you have here,' I say and she walks daintily down the steps, her tight dress impeding her a little.

'Yes, Daddy had to have his way when he built the house for his little girl,' she says airily. 'Finn and I rattle around inside the place. It's much too big for us.'

I open the passenger door and hold her hand as she lowers herself into the tan leather seat.

'Such a gentleman, Ger,' she says.

I wonder if the seat is still warm. When I start the engine the air conditioning wafts her perfume around the cabin. It's delicious and reminds me of Mary Reaney.

'This is a really nice car,' she says.

'What car do you drive?'

'Oh, Dad gave me a car. Some kind of Audi, a big thing.'

'Nice.'

We roll down the driveway and the gates open automatically.

'I'm really looking forward to tonight. I just love Campagne.' She rubs her palms together. 'Do you go there often?'

'It's been a while,' I say. There's a moment of silence and then we both laugh together.

'Look, Ger,' she says, 'I know you're just out of prison but I want you to know I don't think of you as a criminal. That part of your life is over now and this is a fresh start. It's a fresh start for me too, since the divorce. There, now we don't need to mention either of those things again.'

If only she meant what she said.

By the time we've finished our starter course I know more than I could ever want to about Garda Eamonn and why Ella has a court injunction out against him. She comes across as very vulnerable and I feel a protective urge but, at the same time, I recognise her as the type I always fall for.

'So, what was it really like in prison?' she finally says.

'Oh, a holiday camp really. A few unsavoury characters but not too much of a problem as long as I kept out of their way.'

'But it's maximum security, isn't it? You must have had murderers and gangsters, sex offenders, all sorts in there.'

I look at her face, trying to gauge where she's going with it, but all I see in her eyes is genuine interest.

'The sex offenders were kept in a separate wing and the really dangerous murderers were isolated. Other than that, it was a case of fitting in, finding where I stood in the pecking order and letting people know I wasn't a pushover.'

'And where did you stand in the pecking order?'

I decide to tell her what she wants to hear.

'Where do you think? The biggest ever robbery in the history of the State, from right under the noses of An Garda Síochána and the Irish army. It gave me special status.'

My *special status* of the biggest eejit who ever got caught was probably what saved me from ever being properly integrated into Portlaoise's criminal fraternity. That and Officer O'Mahoney. But Ella doesn't see that. She sees a street hero, nationally infamous.

'And what about, you know?' she says.

'How do you mean?' I play the innocent.

'Sex. Nine years locked up with just men. Were you ever tempted?'

'Or the object of temptation?'

She laughs her tinkling ice laugh.

'There were one or two moments when I had to fight off admirers.' Those stories are not for sharing in Campagne, I think. 'I did learn something, though, from those nine years.'

'What's that?'

'I learnt that a man can stay celibate.'

'Not like you had any choice.' She twirls her wine glass.

'Maybe I've lost my sex drive, permanently?' I look into her eyes.

'I doubt that very much,' she says.

A waitress interrupts our flow by taking away the plates. I'm just ready to pick up the thread when I see Bob the Fly across the room. He gives me a nod and walks over.

'Hey, Ger. How are ye, Ella?'

'Hi, Bob,' she says.

He leans down and speaks quietly into my ear. 'I'm supposed to be meeting Mary here for dinner but she seems to have stood me up. Did you see her around today at all?'

'No, I haven't seen her.' And I'm wondering why he's asking me.

'It's her birthday dinner and all. We do it every year, just the two of us.'

'Don't worry. I'm sure she'll turn up, Bob.'

'You're right. Probably just being fashionably late. Enjoy your meal.'

He gives me a pat on the shoulder and walks over to his table. The Fly doesn't look his usual cocky little self, rather more like a worried father.

'What was that?' Ella asks.

'Oh, just a bit of parent child carry-on. You know.'

'Tell me about it,' she says. 'Finn is a nightmare when he comes back from a weekend at his dad's. When he comes home tomorrow night it'll take me a couple of days to calm him down.'

She emphasises *tomorrow night* so I know what sort of window of opportunity we're playing with.

The main course arrives and Ella changes tack.

'You've bought a place in town, I heard.'

'That's right. Just a little cottage, something modest but with a bit of character.' I'm praying she doesn't want to come and see it.

'Oh, I'm sure it has character.' The look on her face tells me she knows it's Old McKinsey's place. 'So, what are you going to do with yourself now, in Kilkenny.'

'Well, I'm working for Bob.' I nod my head in the direction of the Fly, who is still sitting alone. Mary must be really mad at him.

'Yeah, I know that, but what about investments? If you were interested I could introduce you to Dad. He has some big property deals going on and another backer would be welcome.'

'I'll be honest with you. I don't really have that sort of money to invest.'

'Come on, Ger. How much was the drugs haul? Half a billion euro? And they never recovered it. Don't tell me you never saw a penny.'

I see a glint of greed in her eye and suspect she's inherited more than a touch of her father's business cut and thrust.

'Well, I'm always interested in a good opportunity.'

Why not play along? What harm?

'Dad could double or treble whatever you're willing to put in. Tax free, of course.'

The greed is contagious. This is how people end up with mansions. I'm thinking my two hundred and fifty thousand isn't enough for this sort of endeavour. Where can I get my hands on some more serious money? Perhaps the Liffey Valley lad with the dodgy Northern Bank notes?

She's feeding off my greed and it's turning her on. I consider that if it's such a great investment then the Fly would have taken it up. I remember a hundred grand is provisionally allocated for purchase of Krystal's freedom from sex slavery. Both of these are outweighed by the short term gain of impressing Ella.

'Sure, no harm in having a chat with your dad. I'm always interested in money.'

I pick up the tab, which is extortionate, and we wander merrily out onto Gasworks Lane. I notice a blue Mondeo further up the road with the courtesy light on. The light goes out but the driver is watching us.

'Do you have a bodyguard?' I ask.

'You're joking. Watch this.'

Ella walks towards the Ford and the engine starts. The lights go on and the car reverses away from her, slowly at first and then speeding up, before reversing into a side alley and driving away.

She's laughing bitterly when she comes back.

'My ex-husband isn't allowed within one hundred meters of me, by court order. That doesn't stop him turning up and trying to ruin my night out though.'

'I thought you said Finn was staying with him?' I say, scoring myself points for remembering the kid's name.

'Oh, Eamonn's *mot* will be looking after Finn while Eamonn does his intimidation routine.'

'Do you want me to have a quiet word with Andy?' I slip in McAuliffe's name like I'm connected.

'No. I'm waiting for him to do something major so I can well and truly nail him for it,' she says.

As long as that something major isn't me, I'm thinking.

'So, how do you fancy a coffee at mine?' I say. 'I have a great new machine.'

'Coffee?' she says. 'Have you got any vodka?'

I stick my bottom lip out and shake my head. Spirits at home, the road to hell.

'Well, it's back to mine then,' she says. 'Finn's away and I need vodka. And I'm going to let you try and fuck my brains out.'

Day 10 – Renée's ghost

Ella wakes me up in a very pleasant fashion. Another kind of sausage roll.

My eyes feel sore and my head is woozy. I'm still drunk and not particularly in the mood but my morning glory is masking the fact.

Ella is a pale copy of Renée, my long dead lover. She has everything and nothing. Her body is the goal every magazine-reading Irish woman strives for but it's the result of wasting, not genetics or fitness. In Renée's case it was cancer. With Ella it's alcohol.

I don't know how much vodka we put away last night, I lost count. Normally I have a mental ready-reckoner that tells me if I'm fit to drive the morning after but she's blown away any calculation my fuzzy brain can manage. A half empty bottle stands on the bedside table next to a crystal tumbler and I know there's more downstairs.

A buzzing on the bedside table grabs my attention and I pick it up to read while Ella is still busy under the quilt.

Still no sign of Mary. If you see or hear anything let me know. Talk later. Bob.

Like me he's a texter from the last century – grammatically correct.

'Come on, Ger, get with the programme,' Ella says as she emerges from under the covers.

She takes the phone from my hand before I can reply and puts it under a pillow, then places my hand on her breast.

Having sex with Ella is very much a spectator sport. I'm barely needed, more of a mount than a participant. Her thin fingers pin my wrists to the bed as she rides me, bucking and twisting like I'm great. Her face distorts into a pulled mask of beautiful agony and I wonder if she's had work done on it. In the end she slumps onto me with a noise somewhere between a child crying and a dog dreaming.

'That was good. Really good.'

'Yeah,' I say, but it didn't happen for me.

She rolls off to the side and lights up a cigarette from her bedside table. A whiff of weed reminds me vodka wasn't the only thing we did last night. The vodka was straight but the drugs were a cocktail.

The lad is still standing to attention when I step out of bed to go to the bathroom. She gave me a pill for that as well and I can expect to carry him around for the rest of the weekend. That's not good news. Cialis used to be my sex drug of choice and overuse was what pushed my faulty old heart over the edge.

I type a message into my phone while sitting ladylike on the toilet and trying to relax.

Mary, it's Ger. Your dad is worried, please text him.

Then I send another.

Krys, tonight? Ger xx

'Texting your girlfriend?' Ella says as she walks in.

She swills with mouthwash and sprays perfume from a bottle by the sink. I see the name – Light Blue by D&G. It's the same fragrance Mary Reaney wears. I try to commit it to memory.

'Let's go down for some breakfast,' she says. 'I hope you like Champagne.'

~

I toot the horn as I drive my car away from the house and Ella stands in her doorway, lady of the manor.

Her kitchen is bigger than the open office at work. Her bedroom suite is the size of my entire house. What she'll do for the rest of the day, until her son is delivered home, is drink and smoke. Her life is as vacuous as the mansion. When the electric gates shut behind me I have the impression she's locked in there. Somewhere the father, Eddie Cullen, is sitting at a control desk, keeping his princess under wraps.

It's a sad situation. The ex is very likely a nasty piece of work. Whether Ella was a starving alcoholic before or after he left her is difficult to ascertain. I can imagine Garda Eamonn is one pissed off dude, what with marrying out of his league and an early career blemish due to yours truly.

Speak of the devil and he shall appear. En route to Kilkenny there's a routine checkpoint with said guard standing in the middle of the road. Is it just for my benefit or does he stand vigil every morning after? I've no idea, but I'm nicked.

'Well, well, well. If it isn't himself, Mr Famous!' Garda Eamonn barks in my window before I can get a word in. 'Lads, guess who just pulled up for a chat?'

He's talking to himself. The only other *lads* are off on the hard shoulder giving a battered old Nissan the once over.

'I'd like to conduct this conversation in Irish. *As Gaeilge,*' I say to Eamonn. It's my right and, if memory serves me, he's not able for it.

'Ye smart arsed fecker!' he shouts and the other guards turn to see what all the fuss is about.

I put my hands up in surrender.

'Have ye drink taken?' he roars in my face. 'Have ye? Ye have, I can smell it.'

I want to tell him I've drink and ex-wife taken, but he's already performing well enough without any provocation from me.

'Blow into this,' he says, thrusting a breath tester at me and turning to give a grin to his colleagues. 'Mr Mayes has drink taken,' he calls over to them.

Sure enough I register positive. Substantially over the limit.

'You're being arrested on the charge of drink driving.'

'*As Gaeilge*,' I say again but Eamonn ignores me. I tap the horn of the car and he jumps.

'You'll be taken to the station and asked to produce samples for testing,' he says. I see another guard walk over to us from the old Nissan.

'You think you're smart, Mayes,' Eamonn hisses at me through the window. 'Well, you're not. You're just another scumbag. She's too good for the likes of you.'

'*As Gaeilge*,' I repeat as the other guard appears behind Eamonn, making sure he hears me clearly.

'Right, let's have you out of the car.'

Eamonn bundles me into the squad car, making sure my head gets a good bang on the doorframe although he makes it look like he's trying to avoid it.

'I'll bring his car in,' he tells the junior officers in the squad car. 'Go ahead and process him. I might be a little while.'

My Saab flies off with a scrabble of wheels on the damp road. He knows how to hurt a man.

At the station I'm given the courtesy and respect a drink driving ex-con can expect, plus a cherry on top for who I am.

'One phone call,' the desk sergeant says, 'and then it's a few hours in a cell for ye. We have a nice one ready and all.'

I turn into the corner to try and get a bit of privacy on my mobile.

'Bob, it's Ger.'

'Have you heard from Mary? Tell me you have. Ger? Tell me!' The Fly is shouting at me.

'No. I'm sure she'll turn up. Something else. I'm after getting arrested for drink driving by Eamonn Murphy, just outside Ella's house this morning. I'll be needing a bit of legal...'

'She's not at home. She's not at the pub. No one's seen her since yesterday morning. Phone is straight to voicemail. I'm worried, Ger.'

I squeeze my eyes shut. The hangover is starting to thump.

'I need to get out of here, Bob, and then I can help look for Mary.'

'They've taken her. I think they have. Sweet Jesus! What'll I do if they've taken her?'

The Fly is buzzing.

'Get Duggan on the phone, Bob. He knows the Romanians, he'll be able to advise. You can ask him to get me out of here while you're at it.'

'Duggan? Yeah, Duggan. Good idea.' His voice drifts away and he hangs up.

My phone is taken from my hand and I turn to see a smiling Eamonn.

'Scumbag solicitor for a scumbag drink-driver. That's all you are, Mayes. A drunk who belongs in a cell. You're nobody. Take him down, lads.'

The two young guards who drove me in escort me downstairs to a cell.

'Every feckin' Sunday morning the same feckin' thing,' one says to the other.

'Nah,' says the other, 'he takes a week off at Christmas and three in the summer.'

They herd me like I'm cattle. Maybe it's as well. At least they're not abusive or violent like Eamonn.

I have some time to think things over while I'm sitting on the narrow bench in the cell. Hopefully the Fly is just being paranoid. If the Romanians have got Mary then that would be very bad news. She's on the list of people I care about, I realise.

Mary can handle herself but if they get a whiff of what happened to Constantin there's no telling what the Romanians might do. Eye for an eye and all that. Or, good looking girl that she is, Mary could end up on a boat to Spain and be forced into servitude in some knocking shop in Marbella.

I can't think how the Romanians would find anything out, though. Not unless young Bobby is shouting his mouth off around town, which is a distinct possibility. Whatever the state of play, things aren't going to get any better when Krystal does her moonlight flit.

A dry croak makes me cough. I must have fallen asleep, rolling around in a dream duvet trying to get to grips with a girl who is Krystal, Mary and, a bit disturbingly, Nora from the office. Ella doesn't feature, she's probably lying comatose on the floor. My head thumps with the vodka hangover until I realise it's a knocking on the cell door.

A small metal window opens in the door at eye level. Eamonn's malevolent gaze shines through.

'You're to be taken for *interrogation*,' he says.

'There's no need for that,' I say. 'I'll freely admit to all and sundry that I rogered your ex-missus silly, as requested by her.'

It's a gimp-baiting moment. The keys rattle in the door as Eamonn tries to unlock his fury. I stand facing the door, feeling like a knight about to battle a dragon.

Here he comes, all spit and size eleven boots. There's no stopping him and I cover up to avoid damage. Then he's off me. One of the young guards gets an elbow in the eye.

'C'mon, Sarge. Let's not do this.'

Eamonn relaxes, shrugs the guys off and then lunges at me again but I'm too nifty, sidestep behind the lads and out the door to a waiting Andy McAuliffe and his ever present tobacco aroma.

'Time for another little chat, Ger,' Andy says.

The wrong trousers

McAuliffe places the obligatory mug of hot tea on the interview room table.

'Don't worry about Eamonn,' he says. 'Duggan has been on the phone and, as usual, Eamonn screwed up everyone's Sunday morning. You were entitled to be dealt with in Irish. We could technically still get you on your blood alcohol level but I've other fish to fry.'

'The Gimp?' I ask.

He nods. 'You remember I told you McGivney was seen on CCTV with two men? One of these guys turned up again on a camera yesterday so he's still around.'

'Where do I fit in?'

'I want you to look at the CCTV recording.'

'Okay. Do I need Duggan here?'

'Why would you?' he says. 'You're just helping out.'

McAuliffe picks up the phone. 'Bring in that CCTV footage, would you?'

The door opens and DS Cian Purcell walks in holding some sort of flat electronic gadget.

'This is an iPad,' Purcell says. 'It's connected wirelessly to our encrypted network...'

I don't hear the rest. His lack of personality numbs like codeine.

'There,' McAuliffe says, pointing a brown stained fingernail at the strangely trousered images on the screen.

It's Constantin. He looks a little different when he's not wearing a tarpaulin overcoat and a plastic bag over his head. The other guy looks like he's probably his brother. I concentrate on keeping my breathing regular and look vacuously at McAuliffe and then Purcell.

'We think they're involved in organised prostitution in Kilkenny and other cities in the South East,' Purcell says.

McAuliffe puts a palm to his forehead. He looks at Purcell then me and raises one eyebrow. 'Well, Ger?'

'I've seen them before. Yep, those are the two lads we saw on Maudlin Street that night. The ones I told you about.'

Purcell taps the screen a couple of times and another video sequence shows Constantin again, this time at the railway station. He gets off a train. I'm thinking he's been out of town for a few days after the Gimp knifing. He walks past the camera, his face clearly visible, and pulls up his hoodie. Then he walks through the exit and the camera changes to the car park. He gets on a motorbike and that's him speeding off to the Hebron and an early death.

McAuliffe looks at me again. I shrug.

'He's the same guy as in the first video,' I say.

'Do you know him, though?' McAuliffe says. 'Would you know where we can find him?'

'Oh, I'm sure he's not far away. But I haven't seen him where you're thinking of.' Honesty is the best policy. My style of honesty.

McAuliffe and Purcell sit and look at me. I look at them, slurp my tea, look at them again.

'Bob Reaney,' McAuliffe says. 'Word is he's lost something. Or someone.'

I give him the raised eyebrows.

'Ger, if things are escalating into some sort of war between factions then I need to know. This is Kilkenny.'

'Not Limerick,' I say.

'Let's keep it that way,' Purcell says, his face blank as ever.

'DS Purcell was stationed in Limerick, during the height of the hostilities,' McAuliffe volunteers.

'Moyross,' Purcell says, dropping the name of the no-go zone owned by the drugs gangs.

'*Muy bien*,' I say.

The man nearly shows some expression.

'Look,' McAuliffe says, 'these Romanians are a rough crowd. You of all people should know that. My advice; don't get involved. Keep your distance, stay away from their knocking shop, keep your head down.'

'Thanks, Andy, but you know my situation.'

'And stay away from Roisín McGuire,' he adds. 'She's on the warpath again.'

I nod and suck in my cheeks.

'You're free to go.' McAuliffe sits back and opens his hands wide.

~

The desk sergeant returns my phone, belt and shoelaces but declines to give me back the keys to my car.

'Let's not be seeing you in here again until this evening, when you're sober.'

I feel pretty sober.

'And make sure it's after six, else I won't be held responsible for Eamonn.'

I wait until I'm a good bit away from the station before I call Krystal.

'Hey, it's me.'

'Hey you. I'm coming out to yours tonight. Nine okay?' She sounds happy.

'No, listen. You have to get your stuff and get out now. Right now, this second.'

'I have a client in five minutes. I can't just walk out!'

The idea of a client churns my stomach.

'The guards will be round in a few minutes, looking for Constantin. They'll shut you down again, probably put you in the cells. You need to leave now. Go straight to my place. I'll be there in five minutes.'

'God! Okay, okay, I'll do that.'

'Tell them you have an outcall. Big money.'

'Big money,' she says breathlessly and I can hear the noise of her throwing things into a bag. She hangs up.

The streets are full of shoppers and tourists. Everyone walks at half speed on a Sunday. Don't they realise I have an urgent date with a hooker?

By the time I get to Maudlin Street, Krystal is lounging outside my window. She looks like a very short streetwalker, far different from the incognito VIP of yesterday.

'They know I'm here,' she says as we walk into the kitchen.

She puts her black leather backpack on the worktop.

'I had to tell them. They know I'm thinking of leaving.'

'Are we safe?'

I realise I've been walking the streets *sans* stab vest. If they come for us in the house the only weapon I have is an Alessi food mixer.

'I'm pretty sure we're safe,' she says. 'They want the hundred thousand. After they get the money I wouldn't be so sure.'

'So you got away before the guards arrived.'

'Obviously.'

'Obviously.'

We both stand with our backs leaning against the worktop.

'So, what do we do now?' Her smile spreads the beauty across her face.

I so much want to kiss her, and so know she's ultimately unavailable.

'Food,' I say. 'What would you like to eat?'

She puts one finger to her lips in thought. My phone rings.

'Where are you?' It's the Fly.

'I'm at home. Thanks for sorting things with Duggan.'

'You're only home now? What were they doing with you? Never mind, any news?'

'Just walked in the door but I'm on my way out. I'll call you in a bit, as soon as I find out anything,' I say.

'Thanks,' he says and hangs up.

Krystal is looking at me.

'What?'

'Was that your boss? On a Sunday? I thought I was the only one worked a seven day week.'

'He has a problem. We have a problem.'

She raises her hands. No room for any more problems.

'You choose, Ger.'

'Huh?'

'The food. You choose. Italian, Chinese, Indian, anything. You choose. And do what you have to do. I'll be waiting here.'

~

The Edge of the World is quiet. No sign of the owner. Tim from Slaney's is keeping the bar.

'Hey, Tim,' I say.

'Well, Ger. Smithwick's?'

I nod. 'How's Rita?'

'Grand. You know how it goes. The guards were back talking to her, like, about McGivney.'

He places my pint in front of me and won't take any money.

'Mary told me you're family. No charge.'

'Is she about, herself?'

'No. I was expecting her, like, but haven't seen her all day. Time for my break and all. She does that sometimes.'

A draft blows in from the door and a wiry John-Jo walks in.

'Ger,' he says. He looks a bit scared.

'How's the Italian connection?' I ask with a smile he doesn't return.

'Heineken and a Jameson,' he says to Tim.

I wait until John-Jo has necked his Jameson and taken his beer to a table, then I join him.

'What's the story?' I ask.

He shakes his head, lips pursing as he takes a mouthful of beer.

'Come on, John-Jo. I thought we were buddies?'

He puts his glass down on the table and eyes me.

'What have ye got yerself into?'

I give the innocent look. He leans closer, lowers his voice.

'Young Bobby has been mouthing off all over town. He's calling you the Wolf, like in Pulp Fiction. You know, the clean-up guy, the fella who...'

'Yeah,' I say, 'I know who you mean. What's Bobby been saying?'

John-Jo looks up at Tim who is cleaning glasses behind the bar a few feet away. He stares him out and Tim wanders off down the other end.

'He's saying he topped some scumbag and you got rid. One of the Romanians.'

I put down my glass and notice a shake in my hand. I smooth my dodgy hairstyle back into an imagined shape.

'Ger, tell me you've not messed up already?'

I take a long, slow breath and make my pitch of incompetence.

'John-Jo, do you see me as Mr Fixit? I'm more like Mr Breakit. Everyone else knows what's going on except me.

I'm having trouble tying my own shoelaces since I got out. Can barely keep off the drink.'

He looks at the tremor in my hand as I pick up the glass again and I know Ger Mayes hasn't lost his touch.

'I'll drink to that,' he says with a laugh and we toast our pints.

'Another?'

He nods and I give Tim the victory salute.

'Bobby,' John-Jo says, lowering his head again, 'can be a right eejit at times. He's going to cause trouble. The Fly might think about reigning in that crazy talk.'

'I'll talk to him about it. Maybe if Mary said she'd heard the talk? That might be a good idea.'

'Diplomatic, like?'

'Yeah. He'd take it from Mary. Have you seen her about?'

'Not today. Nor Bobby, come to think of it. Although he's probably nursing a mouldy hangover from last night.' He chuckles to himself.

'Was he that pissed?'

'Bladdered. But seriously, Ger, you don't want to be messing with those Romanians. They're organised.'

I look at him seriously. 'This isn't fecking Limerick, you know.'

~

The Indian takeaway in Irishtown is the best but they're slow tonight. I place my order, hover outside the door and dial the Fly.

'Bob.'

'Ger, what d'ye know?'

'No sign of Mary anywhere today. The barman turned up for his shift but she didn't say she wasn't coming in or anything.'

'Tell me something I don't know,' he says.

'Bobby has been talking out of school. He hasn't been seen today either.'

The Fly sighs down the line. 'I'm still waiting for you to tell me something new, for feck's sake!'

I scrabble around my brain for information to impress him. Yeah, that'll do it.

'The guards have raided the Romanians. Well I'm guessing they have by now. They want to speak to them about the Gimp.'

'McGivney? So which one do they reckon did it?'

'Just a minute.'

The guy in the takeaway appears with my food. Out on the street I check there's no one nearby.

'The dead one,' I say.

'And that's all sorted, so I understand from Nora.'

'It is. Untraceable. Sorted.'

'Okay. I'll get on to Eamonn, so, and find out how they went on at our competitors. Or maybe you can call him?'

A beep tells me I have another call waiting.

'I ... eh, um...'

The Fly gives a cackle. 'Just kidding. I saw you with his missus last night, remember?' He gets all serious again. 'No, I'll call him myself.'

And he's gone. This time my battery has run out.

On the walk back to Maudlin Street I'm in a bit of a daze. The urge to please was strong and I had to tell him about the raid. I didn't tell him about my house guest, though. That's my business.

When I get back to number 32 she's gone.

Contrary Mary

No sign of Krystal. Her bag is still there though. Hope she's back soon. This takeaway will get cold and Alessi don't make a microwave.

I have the Fly's absent daughter problem sorted in my head. Mary has done one, headed out of town in a mood with her father over the whole prostitution thing. If she would just text me back. I plug my phone in to charge. The missed call has me worried but the phone will take a few minutes to come back to life.

There's a tapping on the front door. My hand is on the latch when I glance down at that stab vest still sitting in the corner of the hallway.

Two seconds later and I'm backing away from the door, pursued by two smallish, very angry men with shiny knives in their hands.

'She's not here,' I say, unsure if I'm being a coward.

'We're not here for her, we're here for you,' the shorter of the two says.

My house is so empty, nothing to grab as a weapon. I could do with a chair and a lion tamer's whip. Or a gun.

I fumble the key in the back door lock and step out into the rear garden. This is the first time I've been out here. It's begun to rain heavily.

The Romanians, for that is surely who they are, pursue me leisurely.

It's just a back yard. A strip of grass, cinder block walls reminiscent of prison and no way out. I pick up a piece of mouldy looking timber from the ground and hold it out in front of me.

'You come with us,' the short guy says.

'I don't think so.'

Nine years inside has left me no stranger to physical violence. I swing the timber behind my head and aim it fast and hard at the head of the bigger guy. He puts up an arm, there's a cracking sound and the timber breaks in half.

'Ticalos!' he shouts and leaps forward, landing a kick right in my nuts.

'Gnnrrrgh!' I say from my crumpled heap on the ground.

Nine days out of Portlaoise and I've gone soft already. A conversation occurs above me. I can do nothing but let the pain subside, the stars fade and my sweating cool. I hear enough to tell it's one sided, a phone call. I smell cigarettes being smoked. For some reason I expect them to urinate on me, but they don't. It must be tempting.

'Okay, okay. You come with us.'

Hands lift me under the arms and I stand shakily, letting everything drop back into place. When they try and urge me along I stand my ground.

'We're not going to hurt you,' the shorter one says, at which the other growls. I'd say I hurt his arm even though the wood broke on him like a matchstick.

'What do you want?' I ask.

The shorter one lowers his head to mine, which makes me realise I'm still bent double.

'You want to buy the girl? One hundred thousand. You want to buy, right?'

I cough and groan as it makes my balls ache more.

'One hundred thousand,' I say.

His face is too close to mine for comfort.

'You know she's not good for business. You know that? I don't want any complaints afterwards. There is no money back guarantee.'

'It's personal, not business.'

I look at Shorty and he looks at his pal. They both laugh.

'You know she's not good for personal, right?' Shorty says and they laugh again. Seems like joking at my expense is more important to them than negotiating a higher price.

'One hundred thousand, in cash, on Wednesday. Until then she stays with me.'

'We make the deal.'

Shorty grabs my hand and, before I can flinch, slices an inch across the heel of my right palm. He does the same to his own hand and cements the bargain in a handshake of blood. Sharing body fluids with a brothel manager; what a great day this is turning out to be.

'Now you come with us,' he says. 'Boss says we have to show you something.'

The two of them exchange what sound like some stiff foreign words as we walk back through the house. I have the feeling the taller guy is telling Shorty he could catch anything from me and should be more careful who he blood bonds with.

The ubiquitous Volkswagen Passat is parked outside; dark blue with blackened windows. The knifemen sandwich me in the back. A big bald guy who looks like a Turkish wrestler is wedged in the driver's seat, steaming up the windows.

Some words are exchanged and the driver starts to press the screen of his sat nav. I would prefer my kidnappers have some idea of where we're going. The talk gets heated. Baldy turns the sat nav off and we roar away down the street.

My brain lurches from panic to calm. These guys are probably Constantin's brothers. On the other hand I've just made a blood oath to buy Krystal's freedom for a hundred grand in three days' time, so I should be safe.

We hurtle out of town and down country with scant regard for traffic rules. The windscreen wipers thump across the glass. Motorway south and then off after a few junctions. This is darkest Kilkenny County where just a few miles off the beaten track puts you in any number of isolated valleys, visible only from the air.

My stomach gives out a big groan, complaining about the unfulfilled promise of food. The knife brothers look at me and then shout at Baldy as he swerves wildly around a tractor towing an evil-looking farming attachment. Branches bash against the side of the car and the tyres struggle to keep a grip on the next bend.

Baldy throws the Passat into a field gateway and executes a turn, heading back the way we came. Just as I'm about to lose the lunch I haven't had, the car turns down a lane and we squeeze between high hedges. Dirty water splashes up to the windows as the car bumps through deep puddles. An old stone wall looms ahead, the entrance barred by dented black gates of sheet steel. Baldy sounds the horn and the gates open outwards.

A scrapyard, bad news. Slightly flattened cars of all vintages sit in piles within the compound.

The brothers let me out of the Volkswagen and a bad smell greets my nose. There's a hut just inside the gate and two nasty looking dogs lie motionless in a pool of blood and shit. A guy walks out of the hut, an antique looking Uzi hanging from his hand. It works well enough, judging from the holes in the dogs.

'Gerard Mayes from Bagenalstown,' a voice like gravel says from inside the hut. 'Come here so I can see you.'

Ilie Petulengro. I never thought I would hear his voice again. Hoped I wouldn't. The urge to flee is strong.

With a prod in the back from one of my travel companions, I stumble into the hut. A grizzled looking junkyard owner is sitting quietly on the floor in the corner, his ankles and wrists bound with packing tape. One eye has disappeared behind a swollen face, possibly forever. I give the guy a nod and his head drops to his chest.

Ilie Petulengro is sitting on the desk, his crutches leaning against the wall. 'What have you done with my nephew?' he asks.

Ilie's English is still good but he's become even more wizened in the ten years since I saw him. The crippled leg looks worse and his black hair is streaked with grey.

'We didn't do nothing,' the bound man says and earns a blow to the head from Ilie's crutch.

'I wasn't asking you, idiot,' Ilie says in a gentle voice that belies the violence. 'Ger, where is Constantin?'

This man is my nemesis. Ten years ago I threw his identical twin brother's body into the River Liffey, up in Dublin. Ever since, he's been out to get me. And boy did he get me. After all, I did murder Alin Petulengro. Maybe I'm my own nemesis. Can someone be their own nemesis?

'Hey,' Ilie says as he punches me in the stomach with the end of his crutch. 'Where is Constantin?'

It's too much; the hangover, that kick in the balls, Baldy's nauseating driving and Ilie's poking. I throw up over the junkyard owner's bound feet.

'Fer fuck's sake!' the tattooed scrap dealer says.

'Scum,' Ilie says matter of factly. 'Shoot off his foot,' he says to the guy with the Uzi, pointing at my leg.

The knife lads speak up and Shorty shows Ilie his hand. Looks like my planned purchase of a sex slave is going to save me from permanent disability.

'Come with me,' Ilie says and moves off with his crutches.

I'd forgotten how fast he walks for a cripple. Through the rain, past towering piles of scrap that threaten to fall and flatten us into the mud, until we reach a crane with one of those giant electromagnets.

A motorbike stands forlorn in the downpour. It looks like the one from the train station video that McAuliffe showed me earlier today. A trial bike, big wheels, seat and engine high off the ground.

'We found this in the crusher. About to be squashed to nothing.' Ilie lifts the seat with one hand and takes something out from under it. 'Recognise this?'

I nod. A GPS positioning device. Cunning animals. Exactly the same means they used to locate the national drug store. I make a mental note to check Krystal's bag when I get home.

'So, where is the boy?' Ilie raises his crutch and I back up against Baldy.

'I've never seen that bike before and I don't know a Constantin,' I say. True, strictly speaking.

'You bring him back to me,' he says. A phone starts to ring and he pulls it out of his pocket. I recognise the fast dance tune. It's Mary's. He looks at it and shakes his head. 'And if there's a problem with bringing him back then we have to talk compensation.'

He raises his crutch into the air and, with a brain-splitting screech, the crane begins to move. It swings the now buzzing electromagnet over the roof of a dented Transit van.

'My nephew or half a million euro in cash. For that you get back what remains of her.'

The magnet drops onto the van and there's a squeal from somewhere. The crane creaks and the van sags as it's lifted off the ground and into the air. The chains swing and the crane lines the van up with the crusher, then the magnet turns off and the van falls about twenty feet into the machine.

I look to see who is controlling the crane and who might operate the crusher. It's James Bond time. My muscles are taut and the adrenaline starts to pump. I edge away from Baldy and run towards the crusher, trip over his extended leg and land face first in a puddle of mud and oil.

The crusher whines and wheezes as it begins to compress the van.

As I cry through a face full of muck, the truth hits me. She's the one I want. Wanted. The one voted most likely to succeed as girlfriend.

'Very nice. Pretty girl.' Ilie's voice comes from behind me.

'Jesus, Ger. The state of you.'

It's Mary. I can smell her perfume from here, cutting through the oil and grease like a Mediterranean sea breeze. Her hands are tied behind her back and Ilie has her by the arm. He lifts his brown, wizened hand to her face and touches her cheek.

'I don't think we crush this one, Ger. She's too valuable. I could get some big money for her.'

'Half a million is big money. I'll get it for you.'

Mary's face; she trusts me. I'm going to launch a thousand ships to save her.

'Wednesday. Bring it with the one hundred for the other girl, the useless one.'

Mary's face falls. Now she has me down as a scumbag trafficker. I shake my head. It's not how it looks, Mary.

'Six, then. By Wednesday evening,' I say.

'Cash. Used notes, euro, nothing bigger than fifties. Etcetera, etcetera, etcetera,' Ilie says, turning his back on me and walking Mary to the car.

Once he's put her inside, and the car has driven off, he walks back to me and gets right up in my face. It feels like we're a different sort of animal to each other.

'You tried to trick me before, a long time ago. Remember?'

'How can I forget?'

The casualties line up for registration. Friends, family, lovers. All gone, mostly dead.

'You spent how long in prison?'

Here we go.

'Nine years. Ten including remand.'

'How was it for you?'

I look him straight in the eye. 'A holiday camp.'

'If you betray me this time I will destroy everything you care about.'

I laugh. 'That won't take long.'

He laughs as well. 'Oh, I will take a long time.'

'I care about nothing.'

'Liar.' He gets even closer and hisses the word. 'Liar.'

I try to recoil but I'm sandwiched between him and the crusher.

'I saw you look at her. The Mary girl. I saw how she looked at you. I will sell her to some African chief, or maybe an Arab oil sheik. She will be used every day and, when they're tired of her...' He makes a noise like a candle being blown out.

I gulp air, but there isn't enough in the county.

'As for the other one, your lesbian dancer. First her sister,' he blows out another candle, 'then the farmer's wife. Then back to Romania on the streets where she will fuck truck drivers for stale bread until she dies in the gutter.'

'Is that the best you've got?'

'Oh, there are things we could do to Mrs Slaney and the former Mrs Mayes. Don't make me say it. I don't want any of this to happen.'

I decide to take a risk.

'I think your nephew killed our man, McGivney. The guards think so too. That's why they raided your place.'

'It's not *my place*. I'm just down here to sort this out. I know Constantin is dead. I have many, many nephews. Five hundred thousand euro.'

He looks at my oozing hand and shakes his head. 'That won't be necessary. You bring the money, you get the girl.'

'You know who she is, right?'

'You think I am worried about some local hoodlum's daughter? Just because we have some shared interests it doesn't make us equal. These people are nothing. You are nothing.'

He's wrong there. I'm less than nothing.

'Keep her safe, Ilie, and I'll get your money.'

He smiles and calls out a name without looking away from my face.

The fella with the Uzi walks over, phone to his ear. Almost immediately a black Mercedes limousine drives in through the gates and up to us.

'Once again,' he says, turning to me as the gunman opens the door. 'Wednesday, six hundred thousand euro, used notes no bigger than fifties. I will call with instructions. If you fail then there will be blood on your hands, Gerard Mayes.'

I'm left marooned in the scrapyard with the tattooed man. He has a phone in the hut but I don't know any numbers to call. They're all on my mobile back at the house.

'Scissors in the filing cabinet,' my host says. 'Bottom drawer.'

There's a bottle of Paddy's, scissors and a sawn-off shotgun in there. Things could have got uglier.

'They surprised me,' he says.

I cut the tape from around his wrists and let him sort his puke covered ankles out himself.

'Sorry about that,' I say. 'You have the Fly's mobile number?'

'No, but I have Nora's.'

The Ice Queen is connected all over.

I dial and Nora picks up immediately.

'Jack?'

'Nora, it's Ger here.'

I tell her the news and she agrees to call the Fly. It's not like any of this is my fault but it needs to be handled correctly. I feel like I'm walking a tightrope over a pit of Komodo Dragons.

Five minutes later the phone rings and Jack the Scrap picks up.

'Sure, boss, he's still here.' Jack hands the phone to me.

'Ger, is she okay? Did you see her?' The Fly sounds in a panic.

'Yeah, she looked fine, Bob. She's a diamond. Don't worry, I'm going to take care of this for you.'

Except for the money, of course.

Now he knows his daughter's unharmed the anger starts to mount.

'I'm gonna kill Bobby, shouting his mouth off around town like that.'

'Don't be too harsh on him, it wasn't his fault. There was a tracking device on that kid's bike. They traced it to here. None of us were to know.'

Strictly speaking, I should have known. Or at least I should have remembered the Romanians' use of such things from my own bad experiences with that infamous cocaine haul. A shiver grabs me as I wonder whether Constantin had some sort of tracker on his person. Maybe they don't transmit through concrete.

'I'm sending Bobby down to pick you up,' the Fly says. 'It's the least he can do.'

'Thanks,' I say. 'We should meet with…'

'Jim Duggan, yeah. Nine o'clock tomorrow morning, in your office.'

'Right. Good. Just one more thing. Can you tell me my mobile number?'

My car is at the cop shop, my phone is charging at my house and an Indian meal for two is congealing in the kitchen. I call my number three times but there's no answer.

It takes Bobby half an hour to come pick me up. I shake hands with Jack the Scrap and wince as his crushing grip mashes the slit in my palm.

Bobby is remorseful in the car on the way back.

'It's not your fault,' I tell him.

'No, I was pissed and acting the big man. Jesus, Ger, I'm such a hole sometimes.'

All the time, I want to tell him.

'Why didn't they take me? They should have taken me, Ger.'

'You're lucky they didn't. They would have sussed out it was you killed Constantin, then there wouldn't have been any chance of a deal.'

'If they kill Mary I'm going to shoot myself,' he says.

'Yeah, that'll help.'

He looks at me, which is a bit disconcerting as we're on the wrong side of the road, overtaking a string of vehicles at one and a half times the speed limit. Then his baby face folds into a grin and he gives me a whack in the shoulder.

'You're funny.' His laugh sounds demented. I imagine he laughed like that when he killed Constantin.

'We'll get your sister back. I'll see to it.'
'You'd better not fuck up, Ger.'

~

The desk sergeant has my car keys ready and waiting when Bobby drops me off at the Garda station.

It's well past six, as per instructions, and no sign of Garda Eamonn but I can sense traces of him in my lovely car. The steering wheel feels sticky under my hands and the seat position is all weird. I kind of feel a bit sorry for him if this is how he has to get his kicks.

Once parked in Maudlin Street I notice the deep scratch all the way down one side of the body. Now that is annoying.

The house front door sticks as usual. I've just about had enough and I kick it open with a shout.

'Aaaargh!' A mad thing with short blonde hair comes flying at me with a long kitchen knife and just manages to drop it before she stabs me. Instead she ends up in my arms. I hold her away from me. It's Krystal.

'What on earth have you done to your hair?'

We look down at the floor and see the knife embedded in my shoe, the handle and blade quivering. It's gone through the leather and into the top of my foot. I'm halfway to a full set of stigmata. These Romanians.

We both laugh and then she puts her head against my chest, hugging me hard.

'I thought it was them. You've been gone for hours. I thought they had taken you.'

'They did.'

I tell her all about the situation. She takes my hand and kisses the cut in my palm.

'Thank you, thank you, thank you.'

'There's something you are going to have to do,' I say.

She narrows her eyes.

'No, nothing like that. Tomorrow.' I look at her do-it-yourself haircut. She does look like a different person. 'And maybe a trip to the hairdresser's to finish the job?'

The Indian food, sitting neglected in the kitchen, has lost its appeal.

'Hey, how about we go out for a meal?' she says.

I think about it for a few seconds.

'Yeah, why not? We've got nothing to be afraid of. Let's do that,' I say.

'First, though,' she says with a smile, 'there's something I want to do to you.' She leads me upstairs by the hand.

~

The little Italian restaurant around the corner isn't busy, as usual.

'Bella, bello,' Giuseppe the owner shouts as we walk in. 'Try this, I just made it.'

Krystal smiles at me as we indulge Giuseppe's little routine. His wife Ciara gives me a strange look.

'Were you here before?' she says. 'You look familiar.'

I rub my uninjured left palm over my closely cropped scalp and smile at her.

'I was.'

'You look handsome,' Krystal says after we've been shown to our table.

'We make a handsome couple.'

'Bello, bella,' she says and laughs like her name.

The white wine is cold and soothes my body after what has been a very long day. My throbbing stigmata fade to a blur.

We talk and talk. There are no dark turns to the conversation. The ocean's waves are breaking on the sands of our future. It's talk of freedom, sunshine and doing whatever the hell we want to do.

'I like to swim,' she says. 'I was a good swimmer when I was a kid.'

'You can teach me then. I'm rubbish.'

'I can't believe you are rubbish at anything,' she says.

'Oh, you'd be surprised. I have a long list of things.'

She laughs. At me, with me, for me.

'I think you two are very much in love,' Giuseppe says when he comes to share his special Grappa with us at the end of the meal. 'Just like me and my beautiful Ciara.'

'We are very much in love with the idea of being in love,' I say.

Krystal strokes the back of my injured hand.

~

The wine, the Grappa and the elation of a future. Back in the house, in my new bed, Krystal and I fall naked into each other's arms.

In her drunken state she tries to pleasure me, rubbing my good hand on her breasts. She's prepared to try but I know it would be a mistake. Her love is running wild in a field in Tipperary and my lust is locked up, God knows where, with Mary. As a result, and probably not helped by the booze, the lad won't rise to the occasion. We don't need Ella's keep it up drugs; togetherness is what it's all about.

Day 11 – Captives

I wake early enough the next morning without much of a hangover. We didn't drink so much, it was just that we ate late. Krystal is still out for the count as I hobble into the bathroom. Her skin is smooth and golden, asking to be kissed all over, but I leave her be. That was then and this is now.

My hand is aching from the blood oath and my foot is almost too sore to stand on. A good long shower lets the heat of the water take the edge off my pain. The shower gel bottle slips through my hands and I groan when I squat to pick it up. That little Romanian fella might have done some permanent damage when he cracked me in the nuts. I'm spoilt for choices when it comes to limp lad excuses.

In the baker's the ladies' faces light up, reflecting my smile.

It's okay, I want to say. *I'm going to rescue Mary Reaney, daughter of the Fly, and Krystal whatshername, my Romanian girlfriend. This is Ger Mayes and I have a cunning plan.*

'Two chocolate croissants please,' is all I do say.

'How are you getting on?' the lady who last time threw a tray of cupcakes into orbit asks.

'Good, thanks. Redecorating, giving the place a facelift.'

Limping back to Maudlin Street, I leave both croissants in the kitchen for Krystal and put on a pot of coffee so she'll slowly wake to the aroma.

Up on the Hebron the Fly and Nora are already in my office. No pleasantries, they're on edge.

'Here,' says the Fly, getting up out of my chair.

'No, Bob, you're grand,' I say but he insists.

'You're the key player here, Ger,' he says.

Jim Duggan walks in through the reception and across to us.

'Bob, Nora, Ger,' he says, taking off his coat.

I wave for him to take a seat.

'What have you done to your hand?' Duggan says.

'They made me take a blood oath.'

'What the fuck for?' the Fly says.

'As a promise to pay the ransom.'

The best of lies, based on truth.

The palm looks nasty, the cut weeping after the shower.

'I'll get a bandage. You should go and get some shots. Tetanus or something,' Nora says and walks out to find the first aid box.

'Fucking animals,' the Fly growls.

I let Nora wrap my hand. She's gentle.

'Right,' Duggan says, 'what's the situation?'

The Fly clears his throat. 'Before we start, Jim, I want to get one thing clear. Exactly whose side are you on?'

Duggan doesn't miss a beat. 'Yours, Bob. Yours and Mary's.'

The Fly looks at me then growls at Duggan.

'You're pretty thick with them, aren't ye?'

Duggan folds a palm towards his chest then opens it out to me.

'Ger and I know them pretty well.'

The implicating bastard. As usual Double-crossing Duggan has the dirt on me.

'Yep,' I say, 'but it was a long time ago. I recognised the main man, though. Petulengro.'

Duggan winces. Naming names isn't cricket and that's what started the rot all those years ago. I can be sure now that he's batting for both sides.

'Did you do what I asked?' the Fly says.

'Of course, Bob,' Duggan says. 'I spoke with Petulengro and brokered the deal. Half a million euro, used notes, nothing bigger than fifties. He wants Ger to bring the money to Dublin on Wednesday.'

I wonder how much the Fly is paying Duggan to agree what Ilie and I had already arranged.

'Are you okay with that, Ger?' the Fly says.

I nod. 'Whatever it takes, Bob. I'll bring your daughter back.'

The Fly stands and puts a hand on my shoulder.

'You're a good man. It's not your fault. None of this is your doing.'

Things usually are my fault but, in this case, he could be right. It all started with the Gimp and his attempted raid on the competition, probably on the Fly's orders. So the Fly is to blame.

'No one's to blame,' I say.

'Strictly speaking, this is retaliation for their brother,' Duggan says, unhelpfully.

'That was self-defence,' the Fly says. 'They did McGivney and then they tried to get Bobby. Now they've got Mary.'

The little Fly's big fists are bunching. I'd like to see him let loose on the Romanians. With no machine guns, of course. Or on Duggan.

'Bob, Bob. We have to de-escalate this situation. You have two of their girls,' Duggan glances at me, 'and Constantin. I don't suppose there's any chance you can give them back the boy?'

Nora gives a cold laugh.

'Just a thought,' the Fly says. 'If they had a tracking device on the bike there might have been one on the lad.'

They all look at me, like I'm the technical expert. I have a mental image of a red light flashing in Constantin's concrete tomb. My stabbed foot gives a pulsing throb through my shoe.

'I don't think we have to worry about that,' I say.

We all nod. Enough said.

'There's nothing else for it, then,' the Fly says. 'Jim, you arrange the ransom money. We'll take it from the Waterford betting office. First thing on Wednesday we all meet in this office, say at eight, and take it from there. I'll have security escort you and the money up from Waterford.'

'Just one thing,' Duggan says. 'My advice is to do the deal straight. These are heavy people. The only reason Jack, Ger and Mary are still breathing is the money. That's all they're interested in. We pay and the chapter is closed.'

The Fly looks ready to knock Duggan's head from his shoulders.

'I pay, we get my Mary back and then I'll decide if this is over or not.'

~

When I get home Krystal is full of the joys of spring and the house is full of a delicious aroma.

'I'm cooking lunch,' she says.

'Lovely.'

A pan on the hob is sizzling and the worktop is evidence of her industry. Vegetables of every conceivable shape and colour lie in various states of dismemberment and she's hacking away at a slab of meat with the knife that punctured my foot last night.

'I used to cook this for my family back home.' She stirs the pan and throws cubes of meat into it. Looks like beef. 'So, how did it go? You get the girl back okay?'

'We will. Wednesday. Everything will be sorted.'

'Everything?'

'Yep. Do you have a passport?'

She looks at me, narrows her eyes and smiles. 'Of course. I took it back from them before I left. You stir this.'

I take the wooden spoon from her hand. The pan seems to be very hot so I turn down the heat.

'Here.' She places a worn-looking passport on the worktop with her bag. 'Don't laugh at the photo.'

I thumb through the pages and give a little chuckle at the serious face in the photo, but it's not too bad. I'm more interested in her bag.

'Hey, what the hell?' she shouts as I take a scissors to the lining.

'Look.' I hold up a coin-sized disc; one of the Romanians' positioning devices.

'What is it?'

'Something the brothers use to keep track of you.'

'Destroy it! Give it to me and I'll smash it,' she says and grabs for it.

I hold the thing up in the air like a bully teasing a schoolgirl.

'No, I have a better idea. If we smash the thing they'll know we found it.'

'So what then?' she says.

'When the time is right we'll send them in the wrong direction,'

I take a junk mail envelope from the worktop, open a corner and put the device inside. Then I put the envelope in her bag.

'I have a surprise for you this evening,' I say.

'Oh good, I like surprises. But first, we eat.' She serves the contents of the pan onto two plates.

We eat standing at the kitchen counter. My house is still totally impractical – nowhere to sit. Krystal's cooking is totally impractical as well. The meat, beef I think, is fried hard like bullets and the mixture of ingredients is like a mad painting with too many colours that end up being none.

'You used to cook this for your family?'

She laughs. 'A long time ago. I didn't cook much in the last few years. I think I did something wrong.'

'No, it's lovely.' I chew on the beef until my jaw aches. 'Really lovely.'

She pushes her food around her plate until I eventually give up on mine.

'So what is this surprise?' she asks. 'I said I like surprises but I need to know what they are.'

'Then it's not a surprise.'

'Tell me then.' She punches me in the shoulder.

'It's a way to get out of this town with money in your pocket.'

'In our pockets, Ger.'

'That's all I'm telling you for now. You'll just have to wait until tonight.'

She gives a growl that winds up into a yelp. 'You're so annoying!'

I give her my best smirk.

'Come with me,' she says and drags me out by my good hand and up the stairs.

My laptop is sitting open on the bed. The escort website is on display. Before she can close it down I grab the computer and read the screen.

Melody is no longer advertising.

'Look,' she says, taking it from me. 'Aer Lingus flies from Dublin to Perpignan, south of France. And see.' She changes to another window. 'This cottage is for rent, and this one, and here's a chateau. This one is looking out over the beach.'

I nod, taking it all in. I can do this, just walk away. 'First I'll get Mary back safe, though. Then we go.'

'Thursday then. Everything will be sorted by Thursday. Let's book tickets!'

One hour later and we've booked, but not to France. One way tickets to Malaga in southern Spain. It really doesn't matter where, just get the hell out of Dodge.

'I have to go back in the office,' I say. 'A few things to tie up. What are you going to do with yourself this afternoon?'

'Shopping for holiday clothes,' Krystal says with a grin. The Spanish sun shines from her face. 'Let's go out again for dinner tonight.'

'Maybe tomorrow. We'll be having a guest tonight.'

'Oh?'

'Part of the surprise.'

'I can cook.'

'We'll order in.'

~

Nora is having some sharp words on the phone when I return to the office after lunch. I make her a cup of tea and put it on the desk next to where she's standing.

'Thanks,' she mouths to me. 'No!' she barks into the phone. 'From the Waterford betting shop. We'll make sure the cash is there for you to collect tomorrow evening.'

She puts the phone down without goodbye.

'Problem?' I ask.

'Duggan. He's making it more difficult than it has to be. He wants to provide the cash for some reason, but I don't trust him.'

'You're right not to.'

She shuts her eyes and takes a deep breath.

'Here.' I lift the mug of tea and, when she opens her eyes, I place it in her hands. Her eyes crinkle as she sips at it.

'We'll get Mary back, won't we? You saw her, Ger.'

'She'll be fine,' I say with more confidence than I really have.

'Call her.'

'What?' I say.

'They have her phone, right? We'll call her. Give me yours.'

I hand over my phone and Nora's fingers fly over the touch screen.

'Here.' She gives it back to me.

The dial tone sounds through the speaker and after four rings it answers. I nearly drop the phone as Ilie Petulengro's wizened face appears on the screen. He looks like a rat.

'Ah, Gerard. I see you've had a haircut.'

My first ever video call.

'You're calling me to say everything is going okay with the money and you'd like to speak with your girlfriend.'

'Yes.'

'How nice. I'll just see if she's available.' The screen goes dark. I hear Ilie's croak in his mother tongue and then a female voice shouting, coming nearer.

The phone is thrust away and I see her, one of the brothers leading her in by the arm. She shakes him off. As she moves closer I can see a red mark on her face and blood on her lip.

'As you can see, things have not been going smoothly this end,' Ilie's voice says from behind the camera. 'Your girlfriend is not very cooperative.'

The picture turns to one of the lads. He tries to hide the deep scratches down the side of his face.

'Mary? Are you okay, Mary?' I say. The picture moves back to her.

'Yeah, Ger. Just fine.' She gives a little cough. 'Having a nice little time with your friends here. They've told me all about you.'

'They're not my friends. Are you … did they…?' I don't know how to ask.

'Let's just say shaken not stirred,' she says.

Nora grabs the phone from me.

'Mary, we're doing everything to get you home,' she says.

'How's Dad?'

'Under control,' Nora says. 'We'll get you home, chicken.'

Ilie's face appears again. 'I will be letting you know where to meet on Wednesday. We will conclude our little business without any problems, otherwise…' He draws a finger across his throat. 'So, say bye bye for now.'

The camera moves back to Mary's face and her eyes look into mine. Pleading, accusing, delicious. The screen goes blank.

Nora gives a sob and I comfort her with an arm around her shoulders.

'She's like a daughter to me.'

Nora softens into me for a few moments and I can feel the warmth and stress in her. Just when it's getting a bit too comfortable she straightens up, wipes her nose with the back of a hand and walks back to her seat, picking up the phone.

'I have to get that money sorted,' she says. 'We usually have a big float across the shops and Bob keeps a fair bit in his safe. I don't know why it's such a problem today.'

Her straightened blonde hair is hanging forward over the desk. Ice maiden in disarray. I can't help myself and I step behind her, gathering her hair in a ponytail that I lay across her shoulder. Then I walk smartly into my office to fix my own small financial arrangements.

'Ah, Ger,' McDonald says when I'm put through to his desk. I can smell the dust and disorder down the phone line. 'Have you settled on an investment opportunity or do you need some further suggestions?'

'Oh, I've found something very suitable, thanks. I need to get my hands on some of my money.'

'Is it one of the options I recommended to you?' I can hear him lubricating the line so my money can slide into his pockets.

'No. It's a charitable donation for a worthy cause, but urgent.'

'Right, well, how much and when?'

'A hundred grand. And soon, today if possible.'

McDonald laughs. 'This isn't Switzerland, Ger. I doubt your local branch has the funds to fulfill that. It'll be tomorrow if not Wednesday. There's nothing in it for me but I still have your power of attorney so I'll do it as a favour if you want me to.'

It's no great shakes if I let him do it. He'll think I owe him something, which at least keeps the relationship open.

'Yeah, would you? See if they can get the cash ready for early tomorrow afternoon. Otherwise the deal will lapse.'

'I'll let you know if there's a problem. Otherwise go to your branch at 2 p.m. and ask for the manager. He's a pal of mine.'

About two hours later Nora comes into my office and sits down. I close the window on the computer where I've been looking at Spanish villas.

'All done,' she says. 'Wasn't easy but it's all arranged.'

'Shame we couldn't use those notes from up north,' I say.

'You are joking, right? If even one of those notes turn up with any connection to us then we're looking at a life sentence or worse if the lads get hold of us.'

'Yes, I'm joking.'

She looks at me and bites her hand before continuing.

'I'm worried, Ger.' Her voice wavers. 'I'm scared.'

'You've nothing to be scared of.'

'Not for me. I'm scared for Mary.'

'I'm concerned for Mary but she'll be okay. She's a brick.'

'And I'm scared for Bob. He might be a villain but he's not a gangster. These people, you said they had machine guns. I don't think Bob's ever fired a gun. I don't think he even owns one.'

'He won't need a gun, Nora. This will all work out.'

The computer on my desk beeps and times me out of the property website.

'He's not a bad man, Ger. He keeps up the tough façade, but Bobby and that boy really upset him. Then, when he couldn't find Mary, he lost it. Just lies awake on the bed all night, gazing into nothing.'

There's a little confirmation for me that I ought to cross Nora off my list. In response to that thought my mobile buzzes on the desk with a message from Ella.

Hello stranger xXx

Nora nods her head to say read it but I slide the phone away from me.

'This time on Thursday it'll all be over. Back to normal.' I cross my hands on my stomach and lean back.

She laughs without humour. 'You don't know Bob. Thirty-two fights undefeated. He won't give up until they're out cold.'

After Nora's gone I go back to my computer. Time to get the hell out of Dodge, as McAuliffe would say.

~

Ella texts me again and then calls three times but I don't pick up. In the car on the brief drive home I dial voicemail on the hands-free.

'Hi, Ger, it's me, Ella. Listen, I heard about Eamonn's performance yesterday and I'm sorry. I really enjoyed Saturday, and Sunday morning.' She gives her tinkling ice laugh. 'See you soon, call me.'

I'm tempted. Okay, she's twice the drunk I am, she has a drug habit, and her ex is a maniac with a badge, but she's the closest thing I have to a real girlfriend. Krystal is my lesbian Rapunzel, Mary hates me by now because the brothers will have told her all about Krystal and everything else is shite.

I press call.

'Hey, Ger. You're a difficult man to get hold of.'

'Well, you know how it is. Business.'

I let her have a couple of seconds silence.

'You didn't call me yesterday. I don't blame you. Eamonn is such an idiot. He always…'

'Traps your boyfriends when they leave your house?'

She goes for the boyfriend tag.

'So sorry, Ger. He was boasting about it when he dropped Finn off. I've made an official complaint to the station. It won't happen next time.'

So, we're to be fuck buddies, at least.

'I had a really good time,' I say. 'A bit of a hangover yesterday, in the cells, but a really good time at yours.'

She laughs again and I drive on past my turn, through town.

'We did overdo it a bit. I was nervous, to be honest. It's been a long while,' I say.

'I could tell.'

'Oh...'

'I mean, you fair wore me out. You know...' She chuckles, a dirty laugh this time.

The Saab is heading up the hill and out onto the Kells Road.

'Well, let's do it again sometime,' she says. I can hear her breathing.

'How about during the week? I know you have Finn but maybe if I came round after he's gone to bed?'

'Sure,' she says without a moment's hesitation, 'tonight?'

I'm hurtling along the road between the high hedges. Why not now? This feels just like it did with Renée, stolen moments away from the marital home. Except this time it's Krystal at home, not Jo.

'I'd love to, but I have someone coming round this evening. Business. How about tomorrow?'

'Yeah, that would be great. Say nine-thirty? I should have Finn asleep by then.'

'It's a date!'

'I look forward to it. And Ger...'

'Yeah?'

'Save up your energy. You're going to need it. See ya.'

'See ya.'

I slow the car as I pass the gates of An Cloigín Gorm and then boot it on to the next left and the Waterford Road back to Kilkenny.

~

A worried looking Krystal pulls open the front door as I struggle with my key in the lock.

'I had a phone call,' she says.

'The brothers?' I don't like to say the Romanians. Mustn't tar the prostitute with the pimp brush.

'Yes, Silviu.'

'Is he the little guy?

'Yes, the small, vicious one.'

I push the door shut behind me.

'What did he have to say?'

'Just threats. He was complaining about lost earnings and if we don't have the money by Wednesday then the price goes up. And he said hello from your girlfriend.' She narrows her eyes.

'Do you know where they are? Do you know where they're keeping her?'

'Probably at the farm. They have a place, somewhere around here. If you do something wrong they take you there. If you need a doctor they take you there, to the farm.'

'Do you know where it is?'

She shakes her head. 'I can't tell you, but I think I could find it if you drive.'

~

'Why are we doing this? It's crazy!'

Krystal has her eyes tight shut in the back seat of my car.

'It just puts some more cards in our hands. We need any ammunition we can get,' I say.

'Left in about thirty seconds,' she says.

I weave the car through the spider's web of Kilkenny's streets, out the back edge of an old corporation housing estate. The road hits the countryside.

'We do a tight turn and then over a small bridge. Immediate right down a lane.'

'How do you know this so well?' I ask.

'Ten years, Ger. I did something wrong, more than once. And then the times I went to see the doctor. A lot of times.'

She starts to cry.

'I'm sorry,' I say. 'It was a stupid idea. We don't have to do this.'

She sniffs away her tears.

'No, we're almost there. I want to see it. Slower now. Another bend, left, and then take a track to the left.'

I make the turn. 'We shouldn't get too close. I wasn't exactly planning to stop for tea.'

'It's up this hill and down the other side. I think there's a wood in between, I used to hear the sound change. We can leave the car there.'

Sure enough the track crests in a stand of old trees. I pull the car off the throughway and park behind some undergrowth.

The ground is soft underfoot with years of leaf mould; ideal for body disposal.

Krystal walks to the edge of the trees and looks down across the fields to an old farmhouse with a smoking chimney.

'I never wanted children,' she says.

The Romanians' dark windowed Passat sits in the farmyard, innocuous amongst the scruffy outbuildings. No sign of Ilie's limo.

'They'll have her inside the main house. There's a fireplace where they boil water,' she says. 'The house has no electricity.'

I look at Krystal biting her bottom lip to stop it from trembling. I want to storm the stronghold, rescue Mary and return her home safe. Then together Krystal and I will track down the doctor who did the Romanians' bidding over the years and subject him to a horrible death. But I'm not Rambo, I'm finally beginning to realise.

She takes my hand and we just stand and watch the peat smoke curl into the low grey sky.

One time a guy comes out of the farmhouse and smokes a cigarette next to the car. It looks like a machine gun hanging from his shoulder. He's startled by the sound of a shotgun in the distance, followed by the distant cawing of crows in tall trees a couple of fields away. He looks around him but we're safe from discovery in the gloom of the woods. Another cigarette and he goes back inside.

'I'm cold,' Krystal says after what seems like hours.

I take off my jacket and put it around her shoulders.

'Let's go. There's nothing we can do here.'

On the way back to town she says, 'What are you going to do now you know where they are?'

I look at my phone; three messages and a missed call. I don't read them.

'Not sure, I have to think about it.'

Totally out of my depth. Well and truly. I feel like a child in a row boat on Loch Ness with a thousand feet of water beneath me. There's a hole in the boat, the water is coming in, I can't swim and a monster is lying in wait.

Telling tales

Roisín McGuire's little red sports coupé is waiting for us in Maudlin Street. I let Krystal in the house and then walk over to the reporter's car.

She lowers her window. 'Ger. Like the new look. Are we all set? Who's the girl?'

'All in good time.' I inhale her perfume and cigarettes. 'Give me five minutes and then come on over.'

'What's going on?' Krystal says from the front room when I enter the house. She's been peeping out from behind the sheet hung over the window.

'Nothing to worry about, you'll see. Wanna make some coffee?'

Krystal makes the Alessi do its thing and the coffee is just brewed when a knock comes at the front door.

'Hi,' I say, take Roisín's coat and hang it on the bottom of the stairs. When I turn she's picked up my stab vest from the corner of the hall and is examining it.

'What's the story, Ger?'

I put on the innocent look.

'Come and meet a friend.' She puts the vest back down and follows me into the kitchen. 'Roisín, this is Krystal. Krystal, this is Roisín McGuire.'

They seem like two totally different animals; Roisín, normally glamorous and tall, seems pale and awkward; Krystal suddenly seems swarthy and furtive. I wonder if I've made a big mistake bringing them together.

'I know you,' Krystal says, her words dripping suspicion. 'You're that reporter from the TV. What's going on, Ger?'

'Yeah, Ger,' Roisín turns to me, 'what *is* going on?'

At least I've united them with a common enemy. Me, the master of accidental strategy.

'You said you wanted the inside story. Human trafficking, slavery, organised prostitution. Krystal is part of it and she's looking to get out.'

Roisín's jaw drops open as her gaze wanders between Krystal and me. Then she regains her composure.

'Let me guess. You're looking for money?'

An ugly sneer spreads across Krystal's face as she realises it's not a free ride after all. She thinks she's been bought and sold.

'Two-fifty,' I say. 'That's what it'll take. For that you get the complete inside story of Krystal's ten years. Smuggled in, forced to work in brothels across the country. Twenty-four seven, just a few days break each year.'

Krystal tries to hide a gulp and gives a slow nod of the head.

Roisín crosses her arms. 'Come on, Ger. A quarter of a million? You have to be joking me!'

'No joke. Think about it. An exclusive you can sell to TV and newspapers, not just in Ireland. You'll own it. You can write a book about it. You'll be made for life.'

I can hear her journalistic brain processing the possibilities.

'I might be able to get a deal with the tabloids and TV news. But a quarter of a million, no. Not up front. Maybe fifty grand. If I secured a book deal we might manage the rest.'

'We're leaving the country,' I say.

'What! When?'

'Thursday. We fly out on Thursday. You'll still have access to us, to Krystal, but we can't stay in Ireland.'

Roisín pulls her phone from a pocket, starts to press on the touch screen and then changes her mind. She's playing for time.

'Look, I don't know if I can get anything before Thursday.' She turns to Krystal. 'No offence, but your story would have to be authenticated. We would have to do a lot of work. Then there would be a negotiation with the newspapers and news channels.'

Krystal's mouth turns down. 'Let's just forget it. A crazy idea. Fucking crazy, Ger.'

I try to calm her but she looks ready to throttle me. Instead I work on Roisín. 'Krystal has been here for ten years, first as an erotic dancer and more recently in the escort industry. She was an underage illegal immigrant at the time and her family at home in Romania were vulnerable. Abuse, exploitation, sexual slavery, you name it. Now she's buying her way out.'

'I'm sorry, but this sort of thing has been in the news before,' Roisín says.

'Sure, but from a distance. I've seen the reporter running towards the girls and driver, getting a few camera shots and no comment.' I see from Roisín's face that I'm right. 'This is the complete inside story. It'll blow the thing apart, once and for all. Ten years, a personal story. Everyone can make money and we can put an end to it.'

'There will never be an end to it,' Krystal growls.

An idea jumps into my mind. Maybe, for once, me walking away would be a good thing.

'I'm going to leave you two alone now. I'll be back in an hour.' I turn to Roisín. 'If you don't think we have something after that then we're done, but I think Krystal's story deserves to be heard.'

Roisín uncrosses her arms. 'What about the rest of it? Your boss, the money laundering, drugs and all that?'

'No, this is the story you need. This is a story that is leaving the country on Thursday.'

Krystal has her eyes closed. I kiss her forehead, grab my coat from the stairs and walk out the front door.

~

Grass grows tall between the tumbledown gravestones. One of them should have Raymond the Gimp McGivney written on it.

I try reading the names in the fading light. Old names from Kilkenny, families that have weathered the storms of centuries: the scourge of Thomas Cromwell, the surge of the British Empire and the Celtic Tiger's demise. I'll soon be leaving this place to those who own it.

What to do about Mary and the Romanians' rustic hideaway? If I tell the Fly he'll want to know how I found out about the place. Instinct tells me to keep Krystal out of that loop. I have an idea.

He answers on the first ring. 'Reaney.'

'Bob, it's Ger.'

'Ger, what's the story? Nora tells me we should be all set tomorrow. She says you both spoke with Mary.'

'Yep. I know where she is.'

The other end is silent. He's normally on the golf course or in a crowd, but I have the feeling he's locked away somewhere, sitting in the dark.

A lorry rumbles down the Dublin Road at the top of the graveyard and disturbs a flock of sparrows that were hiding out in the trees. They swarm like bees in a fluid formation and land on the grass in the far corner, near the Maudlin Tower.

'How do you know that, Ger?'

'I went to their flat, where they rent the girls. The car they used to take me to the scrapyard was there, a blue Passat. All I had to do was wait and follow it.'

I hear his breathing. He doesn't know what to do with the situation either.

'Were you seen?'

'No, I was careful not to be.'

'So where is it? Did you see Mary?'

'It's out Dicksboro way, a good few miles. Old farm in a bit of a hollow. There was smoke coming from a chimney but I'm sure she's there. It was the same guys, I saw the one with the Uzi.'

He's panting down the line now. 'Fucking hell, Ger. Fucking hell!'

'I know, I know. Unless we want the guards involved? I don't see what...'

'No way. This is between us and them. Thanks, Ger, but it doesn't change anything really. When you come in tomorrow show me on a map where it is and we can keep tabs on them, have someone follow them to the rendezvous and all.'

'Right.'

'Right.' He hangs up.

My scalp itches. I scratch it with my fingernails and am surprised by the stubble. I'd forgotten about my new tough guy look. I need a cigarette or a drink or something.

Roisín's car is still parked across the road from my house. I put an ear to the front door and hear their voices inside. They're not shouting but the conversation sounds animated. A little more time is needed.

The Edge of the World beckons.

Tim is behind the bar again. Perhaps he's been there the whole weekend, raking in the overtime.

My first pint of Smithwick's doesn't even touch the sides. John-Jo stops by and says a few words but I can't engage with him. I don't want to have to answer any questions.

'Same again?' Tim asks and my head dips of its own accord.

I have the second pint half done when my mobile starts to rattle across the bar top.

Ger, I'm in the car. Come and talk. Roisín.

This nervous feeling is worse than having to bury a dead Constantin, staking out a criminal lair or even being a passenger in Bobby's car. I throw the rest of the beer down my throat and go to face the music.

'Nice one, Ger,' Roisín says as I step into the car outside my house. 'The poor girl had no idea. You didn't tell her you were going to do that, did you?'

'I thought she would lose her nerve.'

'You can't blame her. Well, it's not quite the story I was angling for.'

I feel it slipping away: the chance of some easy money (well, easy for me), my friendship with Krystal, Roisín's trust.

'That's okay. I just thought…'

'No, Ger, it's a great story. I mean, it's terrible, but it has to be told and she wants to tell it.'

'Well, it's all I've got for you. How about the money?'

'I've made a few calls. I can get you some money up front but nothing like you're asking. Maybe twenty to start and more later. If we get the book together we could be talking the sort of money you mentioned.'

'She needs a hundred to buy herself out.'

Roisín snorts a laugh. 'Don't be taking her for a fool. Or me, for that matter. She says you're organising the hundred grand. I'll do what I can to get an advance on the story tomorrow. There isn't much time.'

'Okay. How do you want to handle this? Because I have no idea.'

She laughs. 'That's probably the first time I've heard you tell the God's honest truth. What I need to do is interview her at length, get the copy and then you need to get the hell out of the country.'

'Well, that was the plan.' My eyes seem to be searching of their own accord around the interior of the car, looking everywhere except at Roisín.

'The guys she was working for are going to be mightily pissed off when this hits the media,' she says. 'It'll shut down their operation. Unless you get out and far away, my guess is she's one dead woman, and...'

My eyes come to rest on her baby blues. She need say no more.

'Okay, okay. Like I said, we're leaving on a jet plane, just as soon as I've taken care of some other important stuff.'

'And what would that be?'

I stick out my bottom lip and shake my head. The Mary rescue is none of her business.

'Right then, Ger. I'll come round first thing in the morning and spend all day with her to get as much of the news story as I can. Give me every minute she can spare before you fly out and then I'll need access to her for the book. I'll need to know where you go and I'll need your bank account details.'

I pull a folded piece of paper from my shirt pocket and hold it up between two fingers.

'Let's do it like this. Here's my bank info. You make a transfer by tomorrow lunchtime and then you can talk to Krystal all you want, right up until we leave. Then you can come over and see her or Skype or whatever you need to write the book.'

'Okay. I'll see what I can do.'

I lower the paper towards her. She takes it, reads what I've written and puts it in her handbag. Then she takes out a cigarette and lights up.

'Let me know when the money is in and then you can come over. Are you staying locally?'

She sucks hard on the cigarette and nods. Then she blows the smoke out her now open window. It's not a good look. She's going to age prematurely.

'Be careful, Roisín. Watch in case you're being followed. These people are like poison.'

I step out and walk away.

'I'll do the best I can, Ger,' she calls from her car window. 'Tell Krystal that, will you?'

My smile is weak as her red sports coupé zips off down Mauldin Street.

No sign of Krystal downstairs when I enter the house. I find her in the bedroom, curled up on the quilt like a cat.

'Hey,' I say.

'Hey you.'

'Are you okay?'

She sits up on the bed and pulls her knees in to her chest like a child.

'I thought you were going to pay the hundred thousand from your own money.'

'I was. I am. It's all organised, I arranged it today.'

'Then what the fuck was all that about?' Her voice is cracking and her cheeks are wet.

I sit and smooth her hair. What was I thinking? Money is what I was thinking.

'It could make a big difference. It could set us up. I'm sorry I surprised you with it, but I thought you might not agree to do it.'

She sniffs. 'I wouldn't have.'

'Oh.'

'I would have been too scared of them and what they might do to me. But, after talking with Roisín, I know it's the right thing to do.'

Good old Roisín.

'Ten years of my life, Ger. She said no one should have to live through that and telling my story will help others.'

'You're okay with it then?'

She nods her head. 'And you're right, we're going to need money.'

'The more the better. Just think, if we had a quarter of a million more we could buy instead of rent; a cottage by the sea, somewhere remote and private. Every morning you could walk the beach and swim in the ocean. You could siesta in the afternoon and for dinner we'd eat fresh seafood on the veranda and drink the local wine.'

Krystal murmurs and a smile spreads across her face in her sleep.

Day 12 – Cashing in

It's a day I just want done and dusted. And tomorrow. The next week, in fact. I'm used to wishing my life away in Portlaoise prison but this is different. Like a kid who wants some life trial over and done with.

Roisín McGuire wakes me at 7:00 with her first text message.

We have 25k from the Independent. Can I come round?

I text her back that she can come round when we get up to a hundred.

I would go back to sleep but my stigmata half set is throbbing like an omen. Krystal groans in her sleep. I may as well take a shower and get ready for work.

The trickling, tepid water drives me mad as usual but then it puts on an uncharacteristic surge, even getting quite warm in the process. I'm fooled again by the haircut Krystal gave me, rubbing a handful of shampoo onto the stubble. It feels good and the tune of Club Tropicana starts to bounce around my head.

'Club Tropicana drinks are free. Fun and sunshine, there's enough for everyone.'

I'm not a bad singer when the mood takes me. That'll be us on the beach somewhere and soon.

Towelling off I hear voices downstairs. Krystal's deep tones contrast with the tinkle of Roisín. May as well let them at it.

'Hi, Ger,' Roisín says when I walk into the kitchen. 'I know you said later but I have a nibble from a news channel and I think we should start to get the copy together.'

Krystal hands me a coffee and I take a pastry from a plateful Roisín must have brought with her.

'Okay with you?' I ask Krystal.

'Sure,' she says. 'It's not like we have a lot of time.'

They look at each other and I'm obviously not required.

'Hey, I'll see you at lunchtime.' I give Krystal a kiss on the cheek, Roisín gives me a raised eyebrow to say don't try it on me, and I'm off to work with my mug of coffee in the car.

There are a couple of unfamiliar cars parked at Reaney's, together with Bob and Bobby's BMWs. Nora is sitting at her desk, on the phone. She tips her head towards my office where father and son are in conference with four stone-faced older men. The Fly looks up, sees me and waves me in.

'Ger, these gentlemen are going to help us with a spot of surveillance.'

The fellas shake my hand, each of them with a grip that means business. I have them down for retired guards.

'Show us the route you took to the farm,' one of them says, placing an iPad on the table and pointing to a map of Kilkenny with a stubby finger.

I trace the road out past Dicksboro. 'Somewhere out here.'

He taps the screen a couple of times and the road appears on an aerial photo. I see the tight turn and the bridge, then the track to the right.

'It was up this lane. We parked in a stand of trees looking down over the farm,' I say.

'It must be this place,' another of the men says. Stubby zooms in further to see the roofs of the farmhouse and outbuildings. 'One way in, one way out.'

'Should be easy enough to stake out,' Stubby says.

'I'll take first shift,' one of the others says. 'Drop me there and come back in eight hours.'

'You fecker,' the remaining one of the four says. 'I'll end up with the night shift, as usual.'

Stubby turns to the Fly. 'We'll keep tabs on them. Should be able to spot your girl. We'll trail them to the rendezvous and let you know if there's anything strange. I'm expecting this to be straightforward.'

The stone-faced men stand and exchange brother handshakes and man hugs with the Fly. I get my stigmata mashed again.

'They're the best in this situation,' the Fly says when they're gone.

Nora comes in with three mugs of coffee.

'You've done everything you can, Bob. It'll all turn out well,' she says.

We take burning mouthfuls of beverage.

'How's it coming with the cash?' he asks.

'Getting there. We should be sorted by lunchtime.'

My phone buzzes and I glance at the display.

Ger, we need to have a little chat. Andy.

I switch the phone off.

'Got a problem, Ger?' Nora says.

I look from her to the Fly. 'Women trouble,' I say, which is sort of true.

'You still seeing Ella Cullen?' the Fly asks. He's trying to be polite but disapproval hangs in the air between us.

'Yeah, supposed to be seeing her tonight.'

The Fly coughs. 'Well, don't get bladdered. We need you bright and breezy for whatever goes on tomorrow. Any news on that yet?'

I shake my head. 'If I've not heard by say three this afternoon, I'll text to Mary's phone for instructions.'

'Just make sure you keep that phone on. Let me know as soon as you hear something.' He stands up and Nora hugs him, all platonic pretence abandoned. He clasps my hand in his two oversized paws. 'I'm relying on you, Ger. You're in the family now.'

I feel a twinge of guilt. For a second I want to share everything about the Krystal deal and earn their trust, but the urge passes like a groan in the stomach.

The Fly leaves and Nora stays.

'You'd better put that phone back on,' she says. 'What's the story with Ella then?'

'Wouldn't you like to know?'

She laughs, now I'm family. 'Maybe it's something I can help with?'

'Just a balancing act, you know how it is.'

'Well, watch out for her ex-husband. He's a looper.'

'A bit late telling me now. Thanks for the coffee.'

She leaves me to it and goes back to raising her half a million. I just have a hundred grand to find.

The phone buzzes when I turn it on. McAuliffe again. I ignore him and start the engagement with McDonald and the bank, using my desk phone. My mobile continues to buzz intermittently with McAuliffe's calls and texts.

After a frustrating ping pong with McDonald and the bank manager's personal assistant, I get the bank manager on the phone. Unbelievably it's Phillip Purcell, the same jerk I dealt with ten years ago when I had to raise money for the Romanians' drug shipment. A hundred grand it was then too. The Yes Man.

'Yes?' he says. 'Mr Mayes, yes, what a pleasant surprise.'

'Ah, Mr Purcell.'

'Yes, yes, call me Phillip.'

'Thanks.' Mr Mayes to you.

'I understand you want to make a sizeable cash withdrawal, yes?'

'That's right. A hundred thousand.'

'Yes. Goodness, a hundred thousand, yes. Euro?'

'No, Polish Zloty.'

'Well, yes, um, I'm not sure we have much Zloty. Yes, a problem.'

'Euro then.'

He has the sense of humour of a plank.

'Yes, Mr McDonald informed us yesterday. You'll need to come in and bring photo ID, preferably a passport.'

And there it all falls apart. How could I have overlooked the small matter of a passport, not just to get my hands on my own money, but to make good my escape from the country?

My mobile rings. Bloody McAuliffe.

'Andy, stop stalking me.'

'Ger. We seriously need to talk.'

~

We're sat outside my house in an unmarked car. The doors are locked and we have the seatbelts on but it doesn't look like we're going anywhere.

'What's going on, Ger? You know Roisín McGuire is in there?'

'It's my house, Andy. I can have gorgeous crime reporters or whoever I want over to visit.'

He exhales his cigarette smoke without lowering the windows.

'Don't be smart. There are some seriously heavy people in town, Mary Reaney has gone AWOL and you have an investigative reporter in your home. Talk to me.'

'What do you want me to say? Has Mary been reported missing?'

He narrows his eyes at me. 'Are you saying she's not missing?'

'How's it going with finding McGivney's killer?'

'Stop fecking me about, Ger. What's McGuire doing in your place?'

I have to give him something or he's not going to leave me in peace.

'She's talking to a friend of mine, following up an idea she has for a story.'

'Has this to do with Reaney?'

'Nothing to do with any of the Reaneys.'

He puffs on his cigarette again. 'Is this story of hers going to cause me hassle?'

'You'll have to ask her that yourself. All I can say is it's a female interest story from a national perspective.'

'A female interest story?' He laughs with a cough. 'Sure, it's for the money then.'

'A man has to earn a crust, Andy.'

He presses a button on the dashboard and the doors unlock.

'Be on your way, Ger. But mind and be careful. Don't go stirring up a hornets nest here in Kilkenny. No one will thank you for it.'

'Thanks for the advice. I'll bear it in mind.'

I put my hand down to release the seatbelt but he holds the buckle in the socket.

'You were lucky last time.'

'I wouldn't call nine years in Portlaoise lucky.'

'You're alive. What you're messing with this time could get you killed.'

'I won't get killed.'

'There's people who won't ask for help, because of pride or a misjudged sense of honour. When it's time, call me, Ger. This is a small town and we play the game but we look after each other.'

I see McAuliffe's cavalry riding over the hill to a gunfight at the Romanian corral. As reinforcements or to lock everyone up, I'm not sure.

'Thanks, Andy. I will.'

The front door of 32 Maudlin Street opens stubbornly. A steady drone of voices comes down the stairs. I put the lunch rolls I bought at the baker's on the kitchen worktop.

'I'm home,' I call up. 'Some lunch down here for you both if you want it.'

No response. Walking up the stairs, the sound of two other people talking, the house suddenly seems very claustrophobic. When we get to Spain we deserve some space.

Roisín and Krystal are both sat on the bed, surrounded by notes.

'Ah, Ger,' Roisín says, looking up.

'How are you getting on?' I ask.

'Yeah, good. We have a lot of ground to cover but I think we could do with a break.'

Krystal gives me a sad smile.

'How is everything going with you?' Krystal asks me in the kitchen as Roisín busies herself making tea.

'Getting there. I need to go to the bank with the solicitor so he can identify me.'

'What?' Krystal says.

Roisín turns and gives a nothing about Ger Mayes surprises me look.

'I don't have any photo ID, no passport.'

Krystal looks confused. 'But that means you can't … we're flying on Thursday. Can you get a passport that quickly?'

'Strictly speaking, you don't need a passport to travel within the EU,' Roisín says, 'if that's where you're going. You do need photo ID though.'

'No, I don't think I can get a passport or any photo ID that quickly.'

'Then I'm afraid you'll have to change your plans,' Roisín says.

'You could go on your own and I'll follow,' I say to Krystal.

Her face screws up like a child ready to cry. 'I have never travelled on my own.'

'Never? But I thought you used to fly home?'

'Not on my own. One of them always flew with me. And when I was a kid I never left my home town. I wouldn't know what to do.'

'You have two choices, honey,' Roisín says. 'Put off your flight for a week while Ger gets a passport or go on your own and meet up later.'

Krystal turns to her new best friend. 'There is another choice.'

'What's that?'

'You come with me, instead of Ger. Then he joins later.'

Roisín looks at me and then at Krystal.

'I can't leave the country and sell your story. Your best bet is to wait on Ger's passport.'

I don't like that idea at all. Once we get Mary back I have a feeling World War III is going to kick off in Kilkenny. A spark of an idea ignites in my confused brain.

'There is another choice,' I say. 'I could travel by ferry and car. I bet I could get all the way there without having to show a passport. I have a driving licence, the old fashioned paper one.'

Krystal looks at Roisín.

'He's right,' Roisín says. 'That could work.'

'Okay, then,' I say. 'That's the plan.'

Roisín looks at me and shakes her head. 'You are some piece of work, Ger.'

I give them both my best grin. 'Yeah, well this piece of work has to go persuade his bank manager to part with a bag of cash. I'll leave you to it.'

I put a hand out to Krystal's face, half expecting rejection, but she puts her head on my chest and hugs me tightly.

'It'll be okay, won't it, Ger? Promise?'

'It will. I promise it will.'

Over the top of her head I see Roisín with her arms crossed. There's a lecture waiting for me later.

~

McDonald's daughter Sinead greets me in their waiting room.

'Dad's on the phone. I think he'll be a few minutes.'

She leaves and returns with a cup of tea, white, no sugar. Two ginger nuts on the side.

'That's how you take it,' she whistles through her teeth. 'I remember.'

Her father keeps me waiting. Fair enough, that's what this room is for. My tea is finished and Sinead takes it away, the cup trembling on the saucer.

I look at the clock on the wall. A quarter to three. The appointment with the bank manager was supposed to be at half two. I imagine they're on the phone to each other right now, working out how to get a slice of the action. Well they can work away because I'm done with being had for a mug.

'Ah, Ger. Sorry to keep you waiting, come on in,' McDonald says as his office door creaks open.

'Shouldn't we be getting over to the bank?'

'No rush, no rush. The timing of such things is always approximate. That was Phillip on the phone and he has a bit of a delay.'

Approximate timing of such things tomorrow could be fatal. I follow McDonald into his lair, bringing my backpack for the swag.

'Well, this is nice,' he says, dunking a biscuit in his tea.

'You're fond of ginger nuts?'

'No, yes, well, I mean, seeing you on your own two feet, investing in business.' He draws the last word out as an invitation to spill the beans.

I want to say yes, I'm buying a sex-slave out of bondage from the rival brothel. What I actually say is, 'There's a fast food outlet I have my eye on.'

'Very good. When the chips are down, eh?' He laughs at his own joke with a multiple of the deserved mirth. 'Anyone I know?'

'Oh, I imagine you know everyone, Ronald.'

'Robert,' he says. 'The name is Robert.'

The phone on his desk rings and he picks up. A few hushed words and he puts the receiver down. 'They're ready for us now.'

Sinead smiles as we walk out to the stairs. She bends one knee in to the other and twirls her hair with one hand. In fifty years she'll still be here. I want to say come with me, with us. Be rescued.

The bank is just across the road and down the street. A wave of panic washes over me when I see the crossroads. Four soldiers in fatigues are standing on the pavement, holding machine guns and looking around. A blue security company van is sandwiched between two huge matt green military jeeps, their giant aerials bouncing in the breeze.

'This is normal,' McDonald says. 'The military always chaperones any cash deliveries and collections. It makes would-be robbers think twice.'

I'm sure these soldiers are too young to remember me and how, ten years ago, the Army was made to look so stupid by Ilie and his cohorts up at Templemore, but they still make me nervous. I have a terrible feeling that I'm going to do something involuntarily stupid and get shot.

As we walk past I notice one of them is a woman, little more than a girl really. She's quite pretty and looks great in combats.

Inside the bank we're soon ushered into Purcell's office.

'Yes, yes,' he says. 'Ger, do sit down. Robert, how's your Sinead?'

They exchange a few pleasantries and I see a look pass between them. McDonald gives an almost imperceptible shake of the head.

'Yes, very well.' Purcell pushes some papers towards me and holds out a pen. 'Of course I know who you are, Ger. Yes. How could I forget? But we just need Robert to sign as a witness and identify you in his capacity as a Notary.'

I sign and pass the papers to McDonald. He pauses with his pen in the air. 'No charge this time, Ger.'

'Very kind of you.'

Sometime soon I'll be lounging on a beach, drink in hand, far away from this crowd of Uriah Heeps.

'Yes, yes, glad to be of service, Ger,' Purcell says. 'If you can give us a bit more notice of any future large withdrawals … that would be helpful. Are you planning any? Or do you have any plans to put money in?'

Not knowing what I'm up to is driving these guys nuts. I love it.

'Oh, I would expect some large deposits in the not too distant future. Some substantial deposits.'

'Yes. Oh, yes.' Purcell gives a little smack of his lips. 'It determines what sort of account we can give you, you see. Yes. Your account conditions at the moment are very favourable…'

The two creeps exchange a look. When I have my feet up and cocktail in hand I'm going to go through my accounts with a fine toothed comb and see just how much the bastards have creamed me for. Of course it'll all be academic by then.

'...and interest bearing but you do have a withdrawal notice period. Yes, Ger, that's what you should do.' Purcell's lips pop again.

I might have to run outside and grab a machine gun.

'So, the money?' I lift up my empty swag bag.

'Yes, I'll ask Helen to bring it in now.' He picks up his desk phone, makes a quick call and looks to me again. 'Yes, right then, yes. Oh, what did you say you were going to do with the money, Ger?'

'I didn't. A kilo of cocaine, maybe?'

Purcell winces because that's exactly what I did with the money last time, as he well knows.

'You said a chipper,' McDonald says.

'A private investment. That's all I'm going to say.'

'Yes, it would be good if the money is staying local,' Purcell says. 'Yes, indeed. Good for the community.'

'Oh, it's a local investment,' I say. The Romanians will probably put it towards a new knocking shop.

A tap on the door and Helen, presumably, walks in with a large plastic box. She places it on Purcell's desk and leaves.

'Very well. Some papers,' Purcell says, taking documents from the box and sliding them across the desk to me.

I sign and then load the swag into my backpack. It feels like I'm stealing the money. Strange to think it's mine, at least for a day.

'Do you have any security?' McDonald asks.

'Yep. You.'

I know he can't help but comply, desperate as he is for information. I shake Purcell's sweaty fish of a hand and we leave the office to a cacophony of yes's.

The Army has left from outside the bank and people stream up and down the pavement. I catch a note of a familiar perfume and get an urge to shop. A hundred grand can do that, even to a man. I turn left out of the door instead of right.

'Your house is this way. Have you another plan? It's just that I need to be getting back,' McDonald whines.

'I need something from the chemist.' I walk into the next doorway and he follows me.

The phone in my pocket buzzes with a message that comes up as Mary's mobile:

We see you have the money.

I clutch one of the shoulder straps of the backpack to my chest and look up through the chemist's shop. There's a rear entrance opening onto one of the cobbled back alleys that riddle the medieval city centre. So, they're watching, so what? They're not going to grab the money, just keeping an eye on me; they want a successful transaction.

'Is there a problem?' McDonald says.

'Yes, is there a problem?' a woman in an immaculately pressed white coat says from behind the sales counter. She looks at me like I'm a robber or a druggie; either way she can handle it. Then she recognises McDonald who gives a small, embarrassed smile.

'I'm looking for some perfume,' I say.

She slips a plastic smile onto her face and waves a thin hand at the shelves of scent surrounding us. 'Did you have something in particular in mind?'

'I don't remember the name, but it's very distinctive.'

McDonald's teeth click and tut.

'Can you describe it? Do you know the label?' the woman says.

'It's gone right out of my mind. I saw the bottle the other day in a bathroom, but you know what blokes are like. It's intoxicating but pungent at the same time.'

The solicitor is doing a little tap dance of impatience.

'What's the name of the lady who wears it, if I might be so bold to ask?' the woman says with a conspiratorial smirk.

I frown. Not sure I want the High Street knowing my business.

'For God's sake!' McDonald snaps. Then he leans in and lowers his voice. 'Ella Cullen.'

'Oh,' the woman says, 'Ella likes D&G.' She reaches up to a shelf and takes down a sampler bottle. 'I bet it's this one.'

It just looks like another frosted glass perfume bottle to me. 'I need to smell it on someone, to be sure.'

The woman looks at me and then at McDonald who backs further away from the counter. So she lifts her sleeve and sprays the perfume onto her wrist, waves it in the air and holds her arm out to me.

As soon as the scent hits the air I know it's right. I pull her hand gently towards my face and nuzzle the inside of her wrist. She puts the bottle down with her other hand and pushes her fingers back through her hair, which I notice is long, black and sleek, like silk. This is some kind of love potion.

'Is that the one?' A genuine smile.

'It certainly is.'

'*Eau de toilette* or *parfum*? And what size would you like?'

'Parfum. Large.' I'm reluctant to let go of her wrist.

'Come on, Ger,' McDonald moans. 'I told you I have to get back to my office for an appointment.'

'Would you like it wrapped as a present?'

I nod and McDonald's eyes roll to heaven. The woman seems to enjoy his discomfort. Perhaps she's been on the paying end of his services. There's much show made of foil paper selection – I go for the gold – precise folding, curling of the ribbon with a scissors blade and careful placement in a paper bag.

'That will be one hundred and seven euro,' she says, finally handing over the spoils.

I reach a hand into my backpack and notice my solicitous friend chewing his lips. Difficult to imagine him spending any money on his womenfolk. I'm inclined to grab a fistful of notes from the bag and thrust them at him for young Sinead's dental work. Instead my hand finds my wallet and the perfume is bought with my debit card.

'Where now, Ger? Perhaps some jewellery or shall we browse a few ladies' boutiques?' McDonald says on the way out of the chemist's.

I give an eager look at his suggestion but we both turn to Patrick Street and start walking towards the river.

Kilkenny isn't where I spent my years with Jo. That was Bagenalstown, a strange, dour kind of place out on the edge. I never warmed to Bagenalstown. Kilkenny is where I loved and lost Renée. Here, on the bridge where she jumped to her watery death and the Romanian flower sellers tried to frame me for her murder. Ten years ago a hundred grand in a paper sack was placed at my feet as her body floated down over the salmon weir. This time fingers crossed for a better outcome.

'Ger? What's got into you, man?'

McDonald's hand is on my arm, the backpack offered out towards the water. A cool breeze blows up from the river's fast flow and I feel the wetness of tears on my face. He pulls my arm back and I shoulder the bag again. In the corner of my eye a dark blue car pulls out of a parking slot near Tynan's pub, crawling up to the bridge.

I look at McDonald and purse my lips. 'Come on, let's get this over with.'

His face looks confused and more than a little worried.

The walk up John Street to my road is short but I can feel the Romanians tracking me. McDonald takes me by the elbow and fairly ushers me to my front door. The road is crowded outside my house with Roisín's little red coupé, my Saab and, a bit further along, the Fly's corpulent green Mercedes.

'This is it then, Ger. I won't come in.'

Like I was going to invite him. He looks at me, the backpack and the Fly's car up the road. I hear an engine roar behind me and the Romanians' blue Passat flies past my shoulder. I shake the solicitor's offered hand and he walks away sharply, back down past the tower.

When I turn back to my front door, key in hand, the Fly is standing in my way.

The preparation

The Fly's meaty fist thumps me in the midriff, not right through but enough to make me wince.

'Where's your jacket? I need you to wear that jacket at all times. It's not a fashion accessory. Things are gonna get serious in the next day or so.'

It takes a second or two for me to decide I'm not winded by the little man's punch. Time enough to think how to look smart.

'Right. No problem. Just it's a bit conspicuous around town and McAuliffe has been hanging around. I didn't want to make him suspicious.'

'Good thinking. What's in the bag?'

'Just a bit of shopping. Present for the girlfriend.'

He nods, grim-faced. 'They all have their price. Let's make a phone call.' He looks at my front door and then pointedly at Roisín's car and back at me.

'Keeping her sweet, Bob. All under control.'

'You're a dark horse, Ger. I hope for all our sakes you know what the fuck you're doing.'

'So do I. Are you sure you want to make this phone call?'

'Come on,' he says. 'We'll go find somewhere private.'

This is the first time I've been in his Merc. It's one hell of a motor, more like an executive office than a car, and he looks tiny behind the wheel. When he closes his door the chair automatically rises and the steering wheel pushes out towards him. I try not to laugh.

The car whizzes us silently away, up the end of Maudlin Street and out into the countryside. We turn into lane after lane, traversing the railway at old fashioned level-crossings I didn't know existed. He swings the Merc between crumbling stone pillars and along a bumpy driveway, grass growing high in the centre between the tire tracks. Old poplars line the sides of what must have once been an impressive avenue.

'I bought this place a few years ago,' the Fly says as we crest a hill and turn onto a weed-strewn flat area. There, with stone steps leading up to the door, is an old house of classical design. I don't know Georgian from Edwardian, but it would have been a gorgeous building in its prime; what people might call a country pile. The windows are boarded up.

'It's quite something,' I say. 'You'll need the lads working on this for a while to get it into shape.'

'Cost almost nothing except the price of the land. Twenty-five acres. Some old aristocrats were holed up in it. Living in the kitchen and two of the servants' rooms.'

'Are you going to knock it? Probably a prime development site you have here.'

The Fly gives a derisory laugh. 'Knock it? You're joking. It's listed as a heritage site. No, I have plans for it. When Mary gets settled I'm going to make it like new, as her wedding gift.'

He looks me square in the eye. I consciously have to lower my eyebrows. Mary Reaney in the master's chamber of a country mansion. Not bad at all.

'Let's do this phone call then,' he says. 'The way you and Nora did it the other day.'

I pull out my phone and scroll to Mary's number. There are so many ways this could seriously fuck up. The ringing tone sounds. I hold the phone to my ear.

'Put it on the dashboard,' the Fly says, taking the phone from my hand.

'Answer it,' a foreign voice says down the line and a shadowy image appears on the screen.

'Dad? Is that you, Dad?' Mary's voice sounds croaky.

'Hey, honey. How are ye? We'll have you home soon,' the Fly says.

Someone pulls a curtain and we get to see Mary more clearly. She looks dishevelled but beautiful in a grimy way.

'I'm okay. Looking forward to getting home and having a shower. Ger, is that you? Where are you two anyway?'

'Yeah, I have Ger here with me. We're out at Waverley House. Are they treating you alright?'

She gives a hoarse laugh that breaks into a cough. 'This place is a shithole but, apart from that, I'm surviving. You two be careful, these guys have some serious looking guns.' Her face takes on a worried look and the picture scrambles. Then it stabilises back on Mary but from a distance.

'Mr Reaney, do you have the money ready?' I recognise Ilie's voice.

'Of course,' the Fly barks. I put a hand out to suggest he stays calm. His fists are bunched.

'Gerard, you are to do the drop off. A large holdall will be delivered to your house today. Put the money in the holdall and bring it to Dublin airport departures at exactly 11:00 a.m. tomorrow. Mr Reaney will get his daughter back and all business between us will be concluded. We get the money, you get the girl.'

The Fly looks at me and I nod.

'Okay, Ilie. That sounds straightforward,' I say.

Then the Fly grabs the phone and snarls into it. 'If anything happens to my daughter…'

'Mr Reaney, Mr Reaney,' Ilie says in a calming tone. 'There is no sense in us threatening each other. One of my boys is missing, one of your men is dead. We will conclude this business amicably tomorrow. Goodbye.'

The phone display goes dark and the call disconnects.

The dashboard of the Mercedes survives a battering from the Fly's fists as he does a few seconds of berserk punching. Those Germans sure know how to build a car. I'm halfway out the door to escape his rage when he stops and puts those oversized hands over his face.

'It'll all work out, Bob. I'm going to get her back,' I say. People in need make me promise things.

He sniffs and grunts. 'She's a good girl. Strong.'

'The best,' I say.

'She likes you. I can see that.' He starts the Merc's engine and looks out of the windscreen at the house. 'You could do a lot worse, Ger. She's not the easiest woman, I'll grant you; there's a touch of her mother there. But you're a good man. I'd be happy to welcome you to the family.'

The Fly wants me for his daughter. There's no accounting for taste. Now, if he could just drop me back at my house where the crazy crime reporter and renegade sex slave are colluding, I can get ready for my hot date with an alcoholic nymphomaniac.

'I'd like that, Bob.'

~

Back at the ranch the girls are tired but determined.

'We have seventy-five grand in advances so far,' Roisín tells me. 'The money will transfer on receipt of initial copy, which should be tomorrow around midday. I've given them your account details.'

'Good stuff,' I say.

'We'll need to work on through this evening,' Roisín continues. 'What are your plans for tomorrow, Ger?'

I look at Krystal and see something in her brown eyes; it could be fear. 'I have to be at Dublin airport for 11 a.m. So we need to leave here by 9 at the latest.'

'If you let me come up in the car with you then we'll have a couple of extra hours before Krystal leaves.'

'I thought your flight was on Thursday,' I say to Krystal.

'I changed it,' Krystal says, 'and rebooked my flight for tomorrow afternoon. Silviu was here; he brought a bag for you and told me about the meeting tomorrow. I need to get out of here, Ger. You come and join me, as soon as you can. I have some money saved.'

'We'll meet up in Spain, all three of us, and work on the book,' Roisín says with an enthusiasm I don't share. I want this done and dusted, not dragging on.

'Okay then, you can come up to the airport with us, if you promise to stay in the car,' I say to Roisín and signal Krystal to follow me out into the hallway.

'Here,' Krystal says, holding out a large bright blue sports holdall to me. 'The brothers dropped this at the door.'

I take it from her and start to feel around the fabric sides and under the plastic coated cardboard floor of the bag. Eventually I find what I'm looking for in the tail end of the main zip; a disc-shaped stiffness.

'The tracking device is here,' I say.

'We could cut it off. At least then they don't know where we are.'

'No, we have to play it straight. Anyhow, you still have the one in the envelope, right?' I say.

'It's in my backpack, stamped and addressed. Listen, Ger, whatever happens, after this Mary girl is returned, come to me as soon as you can. Do whatever you have to do and come to me.'

'I will.'

'Don't leave me alone out there. I'm not used to being alone. You promise?'

'I promise.'

She hugs me like a long-lost brother and I pet her sister hair.

'Oh, I almost forgot. I bought you a present.' I hold up my backpack and she's in there before I can pull out the package.

She holds up a bundle of notes. 'Don't worry, you'll get this money back. That's my promise.' She puts the wedge back in the bag and pulls out the parcel. In seconds flat the careful wrapping of the chemist's saleswoman is undone. Krystal holds it up and gives a squeal.

'You like it?'

'Oh, Ger! I know this one, it's expensive.' She opens the box, pulls out the bottle and sprays it in the hollow of her throat.

Mediterranean sun, sea and sand.

~

I'm wearing my best clothes for my date at An Cloigín Gorm. Krystal didn't seem jealous and even helped me choose my shirt.

'You deserve a nice evening,' she had said.

I feel good; a spot of aftershave, the hair still looking short and mean in the rear-view mirror, my executive car flying along the Kells Road and a beautiful, sexy woman waiting for me.

The phone buzzes and beeps.

8 at the office tomorrow for the money – Bob

A wave of cold panic grabs at the enormity of what I'm blundering through. Have I packed to leave Kilkenny? No. Do I have any idea how I'm going to head off and find Krystal after? No again. But, as always, I have faith it will somehow all work out. Even though it never does

'Hello handsome.' Ella looks like the lady of the manor as she opens her front door and invites me in. I get a soft kiss on the lips but she pulls back before it gets too passionate and her eyes flash to the sitting room.

The young lad who picked up my dropped phone at the railway station is standing in the doorway, in his pyjamas.

'Hi, Finn,' I say.

'Say hello to Ger,' Ella prompts.

Finn looks undernourished and overtired. Here, in this hall of splendour, he seems neglected. 'Hello,' he says with little enthusiasm.

'Am I early?' I ask Ella quietly.

'No. Finn wanted to stay up and see Mummy's friend. Didn't you, love?'

The boy nods, his hand against the frame of the door and one foot rubbing the back of the other leg. I'm thinking Garda Eamonn is going to line up some more special treats for me when he finds out about my visit.

'Off to bed now,' Ella says.

Finn runs over and hugs his mum, and he's just a normal little boy allowed to stay up late, not a spy or judge and jury over our relationship.

I get a flash of Jo and her son up in Baldoyle, having mummy hugs and walking along the beach, throwing a stick for a running dog. Happy families.

The weight in my hand reminds me of the gift I've brought for Ella – a bottle of wine and some chocolates. Nothing for the boy; I didn't even think.

'Go on in, Ger. I'll be down in a minute.' Ella takes her son up the stairs. She turns to me half-way up and mouths 'Okay?' I give her a thin smile.

I want to run out of here, but I don't. Instead I fill two waiting glasses from a very nice looking bottle of wine sitting on the coffee table – a table that probably cost more than all the furniture in 32 Maudlin Street. The wine smells great and tastes even better. A log fire burns in the huge fireplace making the big room seem homely.

My sorry effort at a gift sits in its bag on the floor by the leather sofa. I really know nothing about wine, about this standard of living.

'Sorry, Ger,' Ella says a few minutes later when she reappears. 'When you want them to go to bed early they seem to sense it and insist on being nosy. You know how it is.'

I smile, a better smile than before, relaxed by the effect of wine on an empty stomach. No, I want to say, I have no idea how it is. Instead I hold out the bag I brought.

'Oh, lovely!' she lies. 'Shall I open the chocolates? Have you eaten?'

'Have you?'

She shakes her head. 'We'd better get something in or we'll be sloshed. Italian okay for you?'

'You mean pizza?'

'No, silly. Italian. What do you like? Pasta? Fettuccine, linguini, tagliatelle? Seafood, chicken or veal?'

'Oh, I like everything. You choose.'

She laughs her tinkling laugh, picks up the phone and dials a number from her contacts. '*Pronto, Luigi? Questo è Ella…*' She goes on to order half the menu in Italian from memory. '*Trenta minuti? Molto bueno. Ciao!*'

'You speak Italian. I'm impressed. Cheers.' I raise my glass and she clinks hers with mine.

'Not really. Luigi and I, well, you know. I only learned the words for food and a few sweet nothings.'

I'm wondering if restaurant owner to ex-con kidnap negotiator is a step up or down the social ladder.

'He has a chain of restaurants across the country,' she says.

Now I know I'm a step down and she's on the slide. Ella curls her legs up onto the sofa next to me.

'Can you stay the night?' she asks, sensing a tension that I'm only just becoming aware of myself.

'I have to be up early for something important. Mustn't get too loaded, have to drive first thing.'

She smoothes a palm on my thigh and holds up her wine glass. 'We'll take it easy, so. I'll get you off to work, safe and sound.'

'Okay.' There's really nothing for me to do at Maudlin Street. I excuse myself and go to the bathroom where I send a text to Krystal:

Will be late home and then have to be in office for 8. Need to be packed and ready to leave at 9. Okay?

She replies almost immediately.

No problem. Very tired. C u 2moro xx

The girl is a star. I walk back into Ella's company with a clear conscience and renewed appetite.

We sip our wine rather than gulp it down like there's no tomorrow, although I know there's no tomorrow for us.

Ella confesses to a long-held crush for me from way back when. I feel a little embarrassed; her memory of our few early encounters in Jo's company is much more detailed than mine. I vaguely recall her being on my list of Jo's tastier friends, but I'm sure we never socialised as couples; I would have remembered Eamonn.

The food arrives and we manage to eat ourselves silly before we get too drunk.

'Do you get takeaway often?' I ask, slightly shocked at the restaurant prices she paid the delivery man.

'Too often,' she says. 'Eamonn and I used to eat out most of the time but now I'm on my own…'

We get into a long exchange about how shit our lives have been. Mine is a litany of underachievement, bad decisions and self-inflicted ill health. She wants to see the scar from my heart surgery.

'I was too out of it last time to remember,' she says.

I feel too bloated and unpresentable to strip off, so Ella slides a hand under the front of my shirt. Her light fingers trace where the surgeon cut in and gave me the life of another.

Her story is sadder than mine. A neglected childhood with a workaholic father and alcoholic mother. Boarding school, starved of affection but lavished with possessions. Eddie Cullen wanted her to join in running his business but it's not for her. It seems Eamonn was expected to do well in the guards but he was her father's choice and a bad one. She's pretty much trapped in her Kilkenny mansion, living off an allowance from her father and with Eamonn still cramping her style. She needs a strong man to provide, protect and love.

This is the point where I normally cave. She's needy, despite having everything. I can provide love, sex and affection. We can help each other. For a few mad minutes the words are on the tip of my tongue: come away with me. Let's get the hell out of Dodge and run to the sun. I'm wondering if it could work with Krystal and Ella, like it seems to with Krystal and Roisín.

'I have an idea...' I begin.

A little voice calls down the stairs. 'Mummy? Can I have a drink of water?'

Ella looks at me. 'Sorry. He does this to get attention.'

She goes up the stairs with a glass of cold water. I just catch a few of Ella's words to him and they're kindly. By the time she gets back down I know running away together is off the menu. I spent ten years thinking Jo was keeping my son from me. I can't play dad to another man's child and, bastard though Eamonn is, I wouldn't deprive him of his boy.

'Now,' Ella says, coming back into the room, 'what's this idea of yours?'

'First,' I say, 'we'll have another glass of wine.' I pour into her glass then mine. 'Then we'll go to bed.'

Her laugh is like a babbling brook. 'But it's only about ten o'clock.'

I lean forward and kiss her. Then I say, 'Ella, life is just too short. Let's make the most of it.'

Day 13 – Fair exchange is no robbery

I'm gloriously tired but clean. We made love with the energy and tenderness of a couple at the onset of war. Then we slept, made love, chatted, slept, made love, on a loop. The alarm went off at seven and we showered together.

'I'm never going to see you again, am I?' Ella said to me at her front door.

'I wouldn't say never.' And I really hoped that I might one day come back.

~

All quiet at 32 Maudlin Street. A bit before eight I creep into the hallway and see Krystal's suitcase looks packed and ready to go.

The kitchen is a mess of handwritten papers, the fruits of their labour.

I trot upstairs. 'Back about half eight,' I say into the bedroom in case either is stirring.

There's a grunt from Krystal and an 'Okay, Ger,' from Roisín. Two of my favourite girls, snuggled up in my bed. Another time, another place.

~

One of the stone-faced men is sitting waiting in my office. He gives a nod and exchanges a brother handshake with the Fly who is close behind me.

'They're on the road already,' the man says. 'We have sight of them.'

'Right. And Mary's with them?' the Fly asks.

'She is. Don't worry, Bob.'

The two of them turn to look at me. I place the empty blue holdall on the table.

'There's a GPS tracking device in here.' I show them the zip tag and the stone-faced man feels the disc through the material. 'It's their signature. No harm in them knowing where the bag is, I guess.'

The man pulls a device from his pocket and scans it over the bag.

'No harm in us knowing either,' he says. The distrust rolls off him towards me.

'Hey, Jim,' the Fly says as Duggan the solicitor walks in.

'Bob,' Duggan says and places a leather pilot's case on the table. 'As promised.' He proceeds to remove bundles of fifties from the case and pile them on the table.

The Fly picks up a bundle, counts it and places it apart from the others. He doesn't count each bundle but flicks through them and measures the size against the first, stacking them together. We all stand and watch while he checks the whole lot.

'It seems to be correct,' the Fly says to himself.

'I've checked it twice,' Duggan says.

'Work away, Ger,' the Fly says. I start to pack the money into the blue holdall.

'Thanks, Jim,' the Fly says. 'We'll handle it from here.'

Duggan takes his dismissal with good grace and walks out after shaking the Fly's hand.

The stone-faced man looks even stonier at Duggan's retreating form. 'What's the plan at the airport?' he says.

'Eleven in Departures,' I say. 'I'm expecting them to text me about Mary's location.'

'We'll know where she is, you don't need to worry about that.'

The Fly says, 'Just make sure they get the money, Ger.'

'Trust me, Bob,' I say. 'We'll get her home safe. This is killing all of us,'

He claps me on the shoulder and then wraps his surprisingly long arms around me in a mafia hug. I pick up the blue bag in my left and stone-face finally yields, giving me the brother handshake in my right.

'Don't you worry,' he says to us both. 'We'll be keeping a close watch on everyone involved.'

The two of them start to talk in low voices as I leave my office for what I intend to be the last time.

'Ger,' Nora says from over by the coffee machine. 'Be careful, won't you?' She gives me a kiss on the cheek and I hug her awkwardly with my free hand.

~

Back at Maudlin Street the girls are busy in the kitchen.

'What are you going to do with all that Alessi stuff in the back bedroom?' Roisín asks.

'Help yourself, if you want anything. I won't be back for it.'

'Thanks. Make yourself useful then.' She throws her car keys at me.

First I take my backpack and transfer my hundred grand into the blue holdall. Then I put on the stab vest.

'Here's a coffee,' Krystal says, holding out a large mug to me. The brew is only just warm so I knock it back and set to work stuffing as much Alessi as I can into Roisín's little red Peugeot coupé.

A quick look around the house that never quite became home. My black leather swivel chair in front of the giant TV, screened from prying street eyes by a sheet for a curtain. The over-sized country kitchen shoe-horned into too small a space. A rear parlour I've never used. The dysfunctional shower upstairs. The back bedroom with my Alessi miscellany. My main bedroom with the huge bed, as yet un-christened unless Krystal and Roisín managed it last night, and the clean patch of carpet marking where Old McKinsey kept his captives. For a decade I yearned to have my own space, now I can't get away fast enough.

'It's ten to,' Roisín calls up the stairs. 'We'll put our stuff in the car.'

I check they haven't left any incriminating notes lying around and then slam the front door shut behind me.

The car smells delicious with Krystal's new perfume.

'Can we stop and get a coffee or something,' Krystal says from the back seat where they already have papers lying all over the Saab's leather. 'That machine doesn't make it hot enough.'

'Sure,' I say. 'We have time.'

At the petrol station I send Roisín in for the coffees. Six hundred grand in the boot of the car, I can't take any chances.

We're soon on the motorway. For Krystal this is a one-way journey, the one she's waited and suffered for. I catch her dark brown eyes in the rear-view mirror and she gives me a nervous smile.

'Have some of this coffee,' she says. 'It's much better than mine.'

I reach a hand around and take the Styrofoam cup with the plastic cover, lift it to my mouth and taste the hot, dark brew.

On the back seat they're deep in discussion again, Roisín making more notes as they talk. I focus on the road and drink the coffee, occasionally taking a look in the mirror at their enthusiasm and rapport. By the time we pass Carlow, Krystal has slipped into a doze and Roisín is chatting on her mobile.

'Yes, no problem, right away,' she says and hangs up. 'Ger, can we pull over for a few minutes? I need to email the initial copy from my laptop to the Independent and then they'll make their transfer.'

I look at the clock on the Saab's dashboard, only half nine. 'Sure, we're making good time.'

At the next parking sign we pull off and Roisín fetches her computer from the boot of the car. I get out to stretch my legs but the cold wind makes me realise I've drunk nearly a litre of coffee.

'All done,' Roisín says. 'That's fifty grand coming your way.'

She closes her computer and smoothes back a few wayward strands of hair from the sleeping Krystal's face. We drive on, Krystal's head now cradled in Roisín's lap.

The M9 merges with the M7 and my toilet urge gets stronger as the traffic slows. In my mind's eye I see Ilie and the stone-faced men watching our slow progress on their computer screens via the tracking device. Krystal slumbers towards her fate and now Roisín drifts away, her job done. I soldier on bravely, alone.

With the beauties in the back asleep the traffic becomes my entertainment. It's difficult to be sure on the crowded carriageway leading into County Dublin but a couple of cars seem to be keeping pace, staying a few vehicles behind. I try speeding up into the fast lane, pushing my way through traffic, and then pulling back in. Past Naas I take it real easy, easing into the slow lane and letting the flow push past. All the time a blue Mondeo and a silver Audi keep pace, about four cars behind. I can't get them any closer so it's impossible to tell who I'm dealing with.

At Newlands Cross the traffic backs up, waiting for the red lights to change. My phone gives a buzz and a bleep. A message from Mary's mobile:

The girl will be at Callaghan Auto Repairs on airport industrial estate, next to cemetery.

I forward the text to the Fly. He replies:

Thanks Ger. Go ahead with the drop.

The traffic moves and we're on the M50 in no time. Everybody rolls along at the speed limit like an American freeway. Through the automated toll plaza, past all the arterial roads heading west and then the water tower which signals the airport back road.

I take the slip road off and see my tails in the background. So what? If it's the guards then they can't arrest me because there's nothing illegal going on from our side. If it's the Romanians then they're just tracking the bag and making sure. Likewise the Fly and any of his stone-faced associates. We've nothing to worry about.

The airport back road hasn't improved during the last decade. Potholes on top of potholes and a mosaic of haphazard repairs. Krystal and Roisín are jolted awake by the bad ride.

'We're there,' Krystal says sleepily, looking at the line of planes in the sky, queuing up to land.

'Which terminal, Ger?' Roisín says.

'What do you mean?'

'Terminal 1 or 2? There's a new terminal, just been built.'

By this time we're in a maze of roadworks and a one-way system that bears no relation to my memory of the place.

'Which is the busiest?' I ask.

'The old one, terminal 1,' Roisín says.

'Right then, that's where we're going.'

We hit a red light and I rattle off a quick text to Mary's phone:

Terminal 1

The car park is the same as it ever was, once I find the way in. Straight up to the roof and I find a parking space near the door to Departures. We have twenty minutes before the rendezvous.

'What time is your flight?' I ask Krystal.

She pulls some paperwork from her black leather backpack. 'In an hour and a half.'

'You should check in,' Roisín says.

I nod. 'I don't want you around when I do the exchange,' I say to Krystal. 'Just in case something goes wrong. You too,' I say to Roisín. 'You can't be there, sorry. In case they recognise you or something. We can't afford anything to go wrong with this.'

Roisín smiles at Krystal and they hug.

'Don't worry,' Krystal says to her. 'I'll be fine. I'll email you when I'm there and we can meet up to work on the book.'

Krystal gives me a ready to go look and steps out of the car to get her bag from the boot.

I turn to Roisín. 'You stay here in the car. I'll come back as soon as the money is handed over and then we'll play it by ear. I can drop you in town or bring you back to Kilkenny for your car.'

She looks tired from all their work. I have half an urge to take her back to Maudlin Street for some relaxation.

'Thanks, Ger,' she says, 'but you'd better get on the ferry and start working your way down to Spain. Don't leave her alone too long, she's very vulnerable.'

'This button here,' I say, pointing to the centre console. 'Lock the doors. I should be back within half an hour.'

~

Terminal 1 Departures is heaving with budget airline passengers. Stressed holidaymakers haul giant cheap luggage around, worrying about having left the oven on and not having packed enough underwear. The armed guards in their dark blue bullet-proof vests cut a routine swathe through the throng.

I look at the departures information but it's a blur to me.

'Malaga, 13:15,' Krystal says. 'Desk twenty-seven, aisle C.'

'It's down this way,' I say, pointing to the signs hanging from the ceiling.

'Oh, I don't need to do that,' she says. 'I already checked in last night. All I have to do is go through security. This is hand luggage.' She points to her small, neat suitcase on wheels. 'But I do need the bathroom.'

'Me too.' I look around and we both see the sign for the toilets.

I'm wearing a jacket over the stab vest and the sweat is starting to run down my back. After fighting our way through the families, hen and stag parties and visiting grandparents, we find a long queue tailing out of the ladies' toilet.

'I'll wait 'til I go through security,' Krystal says.

After all that coffee, my urge is too strong to wait. I heft the blue holdall in my hand. Suddenly everyone looks like a thief and a murderer; I don't want to meet a blood-soaked end in a toilet cubicle.

'Here,' Krystal says and points to an empty row of chairs. A guard stands nearby, cradling his sub-machine gun. Nothing bad can happen. 'I'll be here,' she says, taking a seat. 'You go on in.'

I leave the holdall with her and nip into the toilets. It only takes a couple of minutes. When I come out the guard is giving Krystal his most smouldering look and she's trying to ignore him.

We walk briskly to the security check and she grabs me in a hug.

'I'll text you where I am, as soon as I get there,' she says into my shoulder.

'I don't know if this phone will still be working. Best if you send me an email, like Roisín. But send to me first and then to her a few days later, just to give us some space. I'll pick it up at an internet café somewhere.'

We kiss, a brother and sister who don't want to part. I hold her beautiful face in my hands then push her hair behind her ears. She sniffs back a tear, smiles and walks away. I watch her all the way through the ticket check. Tiny, graceful, gorgeous. She keeps turning back. First a wave, then a smile, then waving me to go away and a final kiss blown as she disappears through the glass partitions to the security check.

~

Ten minutes later I see him – Silviu, brother of the dead Constantin.

On the streets he would turn the heads of the guards but here, in Dublin airport, he's just another immigrant worker sending his visiting family home. He's not a terrorist threat.

I wait in the open bar until exactly the appointed time and watch him walk through the crowds. Then he's at my side, by the high stool. I bend down and pick up the blue holdall, open the zip and show him the bundles of notes. He looks me in the eye, smiles and dials a number on his mobile.

'You can go and get the girl now,' he says.

We look at each other. There's no handshake. I turn away and walk towards the exit. Halfway there a hand grabs my arm and spins me around.

'Ticalos!' he barks. 'What is this?' His hand is full of newspapers cut to the size of fifty euro notes. I look into the bag. There are some fifties in there to make it less obvious at first glance but the bulk of it is newspaper.

When she did it I don't know. Outside the toilet? Surely there wasn't time. In the house when I was saying my little goodbyes to 32 Maudlin Street? It doesn't matter. Out of my hands.

I look around Departures. If they've found the money in her luggage then she'll be dragged off to a room somewhere, I suppose. Or is the money somewhere else? Is Roisín involved?

Silviu is on his phone, shouting. Then he turns to me.

'Your girl is dead. You are all dead,' he says.

Two armed guards walk past and I lower my head. Silviu may as well plunge the knife into my heart now. If he doesn't then the Fly will have his stone-faced friends sit on my chest until I stop breathing. Or he'll use me as a punch bag before throwing me into the concrete foundations of somewhere fitting. I raise my head and look for Silviu but he's disappeared with the bag.

What now? Maybe there's still a chance to save Mary. I pull out my mobile and call the Fly.

'Ger. What's the story? All okay?'

I take a deep breath and go for it. 'They didn't get the money, Bob.'

'What do you mean?'

He sounds confused, not angry.

'Is Mary okay?' I ask.

'Aye, we have Mary, all right. You'd better get down here. What happened to the money?'

'I don't know. I really don't know. I'll be down there in a minute.'

I make it to the car park at a run. The heavens have chosen now to open and wind whips swirling rain across the open top floor of the old concrete structure.

From the doorway I can see the interior light on in my car and the back door is open. Close up I see the damage to the Saab's bodywork, as if someone has levered the door open with a crow bar. Inside, on the cream leather seat, Roisín's computer sits next to a small envelope. It's addressed to Canada. That's where Krystal and I had decided to send the GPS tracking device from her backpack, but it never got posted. No sign of Roisín.

~

Five minutes and I'm pulling in to the industrial estate alongside the cemetery. A small digger is opening a fresh grave on the other side of the fence.

Callaghan Auto Repairs turns out to be a defunct workshop near the back of the site. The Fly's Mercedes is outside, together with a silver Audi, a white Opel and a battered black pickup. I knock on the workshop door and walk in.

Old oil, grease, blood and relief are the odours that assault me.

'Ger!' Mary says and throws her arms around me. She presses the side of her head in close to mine. This gesture is probably what saves my life.

I inhale her scent, a mixture of heady perfume and the mustiness of days unwashed. Even then, she's delicious.

'Well?' says the Fly and Mary releases me.

In the middle of the dirt and oil floor, on a black tarpaulin, are the bodies of three men; Silviu, his taller brother and another Romanian I don't recognise, but it's not Ilie. There's a lot of blood.

'So you lost the money,' the Fly says. He holds out the blue holdall.

'Well, most of it,' I say.

A hollow laugh comes from the shadows of the workshop and the Fly's three stone-faced friends step forward. Each of them holds what looks like a sniper's rifle.

'So who has the money, Ger?' the Fly asks.

I look at him and then Mary puts her hand on his shoulder. 'It's only money, Dad. I'm safe.'

'Tell me.' The Fly's fists are bunched.

'I don't know.' I look at Mary, pleading with my eyes not to tell her dad about Krystal. She doesn't.

'We need to be going,' one of the stone-faced men says. It's the first time I've heard this one talk and his Belfast accent is very noticeable. This is payback to the Fly for his laundering the Northern Bank money.

'Okay,' the Fly says, putting an arm around his daughter. 'This isn't over, Ger. Lads, you take him. Do what you have to.' He walks out to the Merc with Mary and they drive away.

'Right, sunshine,' one of the men says to me. 'Give us a hand.'

We put the bodies in the back of the pickup, wrapped in the tarpaulin. By the time we get around to the cemetery the digger is abandoned. Not a soul about, at least not a live one.

'It's an old trick,' says one of the men to me. I get the feeling he likes to chat. 'You just dig ten feet instead of six. Throw in a body and fill it up to six. No one is going to touch the rightful tenant once they're buried on top.'

My nails bend and break as I drag Silviu's weight by his shoulders, the feet taken by the Chatty Man. The Romanian looks very small in the bottom of the long, deep grave, like a child.

The other two killers look over the edge. 'We could have put two of them in there,' one of them says, 'and saved a few bob on the digging.'

'Aye,' says the other. 'Could have put all three of the buggers in the one hole.'

We move over to the next grave and I reach out to the body of Silviu's brother, just wanting to get this over with, but a gnarled hand grabs my wrist.

'So, where's the money? Where's Mr Reaney's money, Ger?' The Chatty Man has an old looking pistol in his hand, aimed at my guts. 'Oh, don't worry, I'm not going to shoot you in the stomach. Just one knee, and then the other, then your elbows, until you tell us.'

A plane flies low overhead. I see the symbol of a holiday charter airline, no doubt full of burnt holidaymakers. It's very loud. The gun goes off and I hardly hear it above the roar of the jet engines. I wait for the pain but feel none. The bullet is in the face of what's left of Silviu's brother.

'Just a little bit of fun,' says the Chatty Man. 'Now, what did you do with the money?'

'I swear, I don't know. This guy had it.' I point back to Silviu in his squatter's grave. 'He must have taken it out before he got here.'

'We should go,' one of the other stone-faces says.

We roll the remaining two bodies into their final resting places and the Chatty Man uses the digger to half-fill the graves while the other two give me a professional body beating.

~

An hour later we're sat in my Saab, watching the glow of the burning pickup in a field somewhere in County Louth. I think I feel the warmth of the fire or it might just be the burning sensation of my trunk and limbs where they've been twisted and pummelled.

'I really don't think he knows anything,' the Chatty Man says on the phone to the Fly. 'No permanent damage, no. It's either the Romanian who picked up the bag or else that reporter. She's disappeared but I don't see her taking the money. Aye, shame.' He presses the button for speakerphone.

'We were hoping to get the cash back,' the Fly says. 'Listen, Ger. Mary is worried about you. I just want you to tell her you're fine and all, okay?'

'I'm...' my throat feels rough from the vomiting after those stomach punches, '...I'm fine, Mary, not a worry. See you soon.'

'You understand, it's a lot of money, Ger. We had to be sure. No hard feelings, then? You're a sound lad, Ger.'

'No hard feelings, Bob. I might take a few days, if that's okay.'

'No problem, Ger. Mary's looking forward to seeing you.'

The Fly rings off.

'He sounds happy enough,' the Chatty Man says.

'Aye,' says one of the other two, 'but I'm not. Now where is this money, Ger?'

~

They're old, the stone-faced men. It's a tiring task, beating up a man with your fists. Each takes a turn. I don't fight back, there's no point in making it personal. I just try to cover up, taking the punches and making the right noises. Ten years in Portlaoise has taught me a thing or two about playing survivor.

'The Romanian,' I say, spitting out blood. 'The money is with the Romanian.' Honesty is the best policy.

The next assailant steps up to his task. 'You're involved,' he says just before his anvil of a fist lands in my stomach again.

I dry retch; it's all I have left. 'I have no idea what happened to the money,' I gasp.

'Half ... a ... fucking ... million.' He hammers my ribs and plants the last punch square on my sternum. For a moment I panic, worried that my body might finally reject the foreign heart. But no, the beating endures.

'You were shagging that reporter.' Whoever is dishing out the punishment gives me a minute to recover from the foetal position and make a comment, even though it occurs to me he didn't ask a question, strictly speaking.

'She's my girlfriend,' I say. Is wishful thinking lying? 'We've been living together these last few days.'

'Lads,' one of them says to the others. I think it's the guy with the pronounced northern tones, but my hearing isn't too good now. 'This is a waste of time.'

My brain is whirling, trying to suss out the situation. These guys have gone further than the Fly asked them to. They must want the money for themselves.

'Okay, buddy,' another says. 'You have us believing you. No offence, okay?'

I have to laugh. Make it out of this alive and I'm a made man with a reputation and a bunch of new perverse friends. But that's not the world I want to live in.

'None taken,' I say, running my tongue over the salty bleeding gash in my lip. Then everything goes black.

Day 14 – A victimless crime

I don't know how I got here, but here I am and this, if you remember, is where we came in. Sean Walsh Park in Tallaght, Dublin. My predicament has something to do with this thing between my legs. Everything to do with it.

A breeze picks up and rustles the plastic bag at my feet. I look into the wind and see lads loitering at the far entrance to the park. Even at this distance they look foreign. Something about their trousers. Those are the Romanians. Friends or enemies, I'm not sure. Is this their doing? Again, it could be. Doesn't matter now.

The bag rustles again. I have no idea how I came to be here, can't remember. I didn't deserve it. This time I tried to do the right thing. My intentions were good.

A shout makes it upwind from the mother with the pushchair. Two uniformed guards struggle past her at the other entrance. A man in a dark jacket follows and then the wiry, brown-suited figure of Detective Inspector Andy McAuliffe. I can smell his cigarettes in my memory. A day out from Kilkenny, nice for him.

Andy, I should have taken your advice and got the hell out of Dodge.

Before they reach me I have to know what's between my legs. But I think I already know and so does Andy, somehow.

The bag is oozing something onto the tarmac. Clear fluid with traces of pink. I open the top of the bag with both hands and my favourite fragrance wafts out. When a woman wears that it means she's mine. The scorching sun, sea and sand of the Mediterranean, as the ad says, with a hint of butcher's shop.

I put my hand inside and let my fingertips touch, then stroke. Her hair is soft and fair. I always loved her hair.

The youth on roller blades flies past the other side of the lake and continues his circuit. He rounds the guards, making them look slow, swoops low as he passes me again and the bag is gone.

So they thought better of it. Roisín's copy will be front page news by now. A head in a bag would be overkill.

At the east end of the park the lad on wheels is getting a greeting from the Romanians. They peel off and revving engines accompany their departure.

'Ger,' says DI Andy McAuliffe, straining to catch his breath after that run through the park.

'You should give up the cigs,' I try to say but it comes out of my swollen mouth barely understandable, even by me.

'Jesus!' McAuliffe says, looking at my face. I feel what he sees.

Painkillers, car, internet café. Those are my priorities.

~

Fair play to An Garda Síochána. They take me to the hospital and track down my car. In return I give them nothing.

What is there to say? I work for a guy they know, we sometimes make enemies in our business activities and said enemies gave me a bit of a rough time. No, I don't know anything about missing persons, kidnap, extortion or sex slave trafficking. Yes, I know Roisín McGuire and she has been staying at my place. No, I don't know where she is.

The questions go on and on, in a circle. McAuliffe doesn't want gang wars on his sleepy patch. Roisín has stirred up a hornets' nest. What did I do to get a nearly fatal beating? What do I know about brothels and the Gimp's murder?

The foreign heart does me good service. No racing pulse, no impetuous answers. Jim Duggan turns up as my legal support and it's just like old times. I know then that the Fly has forgiven all and I'm safe home.

Day 100 – The quiet life

This is my favourite restaurant. The waves lap at the roots of the tree shading our table. Every day the special is a different fish, caught locally. Great if you like fish, and I do.

Sun, sea and sand. It's everything I dreamed of.

Sometimes I wonder if it was a dream, the head in a bag. I was well out of it. The Fly's geriatric paramilitary friends gave me such a pummelling that it blurred reality.

Here she comes, the woman I saw on the beach yesterday; long blonde hair, slim, a graceful mover. If she takes a table here, today or tomorrow or another day, we might find a common language. She doesn't look British or American; this country is full of escapees of all nationalities. So far I've got lucky once and I will again.

She smiles at me and my companion, her sunglasses hiding her true thoughts, and walks on. My thoughts return to Sean Walsh Park, as they do every day in idleness.

'We're grand, Ger,' the Fly had said to me on the phone. 'The guards will grill you for a bit but there's nothing to say. Is there, Ger?'

'Nothing to say,' I echoed. Half a million missing cash. Crime reporter abducted. Shoot-out next to the cemetery. Ten feet under, little men, bad trousers. Nothing to say.

Tallaght hospital kept me in for four days. 'To be sure about any internal bleeding,' the consultant had said. Then it was straight down from Tallaght to Kilkenny in Andy McAuliffe's ash tray of a car and the best part of two days incarceration, helping with their enquiries.

Andy knew something had happened but he couldn't quite put his finger on it. 'We know you and Reaney have been having a dispute with the Romanians,' he said.

I was flattered at the inclusion, as if I was somehow pivotal or instrumental. Call me a plank or a spanner, I've no illusions now about my role in the proceedings.

'Roisín McGuire exposes a Romanian sex-trafficking operation, citing her source as a prostitute here in Kilkenny. The story gets splashed across the media,' Andy said. I gave thanks on behalf of my bank account. 'And the Romanians disappear off the map,' he added.

'If you say so,' I said.

'I say so,' he said. 'McGuire's source, if she ever had one, has disappeared. McGuire has disappeared. Your girlfriend, gone.'

I laughed at *your girlfriend* because Roisín would have said *In your dreams, Ger*. In keeping with my new-found strategy of only telling the truth, I explained how we had sold the stories to the media, taken the girl from the brothel to the airport and put her on a plane to Malaga. Roisín had disappeared from my Saab in the car park and I had been beaten up by a group of three men I believed to be foreign criminals.

Andy left me to stew for a few hours and was shaking his head when he returned. 'No one matching the description or name you gave us boarded that plane or any plane that day for Malaga. All the passengers have been accounted for.'

Then it dawned on me; a sting of admirable proportions. Krystal had checked in, perhaps, but on another flight. Had Roisín planned to meet her? I didn't know. I still don't know now, to be honest. I didn't get all the answers.

By the time I was able to get to an internet café and check for messages from Krystal it was six days after the cash had gone. I didn't expect anything but there it was – a cryptic invitation to meet up.

I left my Saab at the Fly's office with a note saying I had to take a break and headed for the ferry in a second-hand BMW I had picked up in Carlow. When my wheels were on continental soil I bought a pre-paid phone and made the call. Two days' hard driving later and there she was, sun-kissed and drinking her cocktail on the beach.

Between my money, the payout from the initial news story and the Fly's ransom, we have close to a million. It's cheap here and, as long as we keep a low profile, we should last. This place has seen dictators, revolutions, wars and war crimes, but it's safe these days. The Fly won't touch us, won't hear of us here.

The woman in the sunglasses comes back and asks in faltering English if she might join us at our table. When she takes off her sunglasses she's friendly to me but I see it's Krystal she's interested in. Her features are pretty but vulnerable and remind me of somebody I used to know.

Connect with Ruby Barnes

at Marble City Publishing

http://www.marblecitypublishing.com

http://www.rubybarnes.blogspot.com

Join Marble City's list for updates on new releases:

http://eepurl.com/vek5L

Follow on Twitter:

http://twitter.com/MarbleCityPub

http://twitter.com/Ruby_Barnes

Other titles by Ruby Barnes

Peril - a contemporary crime thriller set in Dublin, Ireland.

Full of sharp wit and realistic characters, this book does exactly what it sets out to do - take readers on an adventure and leave them wondering what could possibly happen next.

Barnes has taken a character's life and spins a web that keeps you reading until the very end.

Like nothing I've ever read before. The story is well written with a fast pace, intriguing plot twists and a good balance of dark humour and human drama.

You won't want to put it down ... it twists and turns like a twisty turny thing.

~

Gerard Mayes is in a bind. He's committed most of the seven deadly sins and is trying to avoid paying the price.

Ladies, don't let your man read this book. You don't want him getting ideas on how to misbehave. Fellas, keep your copy of Peril well hidden.

The Baptist - a contemporary psychological thriller set in Kilkenny, Ireland.

Tight writing, very atmospheric. A chilling tale of real evil.

Dark and disturbing, but oh so good.

Well written and totally convincing, it provides an absorbing insight into the minds of some very strange characters. It's not without humour albeit of the dark kind.

What if you woke up one day and realised you're a serial killer on a mission from God?

He's clever, calculating and uncatchable. If you hear a knocking on your door don't let him in. John Baptist is cleansing a path for the Second Coming.

When God shines a light, it burns. The last prophet must wander, cleanse.

I am not the One. I am merely sent to prepare a way for the One.

I am The Baptist.

The Crucible - a political thriller.

"An insanely evangelicized America ... AIDS is not a global conspiracy ... Love, sex, murder, romance; James Bond meets Tom Clancy."

The world is hungry for energy. Nuclear power, wind turbines and fossil fuels are struggling to deliver and costing the earth. Greg Marshall has developed a revolutionary new way to generate electricity and the hopes of a global corporation rest upon his shoulders, but figures move in the shadows, ready to seize opportunities. When the enigmatic Thomas steals his identity, Greg is lured into a web of global corruption, conspiracy and murder.

Thomas is a shadow, dispensing justice and righting wrongs on a grand scale. His task is to return the billions stolen from Africa by corrupt regimes. Thomas's organisation want Greg's invention to power the continent. Africa will unite and move from famine and relief agency support to superpower status under the leadership of a charismatic and evangelical statesman. But why are millions of Africans still being allowed to die from AIDS?

A collusion of terrifying proportions, this book will change forever your view of European and American intervention in Africa, the cradle of human life.

Allen's Mosquito - The Crucible Part 2 - a political thriller.

The CEO of a pharmaceutical giant is brutally murdered with his family while on holiday at their Swedish island summer home. The authorities attribute the deaths to an unknown, deranged killer.

Thomas wakes from coma to a changed society. The mass European emigration to Africa is underway and a new world order has been established. Governments and industry have united to share the AIDS vaccine with rich and poor alike across the dark continent, and the population is united behind a charismatic leader, Alan Goolden. All looks good for the United African States of Europe in their new land of plenty.

A voice from beyond the grave tells Thomas that all is not as it should be. Is his mental illness just an affliction or a driving force to discover the real horror dressed up as leadership and philanthropy? The secret lies with a murdered entomologist and his discovery - Allen's Mosquito.

The New Author: Writing, E-Publishing & Social Media

A beginner's self-help guide to novel writing, publishing as an independent author and promoting your brand using social networks.

There are three reasons why you should read and digest this book:

1. you want to be an author;

2. you have already written a novel and want to publish it as an ebook;

3. you want to promote yourself as an author.

With foreword by Jim Williams, author of the Booker Prize nominated Scherzo.

Available in ebook and paperback format from all major online bookstores.